KYX

JENNIFER R. POVEY

AITUNE

❧ Created with Vellum

1

THE AIR WAS MUGGY, a sense of oppressive heat that threatened to descend over the town. It felt like it was going to rain, but it never actually did. The oppression just lingered on and on. It swallowed your sweat without letting you cool.

It matched Dhyanil's mood.

They had found the body that morning, washed up on the beach. In that place where they always ended up, all of them.

Once or twice a year, *somebody* jumped off of Maril's Point, knowing that the current would wash them away. It was suicide. Very occasionally, somebody was pushed off of Maril's Point by one who thought they could by this means make a murder look like suicide.

The body was in the morgue. Dhyanil glared up at the Point. It had once had a lighthouse on it, the stub still visible, a broken tooth against the sky. The Preservation Society hadn't bought it, had let it go to ruin. It had not been a beautiful or spectacular light, so nobody had cared. If there was still a lightkeeper up there, it probably wouldn't be a popular destination for suicides.

This one, though, was personal.

No, he had to be honest.

This one was his fault. He had killed Iluhin as surely as if he had pushed her. This had not been meant to happen.

Not like this. None of it was supposed to be like this.

Targeting the rich was one thing, and he'd put the idea into her head. But they were supposed to target property, not people.

And you never involved kids too young to have a suffix on their name, kids too young to know what their gender was.

Who they were.

Not saying they never got hurt. But you never *targeted* them. There would be a Special Investigator sent to investigate the fire now.

And no doubt they would poke into Iluhin's death too, if only because of the timing. He thought of the lovely young woman broken on the rocks. She hadn't even completely finished school.

This was so often a game for the young and fit. He put his responsibility in a little mental box so he could set it to one side. There was no bringing any of them back.

There was no sense to torturing himself over it. That would not serve the cause, would not serve himself.

He glanced up. Orbital hardware glinted as the light began to fail. Kyx had no natural moon, no second body to reflect the sun and light the night.

Instead, it had those hundreds of lights, large and small, and some of it was good. Some of it was not good.

Was one of those dots the alien ship? He didn't know. He didn't want to know. He glared skywards anyway and then went back to walking along the beach, hoping his body language would keep others from approaching him.

He was not ready to deal with people yet. Sometimes he thought becoming a hermit would be a good idea, would keep him away from all of this.

From the crazy.

There was so much crazy.

THE TAVERN WAS SOMEWHAT crowded when Dhyanil decided he could face people again, but the mood was somber. The open windows let in the air, but many people were inside, warming the place pleasantly and filling it with the cinnamon-musk scent of sweat. More gathered under the orange and white awnings.

A lot of people had liked Iluhin. In a small town, people knew each other. She had been considered a good kid.

Somebody who didn't let the excessively progressive influences of the cities go to her head. Not like the girl who had gone off to medical school. A girl in medical school?

Of course, if you went back far enough, tradition would have made him property. No, he didn't want to go back *that* far.

But women were simply not suited to the nurturing professions. Iluhin had been talking about a stint as a ranger in the hunting grounds further north. Much more respectable.

The barkeep poured Dhyanil his usual tankard of vril before he even reached the bar, three slate fingers uncurling from the tankard as he set it on the bar. Dhyanil laughed slightly, taking it and sniffing before pouring a little bit into his maw.

Good.

It was the good stuff, not the cheap mass-produced crap. It made him grateful not to be poor.

It was little things that made life worthwhile.

"Feel better?" the barkeep asked.

"Not really, but it helps." It did, just that little bit.

Little things.

"We're all going to miss her. Don't suppose you have *any* idea why she did it?"

Dhyanil tilted his head in the jerking sideways motion that indicated a no without any vocalization. He didn't trust himself to say more. Everyone knew that he had a connection to her.

He was too old for her to consider as a father for a clutch, but he suspected that she had seen him as a reasonable substitute for her own father, who had not been the best of parents.

Too much strong alcohol, too little proper paternal instinct. Living proof that too much technology affected the bond between a father and his clutch. Her mother was involved in her life, but with a mother's appropriate distance. She cared, but not too much.

One of her siblings had died in the egg, although that wasn't necessarily the father's fault. Such things simply happened sometimes.

You didn't count your hatchlings until they had, well, hatched. In the old days not even then. He knew his history.

"I figured if anyone saw any signs of it it would be you or her lyka, and I haven't seen lin at all."

Dhyanil frowned. He hadn't seen Merilar either, and that was a surprise.

And he finished his drink. "Excuse me. Put that on my rolling tab."

"What?"

"I'm going to go find Merilar."

Because he was abruptly worried about Iluhin's clutchmate. If ly was hiding, then ly was taking it hard.

Perhaps too hard.

Dhyanil did not want to lose both of them. He cared for them almost more than his own long-since-fled children.

The ones who had rebelled.

He *could not* lose both of them.

He KNEW where to look first, but it took him three attempts to locate the young ly'iin.

Ly was sitting on a rock above the beach, throwing stones into the water. Spray had created black patches on lin already dark hide, dripping from lin. Ly had scared off the entire local avian population and was, no doubt, confusing the fish. Dhyanil merely went over to lin, wordless. He waited, the breeze from the water cooling him and lifting his loose clothing away from his skin.

It was a long while before ly stood to talk, and angular anger marked every part of lin.

"You killed her."

"I accept some responsibility," Dhyanil said.

"Give me one good reason not to push you into the ocean right now."

"I like swimming," was all he could come up with. Not that he wanted to take an unprecedented bath with his clothes on.

But he *did* like swimming, always had.

Unexpectedly, bitterly, Merilar laughed. "I know you do. And I suppose that was uncalled for."

"Not entirely. I admit I have some responsibility. But we can't...we have to move on and do what she couldn't do."

"Kill more kids?"

"Not if I have anything to do with it. I swear, they weren't supposed to be there."

They weren't supposed to be there for another month. The unseasonably warm weather had drawn them here faster; the same weather that Dhyanil hated was exactly what drew the rich, who could retreat from it into air conditioning.

"I know. But maybe we need...we should have been more careful."

At least some of the anger was being directed firmly internally, Dhyanil knew. He knew how Merilar felt.

No.

He *didn't* know how Merilar felt. Iluhin had been his trainee, somebody who looked to him as a role model and substitute father.

Merilar and Iluhin had cracked shell next to each other, might easily have each been the first thing the other saw.

Losing a clutchmate was worse than anything but losing a child.

And not just having that child walk away, although he regretted that painfully.

"We should," he agreed. "If we pick another target, we need to do better sweeps, and no more houses for a while."

"I have an idea," Merilar said, finally. "We could make Verahin's life difficult."

Going after Verahin was not what he would have thought of, but if Merilar knew of a good way to annoy her without bringing the military down on them all, he would take it. Merilar must have known that. "Careful. We don't want *her* suspecting who might have targeted her."

"Don't worry. I'm thinking some judicious sabotage. Nobody need even see who did it."

"Be careful of your biometrics then. The rail?"

"The rail."

Verahin's wealth came from shipping ola berries and juice, one of the few fruits ky'iin enjoyed, and a key ingredient in a certain liqueur this area was famous for. She was a staunch progressive, a supporter of the idea of expanding the Council of the World into the Council of Worlds, and allowing offworlders seats at the table.

Once that happened, once the tyrar and the glen were allowed to be equals to ky'iin, there was no putting everything back the way it was. They belonged on their own planets. As did the Ky'iin.

"Do it," he said, finally. "Spare me the details, just make sure nobody actually gets hurt."

There could be no intentional killing. Not right now. Not unless it really was the best way to achieve something. It rarely was.

2

VIYAR STOOD ON THE SHORE. The waves washed up against the stones of the beach. This wasn't a sandy beach like the next cove, and it was gray and black, the colors of ky'iin hide. The wind came off the sea and lin tongue tasted the salt that blew in on it.

It was almost unbearably hot.

This was where they had found the body of a young woman. They had identified her as Iluhin.

A local. This was a backwater, the kind of place where men still put eggs in piles of vegetation rather than incubators, because incubators were expensive and had to be shipped a good distance.

Where people mostly lived off of fish.

The likely official verdict was going to be suicide, but Viyar smelled carrion. Void, ly thought.

Suicide.

She'd drowned herself. It was all but open and shut, no signs of a struggle, except for one thing:

Motivation.

People didn't kill themselves without a good reason. Especially not young, healthy women with full lives in front of them. Viyar walked to the edge of the water. It was shallow here where she had washed up.

The light was fading towards evening, and ly could see the main station glittering, solar panels extended, making it almost like the moon Kyx did not possess. Ly had seen pictures of moons.

Ly glanced up at it for a moment, then over to where ly knew another station orbited. That one was smaller and not visible. At least not yet.

Suicide.

Why had she killed herself? She hadn't been chronically ill, which many traditional ky'iin believed to be a perfectly acceptable reason.

Heck, many modern ky'iin believed that there was still a place for it; the "not able to keep up with the hunt" idea might be outdated, but if one's quality of life was poor, taking the early exit could be seen as a very rational decision.

Not keeping up with the hunt.

They had the body at the morgue. Ly should look at it, as open and shut as the case was per forensics.

No.

Ly would find no answers there. Ly headed, instead, into the village, where ly could talk to the people who had known her.

Tease out why she might have done this.

There was more going on here, or ly wouldn't have been here.

The village was wood and clapboard and worn by the salt of the sea, but there was something about it that still spoke of home.

LY WALKED INTO THE VILLAGE. Three young children, so similar they had to be from the same clutch ran past him, chasing each other. They were barely clad.

Ly lifted a hand to them in polite signal, but was ignored. They were focused on their game, on each other, living in that world children lived in before adult concerns fell down on them like a weight.

Ly felt old. Ignoring the children for now, ly headed for the tavern. In a place this size, it would be the social gathering for everyone, of all ages. An old ly'ir leaned against the wall outside and ly frowned.

The other had a pipe.

Smoking was rude. But perhaps not here, and ly was not, after all, smoking *inside*. And ly was not a community officer to tell them to stop.

No, ly was something much more sinister and less obvious. Ly stepped into the tavern. Like the houses it was wooden walls and a roof that stayed up because they were falling into each other not away from them. Unlike them it had open windows in the walls, allowing alcohol and food to be passed outside to the patio. A brilliant red and blue snake was coiled in the rafters, no doubt *not* a wild snake. Snakes were the best vermin control in this climate.

A woman and a ly'ir were engaged in an animated conversation that was taking up much of the open floor. Others were watching them and ly was pretty sure bets were being taken. Ly was not sure whether this was a conversation that had got heated, a local debating contest or a full out *kila* session.

Ly gave them a wide berth. Ly was leaning towards the last option and while *kila* was meant to prevent violence, it could sometimes turn into violence. Ly certainly did not want to have to demonstrate lir skills in that regard.

Ly made it to the bar, where a couple of women were drinking. Ly pulled out lir badge and showed it to the barkeep.

A small man, he widened his eyes, but managed not to cringe too much.

Nobody wanted a special investigator on their patch. They often found things *other* than what they were investigating. Things people would rather stayed hidden. Like tax evasion, say.

Tax evasion was no doubt rampant in a place like this. They would rather govern themselves and pay for themselves and things like space and offworlders were practically a myth to them.

Ly knew.

Ly grew up somewhere just like this, albeit in the mountains not on the coast.

"I'm just looking for people who knew Iluhin." Ly didn't bother giving her full name; she was no doubt the only Iluhin or similar in the village, if not in the six villages around. Clan names were for disambiguation.

They were unfriendly.

"Shame what happened to her," the barkeep said finally, his accent mostly visible in his hands and shoulders.

"We're just making sure it really was..."

"Nobody would have had..." He tailed off. He swallowed. As if he had just thought of something he didn't want to think of. Finally, "You'll make yourself very unpopular if you press."

"I'm a special investigator. We're *always* unpopular."

As USUAL, ly had stumbled across something larger than one dead woman.

As usual.

Ly swore that the Void had it in for lin. Ly had yet to meet a human to introduce lin to the concept of Murphy's Law, or ly would no doubt have been cursing out that not-so-worthy personage.

Yet, ly had known this was no simple suicide. Then there was the timing. The newest offworld delegation was docked with that station right now. A species that called themselves humans. Bipedal, live bearers like the tyrar, quite aggressive by all accounts.

Viyar would rather deal with an honestly aggressive species. A predator that they could understand and work with.

The timing, though.

Not everyone wanted anything to do with offworlders, which ly quite understood. The question of whether they had myoran was always open, always uncertain.

Ly had only met a couple of tyrar. They did not think like ky'iin, but they were still people. How *could* they think like ky'iin? They had no ly'iin, they gave birth instead of laying eggs, and they lived in bonded groups. They did not hunt.

The timing.

Ly accepted a drink from the barkeep, a local brew that smelled fantastic, then, casually, "Anything to do with the house that got blown up?"

Ly picked up on the tells. Ky'iin can lie as easily as any other social being, but detecting lies is, perhaps, easier for them.

Yes.

A vacation home. It should have been empty. It wasn't. A young woman committing suicide. How had ly not connected the dots until now?

The home of one of the prime diplomats. Ly had not been there.

Just ly's brother.

And ly's brother-children, the nearest ly could have to offspring of lin own. A clutch of two too young to have their adult names. Viyar had no brothers to give him brother-children and sister-children were not the same thing, not really.

The thought of somebody killing even lin sister-children, though, was enough. Then the suicide.

Ly thought ly knew what was going on. And if ly was right it would lead to a small conspiracy, no doubt against the offworlders.

As lin left the tavern, warmed by drink and food, ly glanced up at the station again. Ly imagined ly saw the ships docked there. On one of them there was this human.

Ly wondered if anyone had warned them...her...what she was stepping into.

But for now, ly had terrorists to find.

3

"SPECIAL INVESTIGATOR," the barkeep warned him. "Intimidating. I'm sorry if I gave something away."

Dhyanil laughed weakly. "If you don't give something away to a special investigator then you're made of stone. I'll deal with lin if I have to."

He assumed the pronoun. The barkeep did not correct him. Most detectives were still ly'iin. Most, but not all.

It wasn't something you wanted people to be distracted from, after all. You needed that single-mindedness.

The smell of a woman on the edge of rut would certainly distract *him* even as he got older. He didn't want any more children.

He couldn't guarantee he would be able to make that choice, though, and that was as it should be.

Well, it wasn't unacceptable to give a clutch away to a man who had never managed to sire one, or to one who had no interest in women. It never had been.

"Let's not..."

"Don't worry. I'm not stupid." If the Special Investigator's body washed up on the beach, it wouldn't be Dhyanil's fault. He was quite willing to kill for the cause.

He wasn't willing to commit a high-profile murder that would get everyone involved in a tizzy, possibly bring in the army and *certainly* get a pair of the best investigators assigned.

Oh no.

He wasn't going to be that stupid. "Find out, if you can, if ly has any isolationist sympathies."

Special investigators were supposed to stay out of politics.

Nobody could be completely apolitical.

Knowing his luck they would be a rampant progressive practically wanting to mate with the offworlders.

He would likely have no choice but to put it all on Iluhin, who was dead and could no longer be harmed. Merilar would have to be so careful, though.

He might have to stop lin if ly had not already started lin plan to disrupt rail travel. Dhyanil was assuming a minor alteration to a train here or there, rather than a bomb on the tracks. A bomb on the tracks was simply not lin style.

Besides, lin had promised not to get anyone hurt. Dhyanil believed him; perhaps a foolish decision, but it was a decision he had made without hesitation.

He had to trust people. He was only one middle-aged male who could not be everywhere at once.

He left the tavern into the warm night, the residual heat of the day held by the clouds and humidity. It never got cold here.

Dhyanil had been cold once in his life, during an ill thought-out vacation.

It was not something he wanted to repeat. Above his head jewel-like satellites competed with the stars.

He needed a break. After this he was going to the hunting reserve where the skies were clear of light pollution, and mostly of hardware. Not to hunt. Just to pretend that he was living before any of this, before the world became what it was. To pretend he could exist in that forgotten past. A past in which the idea of a sentient being that was not ky'iin was alien, except for skeletons from the ancient times.

A past in which males and females and ly'iin were what they were and didn't try to be anything else. He wanted that world. Perhaps he would even have been fine with a world where his only responsibility was his children. Right now that appealed. To some people it always would, and perhaps he had found an insight there, but it did not want to go away.

The main space station spun into view overhead. There was a ship docking with it. He couldn't tell what kind, not with his naked eye. He cursed it in his father's language, the old one, not spoken so often now.

The one they wanted so badly to preserve.

DHYANIL SPENT the next three days working. The primary industries of the coast were fishing and tourism, and his work was in the latter.

He acted as a kind of local concierge, working with travel agents and individuals to help them find offbeat locations. It let him steer people away from things the locals really did *not* want to share, and towards things which would make them money. Thus, he worked out of an office on the waterfront, his door always open except when the rain beat down.

Most of the interest right now was in fishing charters. He contemplated what to do with a request from a group of wealthy tyrar. They didn't want to fish, of course, just to spend time on the water and look for wildlife.

He didn't want them on his planet, much less in his town, but he swallowed his politics and gave appropriate advice. Including how they could get food. Tyrar were herbivores and ate very little animal protein, although they could and would sample fish.

He shuddered. They ate *livestock food* as far as he was concerned, yet another reason to keep them well away from him and from those he cared about. Perhaps he shouldn't be disgusted, but all he could see when he thought of them was trin chewing their hay.

Chew.

Chew.

That didn't even go into how they reproduced. Finishing the suggestions and making a note to be firmly somewhere else when the group showed up, he pulled up the news.

Some of it was good. A local artist had mated and was now dealing with a clutch of three eggs and still trying to make his deadlines. Dhyanil made a note to send tips and sympathy. Yes, it had once been much easier, but even he had to admit that Sheril's art should not be interrupted even for potentially-talented offspring.

Most of it was bad. News was *always* mostly bad, that was a law of nature and the way of things. Always.

The ship that had arrived carried the ambassador of the newest offworld race to be contacted. They called themselves humans, although she was also representing a second species, dolphins. Who were apparently aquatic and thus had managed to coexist.

Ky'iin would never have let them live. He shuddered a bit, looking at the picture of the human. Pale pink skin, thin tendrils grew out of its head. Fur, like the tyrar, but *only* on its head. An oddly curvy body.

Supposedly it was a woman, but she seemed too small for that, too fragile.

And the next piece of news was a train going off the rails. The driver had been killed.

Dhyanil was going to *kill* Merilar. Ly had *promised* and you didn't break promises.

No, he wouldn't literally kill lin, but by the time Dhyanil had finished with lin ly would be seriously considering following lin sister into the ocean. Then he thought about it.

Perhaps they would get lucky and this would distract the special investigator. Send lin off in another, wrong direction. He could hope. But still, Merilar could not get away with this, even if it had been an accident. Lin leash would have to be tightened no matter how much ly snarled about it.

MERILAR WAS WHITTLING, making some shape from the wood that had yet to emerge. Ly sat with lin back to the land, face to the water. Dhyanil came up behind lin and growled.

It was a hunting growl, and intimidating even from a man. It had the desired result of making lin jump almost lin own height into the air.

And cut lin hand on the knife. "Void it!" Ly stood, setting the knife down and glaring at Dhyanil. Behind lin, the waves crashed quietly against the shore.

Dhyanil fixed his eyes on lin. "You promised nobody would get hurt."

"I didn't do it."

"You said you were going to mess with the trains. I stupidly trusted you to have a good plan for doing that that wouldn't involve any killing."

"I did mess with the trains. I sabotaged the refrigeration system so the juice would go bad in transit." Lin tone was defensive, upset. Miserable.

If that was true, Dhyanil had to give lin points for cleverness. "Then who caused the derailment?"

"Are there no accidents in your world?" Merilar snapped. "You should have been an investigator."

Lin clearly did not mean it as a compliment. "In other words, you claim not to know." What other conclusion could he come to?

"I don't know of any sabotage that would have led to a derailment, no."

Could he have somebody else in his territory working at cross-purposes. "If I find you've lied to me..."

"You'll do what? Kill me?"

Dhyanil cared too much to do that. "You'll wish I had."

He was already coming up with some creative tasks to set Merilar to. Tedious, time consuming and unpleasant.

"I'm too old to ground."

"You aren't too old to put on punishment duty. Or you can say you're outside my authority and then I won't protect you when the Special Investigator pokes around."

He was gratified to see Merilar's slate skin lose some of its warmth, turning cool and blue.

"I see you get the picture."

"You have my word that I didn't derail the train."

"Go over what you *did* do and see if you did anything that could have, for example, caused a short circuit back into the brake system."

Merilar turned even bluer.

"You didn't think of that. Think of it." And then he turned and walked away, leaving the other to stew on that thought for a while.

He half hoped that would turn out to be the answer. Merilar got careless. Or perhaps lin was right. Perhaps it had simply been a rail accident, and he had become paranoid. He analyzed himself and his own thoughts. Yes, he was definitely paranoid. But people had been out to get him in the past and likely would be again. He decided he was allowed to be paranoid and walked down the waterfront to his home.

Where he lived alone, as a good man whose children were grown always did.

4

Ly'iin did not engage in sexual relationships. They did not come into rut like women, nor were they vulnerable to pheromones like men. Okay, there were rare exceptions. Viyar was not one of them.

In fact, ly often felt that was an advantage. Ly certainly felt it was one now. The woman walking down the street was either on the edge of rut or wearing pheromone perfume, a trick some might use to trap a specific man for later use, as it were.

If the latter, it said things about her that were not particularly flattering. Or perhaps Viyar was simply a prude. But ly was suspicious. In addition to the pheromones, she was dressed in cut back leather, revealing every bit of muscle she had and screaming "I am a good hunter." The teeth ringing her maw sparkled and ly was sure she had polished her scalp. Inwardly, ly sighed. Ly was not vulnerable to her tall, lean form, but her behavior was setting lin teeth on edge.

She stopped, a little bit away, tilting her head and then regarding lin in a way which might have made a lesser ky'iin feel like prey.

Any kind of prey.

Viyar had dealt with the type before. Ly stood lin ground then finally asked, without raising lin voice or exaggerating lin gestures, "What do you want?"

"I have information about that poor girl who drowned herself."

Ly didn't want to believe her; of course ly had to pursue any lead ly had, but there was definitely something about her that told lin she was no lady, as it were. "Then we should go somewhere we can talk more privately."

She nodded. "I know..."

Ly lifted a hand. "No. I have rented a temporary office. We're going there."

Ly was no fool. Following a strange woman into an unknown place was how investigators washed up on the same beach they found the victim on.

Not that she was giving lin that vibe, quite, and she acquiesced quickly enough to reduce, but never remove, lin suspicion of her.

She followed lin to the office, the faint scent of heat still coming off her.

Pheromone perfume. It could distract ly'iin even if they weren't affected by it, simply because they noticed it. She wasn't acting as if she was cycling.

Or she had Myr's syndrome, but Myr's syndrome was pretty rare. Ly wouldn't expect to run into it at random, although this was the kind of place where getting treatment might not be easy.

Ly didn't ask her about it. Just led her into the office and closed the door. In the confined space the scent was stronger.

"So, tell me what you want me to know."

Ly phrased it in a way designed to test her. What she wanted lin to know could be one of so many things. It could be information about the case.

She leaned in towards lin. "What I want you to know is that Iluhin killed herself because she was sick. Nothing more, nothing less."

It was a threat. Not in the words, but in what lay behind them. The importance of lin knowing this. The importance of lin dropping the case. That was what she wanted lin to know.

That ly should drop the case. That ly should rule it a suicide while the balance of the mind was disturbed and leave.

Ly responded, "How do you know this?"

"Iluhin was my daughter."

THE WOMAN LEFT. Viyar had no grounds to hold her.

No grounds to ask further questions. She explained that Iluhin had been secretly unstable for months, if not years, had held things together so well on the outside that it had destroyed her on the inside. It happened that way sometimes.

Sometimes you functioned until you didn't, and people who fell apart more obviously got the kind of help they needed. By intervention if necessary. And girls in the throes of puberty and first rut were...often more fragile, as little as they wanted to admit it.

It sounded like Iluhin's mother, who called herself Erehin, had tried and tried to get her daughter some help.

Medication. Therapy. Whatever she had needed. Ly didn't buy a word of it. It didn't explain the distracting perfume, in fact it explained it less. It certainly didn't explain why she had come in intimidating, hardly the image of a grieving parent.

They were more traditional here; she might not have had that much contact with her children. But even here, even on the coast, women took more of an interest in their offspring than back in the day. Back in the history books where some children might not even know who their mother *was*.

No. This place was not *that* traditional, despite their weird habits and odd ways of keeping track of things. Men still had rights, unlike some of the most distant communities in the south, where the old ways were far too strong and far too scary.

Viyar decided ly was going home for a bit after this case. Check on lin sister and her children. Check on family and the culture ly had been raised in, which wasn't that of the mainstream. Wasn't that of this place either. But far from making lin want to drop the case, she had raised all of lin suspicions.

Maybe she really was Iluhin's mother, but she had not set lin mind at lease. No, ly was going to do what was necessary.

Ly was going to find out why Iluhin had killed herself, and ly was not going to rest until ly had the answer. And how it was connected to the bombed house.

THE NEXT DAY ly went to the bombed out house. It was the logical next step. Nobody told a Special Investigator of Viyar's experience what was and was not in lin purview; that was why the barkeep had been so worried about lin presence.

Lin stomach full of a breakfast of fish and sausage, ly made lin way along the cliff on foot, having parked lin vehicle at the bottom.

Viyar always liked to approach a scene on foot. It gave it an immediacy, let lin get the scent of the place. There was not much left of the house. The smell of fire had long gone and most of what touched lin tongue was the scent of vegetation already starting to take over the abandoned site. Not that it would stay abandoned. Somebody would build over the site and the entire tragedy would be forgotten. The bomb had, lin suspected, been intended to destroy the building. It had been intended to be expensive for the owner.

Lin doubted they had intended to kill children.

Which might...if Iluhin had been involved somehow, perhaps she had killed herself rather than face the fact that she had harmed children. Ly shook lin head. Jumping to conclusions again. Or seeing patterns, something lin was almost too good at.

Hunches.

Lin walked over to the wreckage. Forensics got everything they could out of it. They knew exactly where the bomb had been planted. On the outside of the building, when things were quiet. Right outside the room the kids had been sleeping in.

They hadn't stood a chance.

Nobody wanted kids dead. Nobody sane anyway.

Unless, of course, they were another tribe's kids or offworlder kids.

Ly studied the blast pattern for a long moment.

They had come up from the beach, lin decided. There was a staircase there, a wooden one, somewhat rickety. A quick route from the summer home to the water on those hot days when you were reminded why you had fled the city.

The people who owned this house were rich. And pro offworlder. This had been aimed at one or the other of those things or both. Likely both. Nobody here was rich. The best houses were all second homes, owned by people who came in the winter to enjoy the warm beaches and fled before the summer heat.

If lin lived here lin would be tempted to do something to the rich folk too. Not this, but something. Maybe something involving trie eggs. Trie eggs were cheap and made a very satisfying mess when smashed.

Tasty too. Ly would have made linself hungry, but ly had eaten a big enough breakfast that even the thought of fried eggs wasn't enough to make lin feel anything like that. Ly walked over to the stairs. Hesitated. Then walked around the promontory.

Yes.

Here.

Ly had to check the currents, but ly had another hunch. One which could actually be proven with science. Ly would know soon enough if ly was right.

5

FINDING out what had happened with the train was not going to be easy. For once, Dhyanil was not entirely sure who he had to bribe.

Bribing the Special Investigator might have done it, *if* that worthy was paying attention and *if* bribing a Special Investigator wasn't dangerous.

If he got an honest one it could get him into huge trouble, even if it was only a fishing expedition.

They were more likely than the local peacekeepers to be honest. There was a zero tolerance for corruption. Made them hard to bribe. Not impossible, of course. They were still ky'iin, still fallible. But the consequences of being caught were heavy enough...

Easier to go for blackmail if you could get something on them. He wasn't sure he could. Ergo, he had to do his own legwork.

Passenger trains came along the same route but not the same track; nobody wanted to get stuck behind a freight train, so they were kept appropriately separate.

Had it been the train hit or the track? Public records indicated that the locomotive involved was older, which actually might have made it safer. He wasn't sure about the sheer level of automation of modern trains. They didn't need a driver any more.

He rather thought they should have one anyway, just in case. Just as a backup if the worst happened. It wasn't an entirely unpopular viewpoint. More jobs was good, especially if you disagreed with putting too many people on public support.

Artists and the like, sure.

Men who wanted to spend all their time with their kids, sure.

But people needed to be doing *something* with their time that wasn't sitting around playing games or whatever.

Which meant you kept jobs, even if they were supervising the automated systems.

You didn't build machines to take jobs. Because you didn't want people to get bored. People like him, of course, benefitted from bored people. That didn't mean he thought it was a good thing in the long run.

An older locomotive. It had a driver. Could it have been driver error? That certainly happened sometimes. People would make mistakes. Go too fast. Override the automatics because they thought they were wrong when they were right.

People were imperfect, but so were automatics. If he could get hold of the logs. He didn't want to wait for the official word to be released.

If he could look at the track. Wait. He *could* look at the track. Given where it was, a vehicle could get there, and no doubt there would be enough rubberneckers for his arrival not to be particularly suspicious.

He frowned, then he looked into renting a car. He didn't own one; he seldom had any desire to go past walking distance *or* he was going far enough to want to take a train or even fly. But he could rent one easily enough. If it was the track, one look would satisfy his curiosity. He was pretty sure it wasn't the track.

THE CAR WAS AUTOMATED. He kept an eye on it rather than relaxing with a video as some might. Just like the trains. Exactly like the trains.

You didn't trust unsupervised AIs. The tyrar had sentient AIs, it was rumored, which might be more or less trustworthy. He rather thought more. Something with emotions could make decisions that *weren't* entirely rational and thus could make better decisions. But he still let the car drive itself. Dhyanil was a backup system, but he was a backup system that would pay at least some attention; he wasn't going to fall asleep.

The road was decent, but not well trafficked. There really wasn't much out here. The settlements were on the coast, and inland was the jungle. Various plantations spread across the land and at one point he had to wait while farm machinery, some kind of harvester, sluggishly crossed the road in front of him. He recognized most of the trees being grown.

Recognized, also, the carefully positioned patches of natural jungle, habitat for wildlife and for game. This wasn't a hunting reserve, but these corridors and patches helped animals move around and avoid people. From the spindly kryl trees, thy'iin squawked as they coordinated their hunting. They were the loudest of the animals. They avoided people.

Avoided other predators. Ate. Lived.

Sometimes he envied them. All they had to worry about was eating, mating, and clutching. Yet they were animals. They had no myoran, no true abstract thought, no ly'iin to guide them through childhood into maturity and wisdom.

Only ky'iin and their two closest living relatives had three sexes. He was no biologist to wonder about it. He knew what he had learned in school about the origin and the reality of ly'iin. But he didn't care except...except that they mattered.

Rather, he assumed that it was a gift of sentience...and proof that the offworlders had no true myoran. Tyrar had two sexes. Glen had none or one, depending on how you wanted to look at it.

Humans, apparently, had two. A binary without the third leg to support it. Ly'iin were needed, even if he was glad he wasn't one. He loved his children, the one thing ly'iin could never have.

The car hit a pothole and he realized that he was breaking his own rules, not paying nearly enough attention to the road and what the autopilot was doing.

Then he realized it was raining. A sudden rapid storm, no doubt it would not last long. For safety's sake he had the car pull over at an overlook to wait it out. Stationary, he pulled out his personal terminal and started looking at the news again.

The memorial service for the ly'iin who had been killed negotiating with the humans was in two days. He scowled, thinking about how much pomp and circumstance they were giving lin...even as they negotiated treaties and arrangements with the offworlders who had killed lin.

At least he assumed that. He had not bothered reading the articles on what had happened. Of course omnivorous offworlders were dangerous.

After all, ky'iin were dangerous. Anyone who could go toe to toe with them was as dangerous.

And that was exactly why they should stay on their own world. He would not agree with those who thought the only good offworlder was a dead one. He just didn't want them here.

The rain beat down harder, and he was going nowhere any time soon. He decided the best course of action was a nap.

HIS NAP LASTED SLIGHTLY LONGER than planned; there was still enough light to get to the place and see what was going on, but the tropical night would fall before he could return. He had the car look up a place to get food before heading back. He wasn't fussy, just somewhere affordable and clean.

The rubberneckers had been and gone. There was still a crane, which had presumably been used to right the fallen locomotive, but the train itself was already gone. It wasn't, as he had suspected, the track. No sign of damage to the rails, no sign of debris on the rails.

He sat in the car staring at the curve. Brake failure? Most likely. But he found himself believing Merilar. True, the young ly'iin could have sabotaged the brakes, could have weakened them so when the train hit this curve...

Or it could have been the accident ly claimed. At least it hadn't been a passenger train. True, nobody had been killed in a passenger train accident in decades. Or in a freight accident in years, which brought up another possibility. Had the driver had a medical emergency while she had been in direct control of the train? Modern medical monitoring made that less likely. So did automation.

It still happened, and not everyone had a medical implant. Void, Dhyanil had always refused one. But he still got his vitals checked regularly for any warning signs, especially as he got older.

It was merely the smart thing to do, even if some people would insist on politicizing the situation. They would scream about their privacy rights, but only theirs. Mostly it was central valley folk, the people of temperate areas and calm climates. They had never understood what it was like in the mountains, where men had long held the true reins of power. Or on the coast, where men had once been property and had fought to balance their rights with the traditions of the people they loved.

He was one of those men; he didn't want to be owned by his father's sister or lyka, rented out to women for breeding, used as a servant. But he still didn't want every part of the past to be thrown away. He drove away to the restaurant the car recommended, based on aggregate reviews. It was good enough that anyone who was monitoring this would think he'd taken the day for a drive and a good meal.

Inside, it smelled as good as the reviews said. And tasted that way. He might not have achieved anything but elimination, but he hadn't wasted his day. He made a note of the place for future recommendation and then relaxed to enjoy his meal.

There were worse ways to spend his time.

6

VIYAR WALKED DOWN THE BEACH. The stones crunched under lin boots, and the scent of salt was so overpowering that ly more than once scrunched lin maw closed against it.

Ly was not a coastal ky'iin, ly was not *used* to the salt.

Ly could find no actual evidence connecting the explosion and Iluhin. The barkeep had been the most willing to talk to lin and that had not exactly counted.

The barkeep knew far more than he had said. But even plying him with currency had not resulted in anything useful.

He was afraid. That much Viyar knew.

They were traditional here to a point. Only to a point. Lin was pretty sure that women in rut were not taking men as they chose without regard to consent or anything else.

But men were definitely the lowest status, confined primarily to caring and nurturing jobs and to childrearing.

Women did the fishing, gathering what was both sustenance and what there was of a cash economy here. These fisheries had collapsed once, but been brought back from the brink.

Ly liked what ly saw there. The ocean was healthy. Tourism was also growing. But this was never going to be lin place. Where ly came from, the reins of power were held primarily by the fathers. Including lin father, who lin loved.

Ly knew lin life was in danger. Ly had heard a name whispered, although lin did not have a clear knowledge of it.

Dhy something.

What ly could hope was that they would be too afraid to actually kill a Special Investigator. No, they would, having failed to scare lin off, try the next thing before that.

They would mislead lin.

Ly had to be very careful. Ly had ordered an audit of Iluhin's accounts, for what it was worth in a society that often still used cash.

Nobody in the big cities used cash anymore, not even the poor. Out here on the fringes of civilization, in one of the last places ky'iin had reached.

There were even rumors of my'iin sightings in recorded history here; the ky'iin's defeated semi-aquatic cousins. Lost to civilization and time.

Ly hit the sand. Ly did not register why until afterwards. The pop of a weapon. So, apparently, somebody wasn't going to mislead lin after all. They'd gone right to trying to kill lin.

Ly rolled away, diving into the water. Ly could hold lin breath for a while; a skill ly had long practiced. It might not be long enough. Maybe. Ly dived into the water. Started to swim out to sea. Shallow water fish gathered around lin, curious. They would make chaff to distract the shooter. Whoever they were.

Another shot, the sound of it altered by the water. Old school firearms. Hunting weapons. Maybe this was another attempt to scare lin off. Ly dived as deep as the water would let lin and swam along the shore.

There were no more shots.

VIYAR CLIMBED out of the water and shook linself off. Lin clothes were wet, but they would dry quickly enough in this heat.

Lin heart rate was slowly returning to normal. Slowly. Ly had been shot at before; it was an occupational hazard of lin job.

Most people wouldn't dare.

Somebody had dared.

Lin had to find the person behind all of this. If they were a danger they could be removed. If they were not, then they could be leveraged.

Used to keep their people in order.

Dhy, whoever they were, could be a mortal enemy or a natural ally. In a place like this, there was almost always somebody in the shadows.

Almost always.

Ly went back to the tavern. Ly took care *not* to get to dry on the way. Ly had a point to make.

As Viyar walked in, the place went silent. Ly was wet and smelled of brine, so there was no surprise ly caught all of the attention. Ly waited that moment and then spoke, "Somebody tried to kill me. I'd like to know who it is."

Silence.

The barkeep wasn't even cleaning glasses. Just staring.

"I'll be waiting. I would also like to know who killed Iluhin."

More silence.

No, ly knew she had indeed committed suicide, but it would tell lin something.

The barkeep poured a drink. Offered it to lin wordlessly. It was warm.

Ly took it, unafraid of poison. Ly had made lin point. Ly did not, however, pay for it. It warmed lin up, perhaps it was indeed something the locals drank after a shock.

Then the barkeep muttered to lin. "You need to talk to Dhyanil."

Dhyanil.

The name lin needed. The name was going to be enough, in a place this size, to find the person. A man, from the suffix.

This was a place where men had been property not all that long ago. Ly was, thus, not surprised that the secret mastermind was a man. They had to learn to hold power subtly, unsupported by either legal position or physical might. Shooting lin on the beach? That was a womanly thing to do. And here, in the back of beyond, that still mattered.

It was also not entirely an honorable thing to do. That mattered too.

7

"SPECIAL INVESTIGATOR'S ONTO YOU."

Dhyanil glared at the barkeep. "Because you mentioned my name."

"I *muttered* your name. Lin can't have hearing that good." The barkeep was lying. It was in every motion of his hands.

"This is a small town. There's only one Dhy in town. He's going to find me soon enough." And there was only one tavern in town. Which meant that he had to put up with the barkeep lying. No doubt the special investigator had bribed him. Or scared him.

No other place to get the microbrews he preferred. But it was, at some levels, fine. He was always going to have to confront the ly'iin.

Always.

He just would have preferred a little more time to plan for it.

"I did warn you I intimidate easily."

That was a point. "You sure do," Dhyanil said with a slight growl, and was gratified as the younger man flinched away.

Flinching from another man *definitely* meant he was easy to intimidate. But then, Dhyanil could probably get him fired.

Did he care enough to do so? He decided it was best to let the man stew for a bit. Let him wonder if Dhyanil was going to go after his job.

Worse punishment than actually doing it; besides he sympathized.

He'd seen the ly'iin from a distance. Ly was huge. Ly was bigger than most females, and that was relatively unusual. Far from unheard of, but unusual.

Dhyanil could not swear that instinct would not take over and make him quail from a ly'iin *that* large, especially one trained in intimidation.

"You owe me," he growled finally and slipped out of the building. Or tried to.

His mother was there. "We have a problem." She was old, wrinkled in places, but still formidable and huge and dressed for the hunt.

If there was anyone who could intimidate him even more, it was his mother. "What problem?"

"Meruhin ran away."

Dhyanil felt a headache start behind his eyes. "Ran away?"

"Ran away. Screamed at her dad about how he was wrong about everything and left."

A young girl's wanderlust combined with...combined with who knew. "Do you need my help finding her?"

"Please. She may have hopped the train."

Kids hopped the trains. Usually they got caught and sent home. Sometimes they got killed. That fact didn't, ever, stop the next batch from doing it. It was the way kids were, he thought wryly. They would always hop the trains. Some things would never change. He wondered what they had done before there were trains. Just ran, he supposed.

"May have? We know she has. And...don't tell me she was looking for offworlders."

"Who knows what she's looking for. You won't understand. But I think, yes, she hopped the train. It's what I would have done."

It was almost always girls. Occasionally ly'iin. Boys were never that reckless.

Modern science tried to claim there was no difference. He knew better.

HOPPED THE TRAINS. And he thought about the derailment; which had now been ruled driver error combined with mechanical failure.

The driver had failed, the automatic backups had failed the driver. People couldn't use this one to argue either way.

It hadn't been anything to be mad about.

Dhyanil felt as if he was being mad far too much of the time lately, but he also wasn't sure what he could do about it.

Now Meruhin. She was the daughter of his maternal half sister, a relationship that wouldn't even have been tracked in the old days. Of course, it was good to track those relationships. Reduced inbreeding.

But it didn't really make her his niece, not really. A niece was the daughter of a full or paternal half brother. It didn't make her his responsibility.

Except, of course, she *was* his responsibility. Her father's goal of keeping her out of things until she was an adult had backfired; she was curious and she wanted to know everything about the world.

He knew where kids hopped the trains. She would have walked quite some distance to do it, but a girl in the throes of wanderlust would do such things. She wouldn't even realize her hormones were shouting louder than her reason right now.

He had to find her and bring her home. Possibly get her on ovulation suppressors now rather than later; almost all women took them when they weren't planning on children. But the question was whether... She had to have gone north. If she was looking for offworlders, then she was going to the spaceport.

Dhyanil sighed. He might have to go to the spaceport to find her. Not a trip he was looking forward to. Of course, it was rare for offworlders to get permits to land. He wished it was impossible, but at least it wasn't a floodgate. Most of them were on the main space station. Sky City, they called it.

He turned back to town. Thinking about the trip made him remember that even this place had a name, a moniker by which it was referred.

White Fish.

Because that was what the fisherfolk commonly caught. The old ways, the women out on the boats, the men back with the nets, the ly'iin selling the fish to the next town. Those ways were gone and Dhyanil knew they couldn't be brought back.

Meruhin had to be found and dragged back before she got to talk to any offworlders. Who knows what she would let slip.

———

HE TOOK a car to the place where the kids hung out, not the good kids, but the troublemakers. The ones who might hop a train. He'd never hopped the train; he'd had friends try to talk him into it, just for a joyride.

He'd resisted the temptation and now they remembered him as the smart and sensible one. Probably why he had ended up in this unexpected position of leadership.

There were some kids on the verge of adolescence hanging around. A mixed group; they wouldn't start splitting by gender for now. One was starting to turn female; he could both see it and, slightly, smell it. Soon she would hit her growth spurt and tower over her brothers. Her hide had that peculiar mottling often associated with puberty, especially where her small crest would grow.

"Hey," he called to the kids.

"Hey grandpa."

He didn't take it as an insult. To them he probably *did* look old enough to be somebody's grandfather.

"Looking for a girl. Any of you know Meruhin?"

"She left," the half-female said in a voice that hovered between childhood light and adult deep, every gesture of her body language defensive. Her hands kept lifting towards her face between words.

"Gotta find her before she gets herself hurt."

"You mean so you can haul her back and get her dad to ground her for life."

"What her dad does to her isn't my choice." She was female, but she was still a child; there was nothing intimidating about her. "We're concerned."

"She didn't get hurt hopping the train. But I'm not telling you where she went."

"Wasn't expecting you to. Wanted to make sure she *did* hop the train before I tried to work out where she hopped off."

The girl lifted her hands to her maw.

He smiled. "Age and treachery," before turning away. It was honestly more information than he had expected from them.

It was the answer he had expected. Unless, of course, she was lying, but no. That chagrin couldn't be faked. She felt as if she'd let Meruhin down.

But she'd also wanted to reassure a man that the girl was okay. Instinct and socialization.

And it was mostly instinct. Things might be different in the tyrar, who's men had external genitalia visible from birth.

But you didn't know with kids

And it was bad to know. If you knew, you would change how you raised them.

Or would that be better? When you realized the others were growing faster than you, their voices changing. When you felt the ache around your pelvis and realized this was it; you were going to be the least powerful sex, the one who cared, the one who nurtured.

You had to accept or rebel, those were your two options. Except it was more complicated than that.

He glanced back. The passenger train roared through. That wasn't the one you hopped. It went so fast, streaking across the countryside. Uniting the planet, taking people to the airport where they could fly.

Meruhin wouldn't fly. She needed an ID for that.

She'd ride the freights like the kids always did, hop off when she thought she was in the capital or the spaceport. His mind went over the route. He *thought* he knew where she had gone.

8

IT POURED WITH RAIN. This was not unexpected, and Viyar had made plans to spend the rest of the day indoors, the storm shutters closed. It was the very start of the wet season.

There was a lot of tension, so much so that ly was not entirely sure what to do about it. A girl had gone missing, although that was not unusual.

There had been a report of gunshots on the beach.

...and there was a bang on the door. A loud one. Ly stood up to open it. The rain came charging in, wrapped around the form of a middle-aged man who stumbled into the office.

Drip.

Drip.

"Are you alright?" Viyar asked.

The man didn't answer right away, being too busy dripping. Then he shed his light purple, waterproof coat. "That will teach me to look at the weather forecast."

Drip.

"Hold on." The temporary office was only really a shack, but it did have the facility to make a pot of min. Viyar put one on.

That caused the man to visibly relax. "You wanted to talk to me. I figured I would save you the trouble of tracking me down."

"You're Dhyanil."

He turned his head in a ky'iin nod. "Yes."

"And you don't like me." Viyar was not stupid.

"I don't trust Special Investigators. You must be at least somewhat used to that by now."

Truthfully, Viyar *was* more than somewhat used to it. It was part of reality, and part of the job. "I am. But you also don't trust offworlders."

"Do you?"

Viyar considered the question with more honesty than ly might otherwise have given it, mostly in the interests of giving the man a fair hearing. "I suppose it depends."

"You probably don't trust anyone in your job."

"It's not how we're trained, no. But the answer is that I would trust an offworlder as much as I understood how their motivations were likely to work."

"And can we ever understand that? I don't even understand women most of the time."

Viyar laughed a bit. "We can try. And we can accept they aren't going to be us or think like us. But I'm guessing you'd rather they all went home."

"I would rather they stayed home and we stayed here rather than exploring further. We just got our nose bloodied."

"And now we have a treaty."

"With the people who attacked us for no reason," Dhyanil pointed out.

"They must have had a reason. Perhaps not one we understand, but a reason.

Dhyanil shifted uncomfortably, "Okay, bluntly. I didn't kill Iluhin. I grieve her as much as anyone else, if not more. And you are safe from me."

Viyar poured the min, offered the man a cup. "I believe you."

"Don't get me wrong, the idea of killing you crossed my mind, but I knew that would only bring down more attention."

Viyar took a sip from his own drink. "And the explosion."

"It was all Iluhin's idea," Dhyanil said, finally. "Blowing up that house. She was young, she wanted to strike a blow for us. It was supposed to be empty. She..."

"Couldn't live with what she did." Viyar sipped lin min, then turned back to the male. "I already worked that out. The question is what she thought she was going to achieve."

"It's about..."

"Annoying people? That doesn't work. You need to scare them. Or you need to convince them which side their bread is buttered on." Viyar studied the man. "And we as a society need to work out exactly how much we're going to trust the offworlders."

No, ly wasn't an isolationist. But ly could pretend to have sympathy for them if it would help lin find out the truth. And there *was* a point to being wary of aliens. There always would be.

AFTER THE MEETING WITH DHYANIL, Viyar felt both more and less comfortable about leaving the office. The rain had stopped, leaving everything fresh and damp, water pooling under lin feet where the sidewalk dipped. The sky and sea were still gray. The beach, no doubt, was quite slippery right now. It would be better if it was sand, but those stones... Anyone who went down there was likely to get wetter than intended.

Ly walked along the waterfront nonetheless, staying on the still wet boardwalk. It felt like a moment out of time. A moment that could have happened any time in the last thousand years. Most people would be working or, in the case of the fisherwomen who had gone out before the storm, resting.

Ly was alone.

Ly knew Dhyanil wanted him dead. The man had as much as admitted to it. He wanted the offworlders gone.

He was too dangerous to leave in place but also too dangerous to remove. Taking him off to rehab would only cause his replacement, likely with somebody less reasonable.

Turn him? That would take more resources, Viyar suspected, than ly had.

It would take something Ly didn't have, but perhaps could get. Ly glanced up at the space station again. It was possible. It was very possible.

The ground shook.

Ly looked around.

The ground shook again.

Ly looked at the ocean. It was slowly retreating, drawing back and away. Ly ran. As ly did so ly pulled out a device from lin pocket. Time to use lin Special Investigator powers for good.

"Override local broadcast, code B71657. Tsunami! Get to high ground!"

Everyone who grew up on the coast knew that if the ocean left you didn't go looking for it. Ly didn't have to worry about them not under-standing.You ran inland, you ran for the highest ground you could find. Because the ocean was coming back.The ocean was coming back and Viyar ran with everything that was in lin. Then ly turned.

Dhyanil had obviously not gone far. He was running too, but he had apparently injured himself, he limped, he hobbled. Viyar measured the time. Tried to measure the wave. Ran. Grabbed the man and threw him over broad ly'iin shoulders, then ran inland once more.

Ly kept running until the wave washed inwards...then lin grabbed a sturdy tree. The water washed over them, a roar in lin ears and then darkness. Silence.

VIYAR WOKE UP IN A BED. It was obviously a clinic, white walls and a decidedly uncomfortable mattress. The faint smell of antiseptic touched lin tongue. Gingerly, ly felt lin scalp and was unsurprised to find a bit of a lump.

Lin tried to sit up properly and coughed. Ly had no idea how ly got there, but had to assume ly had been pulled out of the water by somebody.

A nurse entered, a small man with a reddish tinge to his hide that spoke of an ancestry on the western continent, "Awake."

"How long was I out?"

"Not long. A couple of hours since we pulled you out of the water. Thanks, by the way."

Lin warning had, then, saved lives. That was... "There was a man with me."

"He's in the other room, still out."

"Any chance you can discharge me before he wakes up?" ly asked, wryly, sitting up the rest of the way so ly could talk properly.

"You know him, then."

"Let's say we aren't friends."

But that hadn't kept lin from grabbing him. Ly analyzed lin own feelings. Was ly just being a decent person? Had it been instinctual? "I don't want him to know he owes me," ly said, finally.

"Unfortunately, we have to keep you until tomorrow for concussion observation."

Viyar sighed. "I know."

Ly had mostly been joking. And hopefully, Dhyanil would be alive, fine, but in no condition to talk or at least to want to talk for a while.

"Do you have an appetite?"

"Not really. I suppose I should eat something." Or maybe ly didn't have an appetite for hospital broth. Who did?

"Let me check with the doctor."

He left. Viyar was not restrained, they were trusting lin to know how to act. Ly was wearing a gown. Lin possessions, those not ruined by the water, were presumably around somewhere. Hopefully the buildings had held against the tsunami. Earthquakes were common enough here that people knew to build for them.

Everything was backed up anyway. Ly was sure lin portable terminal was a dead loss, not to mention lin clothes.

The nurse came back. With a bowl of broth.

Sigh.

9

DHYANIL WAS RELEASED from the hospital after a couple of days, although he was still a mass of bruises. The smell of the air after the rain might have made him feel better, but he was not sure anything would.

Thanks to the investigator he wasn't broken.

Just angry.

There was something about being saved by somebody he considered an enemy that was just painful. It didn't help that the investigator was ly'iin, stirring old instincts.

The ones that wanted to let people protect him. Were they instincts or socialization? He figured he would never know, and he didn't want to. Men were *supposed* to want to be protected.

It was that he wanted to choose who got to protect him. But had he been the larger and fitter of the two, he would have done the same thing.

He just...

He didn't want to owe the ly'iin. He didn't want to, because that could be used against him, and put together in ways he didn't like.

You definitely didn't want to owe a debt to a Special Investigator. They weren't like the local peacekeepers, who were part of their community and spent more time talking old Priahin out of her latest stupidity than anything else. She refused to go into a retirement community and would not acknowledge that her mind was not what it had once been.

Dhyanil couldn't entirely blame her. He couldn't swear to the fact that he might not go into denial himself in the same situation. Nobody wanted to admit they were losing their mind.

He stalked along the waterfront. The tsunami should have been recognized. There should have been warning. But this was an unimportant place and it wasn't tourist season. Nobody cared.

He knew where she had gone, but he had lost three days. By now she would have vanished into the capital city, unnoticed amongst a thousand other girls. They would have to involve the authorities, get her hauled back that way. Far more embarrassing for the child. She could go haring off to the capital when she was of age and out of school. Or she could apply to university there.

He hoped she wouldn't, too many foreign ideas. But she could, and she *was* a smart child. She could be a doctor. But they had to find her.

His plan of going to the capital to find her himself was on indefinite hold. He was afraid to leave. He took that fear, examined it. The Special Investigator knew exactly who he was. Suspicion would fall on others if he took off.

Unless he told the ly'iin what he was doing. There might be sympathy. Surely the Special Investigator, who was older than Dhyanil, had chased down a wayward girl in lin life.

He would tell lin. Just not anything more. Play it as just a girl with wanderlust running to the capital for adventure. Just make sure he didn't find out how much Meruhin might know.

NOT RIGHT AWAY, though. Right away, Dhyanil knew he had to start planning his next move; and he rather thought his next move would also take him to the capital.

The human ship that had arrived. That would be a target worth taking on and more than worth taking out. It would be a target he could be proud to deal with.

But how?

They had their own dark network. He found his way back home, which had thankfully been closed up. There was salt water and seaweed all over the exterior, but inside was fine.

Albeit smelling a little of salt.

Well. He was used to that. His computer worked; he wasn't trusting this to anything but old-fashioned wires.

Checking the boards. Finding out what his rivals and questionable allies were up to.

One of them had an insider on the station. The plan was to poison the human ambassador. Apparently, humans could eat ky'iin food, albeit with some supplementation as they were omnivores, not carnivores.

He frowned. He wouldn't try to poison an alien, but the plan didn't look like it would endanger anyone other than whatever chef they were bribing or blackmailing to get it done. Probably bribing.

He thought about that. Living on the station. Cooking food for offworlders. They had to be something of a radical. They also had to be desperate. Probably he. Even there, probably a man. Many women were still above learning that particular profession.

Dhyanil wondered if he would take the money. He supposed it depended on how much he cared about getting on with the offworlders. He wouldn't throw out his own principles in return for money.

Then somebody called him. He pulled them up on the screen. His mother.

"Are you better?"

"Mostly."

"They aren't funding the seismic warning system properly." Her tone was dry and aimed squarely at a provincial government that did not always care about small towns.

Of course she would put it at their feet, but as he had been inclined to do so himself, he could hardly criticize her for it. "I'm going to see what I can do about Meruhin."

"The little so-and-so's on the space station!"

"What?" Dhyanil jumped about a foot in the air, the desire to pounce and rend flowing through him. "How did she manage *that*?"

"Stowed away on a shuttle, apparently. And went right to the human ambassador and requested formal sanctuary. She's going to tell them everything!"

Meruhin was a child. Somebody was going to poison the ambassador. Dhyanil felt a coldness flow through him.

He would not even *contemplate* that. In fact, he sent a warning to the poisoner, anonymous, telling them there was a ky'iin child in the embassy and to be careful.

"We have to go get her. Bring her back."

His mother's shoulders fell. "She has me mad enough..."

"She's a star struck child who dreams of spaceships," Dhyanil said. "We make sure whatever she tells them is worthless. And we bring her home."

He was going to have to go to the space station.

He wouldn't trust anyone else to do it.

He couldn't.

HE QUIETLY MADE preparations for a trip.

The idea of going into space terrified him. He wasn't afraid of seeing an offworlder; he had before, albeit not a human. Tyrar came to the coast sometimes. Even more rarely, glyn, who would would stalk along the beaches like living and moving sculptures and buy whatever kind of fruit juice anyone would sell them, sucking it through their mandibles. Like nothing which had ever walked Kyx before.

It was the idea of doing something as frankly unnatural as flying out of the atmosphere in a spaceplane, docking with the station. Breathing canned air. Drinking...he didn't even want to *think* about recycled water.

Everything on a planet was recycled, but it was a long cycle. You didn't need to think about where the water came from.

Oh, he knew with filtration it was perfectly safe.

He still didn't want to think about it. He checked the rules. He checked the ticket cost and flinched slightly. It wasn't the ridiculous amount it had been ten, or even five, years ago, but it was still an expensive flight, and that was on top of flying to the capital. Or taking the train.

He weighed those two things in his mind as he finished packing and checked the news. No mention of a girl seeking sanctuary with the humans.

Good that they were keeping it quiet.

There was some talk about the human ship. And about the memorial service tomorrow. He would have to watch that.

Train was better, he decided. Slightly slower, but with the shuttle schedule he wouldn't really lose any time. More comfortable. You could spread out more on a train. You could watch what you wanted to watch. Or the scenery.

There wasn't really scenery from a plane, especially as the rainy season closed in. The skies were cloudy more often than they were clear, although not so much near the spaceport, which had been built with that in mind.

He bought train tickets. Open return, as he had no idea how long this would take.

He optimistically bought a second return ticket for Meruhin. He was worried for her. He was worried somebody would ignore her age and take her out as a traitor to the cause. Which she was.

When they got her back, he wondered if the best thing to do was talk to her father about boarding school. Call her a loss, send her to the capital for education. Make sure she never heard anything else she could use against them. Let her lead her life. When they finally got rid of the offworlders, she would understand. Or it wouldn't matter.

That was the best course of action.

Meruhin probably didn't want to come home anyway. If he planned this right, everyone could be happy.

Assuming she didn't get poisoned.

Assuming that.

10

THE OFFICE HAD SURVIVED, thanks to Viyar remembering to properly lock and seal the door on lin way out. It was, however, covered in seaweed.

Which was pretty much the state of the town. People were already cleaning up. Ly had heard of only one death, somebody who had been fishing when the quake hit, out on a remote beach with her phone turned off.

There were questions as to why it had not been predicted. Seismology was not an exact science, and predictions were as weather predictions had once been. Not quite something you watched to see what wouldn't happen, but not something you could count on.

As it happened, Viyar hadn't been the only person who had seen the sea leave and given warning. That made lin feel better. Ly would have hated to feel as if if ly had not been there, more people would have died. Lin didn't like that particular kind of responsibility.

Dhyanil was also recovering, although Viyar had not heard from him. No doubt the isolationist was embarrassed to owe lin a debt and ignoring lin.

Right now, ly sat in the bar, watching people drink. Ly wanted a drink or two, but ly knew better. Ly needed to keep lin head clear.

Instead, ly watched from across the room, at least until lin (new) personal terminal beeped. Checking it, ly stood up and stepped outside. It was raining lightly, just that faint warm drizzle that most people would hide from, but which had never bothered those used to these climes.

Lin checked the terminal again.

They had to be kidding lin. A missing child, something which had not warranted the bureau's attention, had suddenly blown up. The child had been a girl going through puberty and it was thought she had most likely run away...that was often a risk with young women. They generally came back, but there was never any certainty that they would.

Wanderlust.

Good fathers found an outlet for it, for that memory of the time when girls left at puberty to join other communities. But *this* girl had managed to stow away on a freighter and showed up on the space station. In the human embassy. It all tied back to the isolationists. The human ambassador had given the child sanctuary.

Sanctuary. Which no doubt *somebody* had explained to her. Abuse, perhaps? But no, why run to an offworlder. Unless it was all tied in with the isolationists. The child's father was, needless to say, up in arms. In fact, her entire family was furious. And she was from here.

Viyar wanted to let lin head fall into lin hands. Ly had just solved this case. No. Ly had just resolved this part, this tiny section, of the case.

The case was a lot bigger than this.

Viyar closed down the office. But before ly left, ly had to talk to Dhyanil.

Ly found the man in his house. Surrounded by suitcases. He was packing. They formed a wall around him. Even for a man, Dhyanil was tiny. Heck, he wasn't that much bigger than the tiny human ambassador, literally the smallest adult sentient Viyar had ever seen, if the videos did her justice.

"What?"

"They found that girl who ran away. She ran to the *humans*, Dhyanil. What is going *on* on this coast?"

Ly wasn't even angry. Ly was confused.

"A movement to make sure we keep our myoran pure." Dhyanil closed the last of his three suitcases.

"That scared a girl so much she ran to offworlders."

Dhyanil took a deep breath. "We don't need the offworlders."

"Where are you going?"

Dhyanil took a visible deep breath. "She's kin to me. I'm going to the station to talk her into coming home. Before she embarrasses herself or her family further.

"I don't think you want to do that.

Ly could sense it, smell it. This was going to go south in some very, very bad ways.

"I don't trust anyone else to do it without causing a scene on the station or worse." He paused. "Well, more of a scene than one generally associates with girls doing stupid things."

There was a connection. Ly could smell it. The timing. Ly might even have to go up to the space station. Ly shuddered a bit. No, ly was no isolationist, but space travel made lin uncomfortable.

Landing was worse than leaving, though. But leaving inevitably led to landing. Ly sighed. "I have to go there too. And I hate space travel."

Dhyanil froze for a moment in shock.

"What, you thought you were the only one?"

He relaxed. "No, but I thought they trained you to completely eliminate all traces of fear."

Viyar laughed. "They try."

Ly watched Dhyanil's face. There was more relaxation. No doubt at the timely reminder that Special Investigators were, after all, only ky'iin.

"Seems like case closed to me," Dyahin said. The video screen had a slight flicker to it, but it didn't interfere with the woman's ability to talk or lin impression of her, familiar and yet still slightly intimidating. Dyahin was broad shouldered, if not overly tall, and ly knew exactly what she was capable of.

Viyar nodded. "Oh, definitely, but there's..." Ly tailed off. Ly paced slightly before saying more to lin supervisor.

"There was a girl who went missing from the next town down at exactly the same time. She showed up on the space station. Stowed away."

"That takes talent. We should hire her when she grows up."

Viyar laughed silently. "Perhaps we should. Her family is sending somebody after her. They're isolationists. And she went to the human ambassador. Took sanctuary with her."

"Well, *that* is interesting."

"I think people may be particularly afraid of the humans. They did start a war with us," Viyar pointed out. "And unlike the tyrar and the glen, they're predators."

Dyahin fell silent for a moment, although the slight twitching that went through her indicated that much thought was going on. "They are indeed. Are you asking me to send you up there?"

"If the two cases aren't linked then you're right, and the Iluhin case is closed. If they *are*."

"I know you're serious."

Dyahin knew how much ly hated space flight. She knew ly wouldn't make this request unless ly was being serious.

"I am." Their eyes met. There was no challenge in it, at least not directly.

"Alright. Go ahead and book...do you think commercial tickets will be safe?"

"Safer, if anyone's going after me. They'll be expecting me to take a private shuttle."

And ly would have to notify the ambassador and her liaison that ly was coming. There was also a human ship in system.

If everything blew wide open.

And then something else hit lin. The poisoning. The timing. They'd intended for her to collapse during the memorial for Ambassador Haniyar.

The one who had negotiated the peace.

Ky'iin did not put up statues of people, but lin name was going to be on the wall for sure.

This had been aimed, in part, at lin memory. And somehow, that made Viyar angrier than any other part of this.

11

THE TRAIN GLIDED through the countryside. This far inland and south, the plantations gave way to grazing land for livestock and to hunting preserves, the latter marked by heavier tree cover. It was beautiful country, even seen through the almost sterile windows of a modern train.

Six hours and Dhyanil would be in the capital, Hunter's Mist, at the spaceport.

Regional capital, regional spaceport, but he was provincial enough still to think of them as the capital, the spaceport. He had been into space once.

It had been a school trip, one he had earned a place on by having good grades. His teachers remained disappointed he had chosen to stay home, not go to the university and become a scientist. He hadn't wanted it. He didn't want it. And he had certainly never wanted to leave Kyx again.

Given the choice, he would never leave White Fish again. There was everything there he could possibly want. Good food, good beer, good people. If they could just make sure it was preserved.

He was half watching the scenery flick past at full speed, half watching the memorial service. The human ambassador was speaking as a friend. She was tiny, dwarfed by the ky'iin around her, and very pale.

Ugly, he decided, and started to turn away. She left the podium, and a fleet captain, kin to the deceased, took her place.

At least they were all keeping it short. There was little less fun than somebody who droned on for an hour at a memorial. Nobody could leave until everyone with the right to speak had. It could go on for hours while everyone got hungrier and hungrier. He always kept it short.

He prayed he would not be doing it for Meruhin. The service ended and the channel switched to a game of eyar. He turned it off for now; he had no interest in watching grown people chase a ball around. The train shook very slightly, going across points. A shadow loomed behind him. Viyar.

"I thought you would take the plane."

"No point with the shuttle schedule."

Brilliant. They were going to be on the same shuttle; they were going to breathe each other's air. He thought about water recycling again.

"What do you want?"

"Somebody tried to poison the human ambassador."

"Looks like they failed."

"Only because humans apparently consider *bili* berries to be a tasty seasoning."

Dhyanil tried not to laugh, but couldn't help it. "They can have the global supply!"

Viyar rested a hand on his. "Meruhin ate some of them."

Oh.

Void.

"Is she going to be okay?"

"It wasn't a particularly dangerous dose. The ambassador gave her what was left of her breakfast. She'll be fine, although she's in sickbay right now."

Having her stomach pumped and other such unpleasantness. Dhyanil flinched. "I swear I had nothing..."

Viyar interrupted him. "I know. You would have called it off the second I told you the kid was there."

"Family comes first." Dhyanil took a deep breath. "I..."

Did he tell Viyar? It was betraying the movement. No, it was betraying somebody who had continued with a plan even after being told it could harm a child. He would find out more information first. Then he would decide what to tell Viyar.

It was the only sane thing to do.

DHYANIL HATED CROWDS.

Honestly, even with no other considerations, he would choose to live in a small town for that reason alone. He wasn't practiced at the skill of studiously ignoring the body language and scent of strangers the way city folk were.

His anxiety rose as he tried to shepherd his luggage cart through the crowds to the monorail to the spaceport. The elevator didn't help, and he envied those who were unburdened and could just take the stairs.

Thankfully he hadn't seen Viyar again. It was clear what the Special Investigator wanted. There was an unspoken deal.

Ly hadn't said, "I get that you're an isolationist, but I know you won't hurt kids." Ly hadn't needed to.

Dhyanil would never deliberately hurt a child. And he understood something. The human was about the size of an adolescent, and a boy at that. Smaller even than himself, and he was generally considered petite. Were people seeing her as not a threat, because she looked like a child? It wasn't impossible. No doubt she didn't smell like one.

But she looked like one and the fact that she had stumbled over a word or two in her speech enhanced the image. Especially amongst monolinguals. He saw it as the struggle of a multilingual person speaking a less familiar language.

One which might not even have all the same sounds. In fact, he suspected it didn't. He felt, for a moment, almost sorry for her. The fact that most humans couldn't, apparently, be in a room with ky'iin without wanting to punch them meant she had to be isolated. Maybe he could convince *her* that humans and ky'iin should go their separate ways, never to meet again?

It was a thought he wasn't quite able to escape. Instead, he made his way through the crowd. He heard music. Somebody playing a herta, dextrous fingers moving over the strings, claws plucking them.

The busker was actually pretty good. Broke music student, most likely. He could not get close enough to transfer any money, so he surreptitiously took a picture that he could use to track them down later. He was feeling generous and they were making the crowds more...tolerable.

There. The entrance to the monorail. He wasn't going to linger in the city. He wasn't going to sightsee on the way back either. Meruhin was going straight back to her father with no detours. Assuming she survived.

Viyar probably hadn't lied on that front. *Bili* poisoning was often lethal, but if the dose had been low and she had been found quickly, it was quite treatable.

Humans thought of them as tasty seasoning. Of course. A neurological poison, a different evolution. The joke about them having the entire global supply?

If humans wanted them... He shook his head. No. Humans did not get them. Humans got nothing except to be sent back where they belonged, along with the tyrar and the glen and whatever other species might be discovered.

The universe would be better, Dhyanil thought as he climbed onto the monorail, if light speed was the absolute barrier it had once been believed to be.

The universe would be a lot better with that quarantine, that separation between sentient beings.

But he had to live in the world as it was, not as he wished it was. Which meant he could fail.

But he was determined. The monorail. His luggage. Safe.

THE SPACEPORT WAS MUCH LESS of a mob scene. Truth was, the vast majority of ky'iin would never leave Kyx.

Not all of those who left came back. There were enclaves on the tyrar homeworld, there was the colony world of Horix, and others perhaps in the works. But most people had no interest in leaving the planet. Dhyanil counted himself amongst them.

He counted himself amongst those who thought space was something of a waste of time and definitely a waste of money. Now he was waiting in line for a ticket and identity check to get on the shuttle. He didn't see Viyar, but he suspected the ly'iin was around somewhere.

They had to be on the same shuttle. Orbital economics had become such that it was cheaper to send large ships infrequently. Of course, this meant that when something went wrong it was a worse disaster.

There hadn't been one of those in years. He swallowed a bit of nervousness. No, this was as safe as a transcontinental flight, just a lot less comfortable. It was the acceleration he wasn't looking forward to, not at all. The acceleration, the vibration. All of the reminders that you were throwing yourself off a planet's surface and out into the void of space, where life was not meant to exist. Beyond a few very hardy microbes, at least.

Even the glen, very different from ky'iin, needed air and light and heat to live. Where, though, did you draw the line of what was "natural" and what wasn't? Some people drew it at trains. Tyanar drew it at, if he was going to be honest, interacting with aliens.

The line moved forward. A very young looking man checked his electronic ticket and his biometrics and waved him onto the shuttle. He took his assigned seat, studiously ignoring those around him.

He reached for the VR helmet that would distract him, then hesitated. Instead, he took out his personal terminal, hooked up some headphones and put on an episode of his favorite show he hadn't had time to watch yet.

Somehow, he wanted something older, more traditional.

He had a memory stone in his bag. He abruptly wished it was in his pocket, wanting the rough feeling of what his people had once made to store their tallies.

And other things.

Nobody used memory stones any more. But some people still made them, just to say they existed.

Just to, well... Remember.

12

Viyar was glad to take the commercial transport. There was nothing to indicate ly was any kind of law enforcement officer, let alone a Special Investigator.

Ly could, briefly, pretend to be a normal ky'iin. And ly needed that break before things got bad.

Ly distracted linself from the flight by pulling on a VR headset. Ly was not playing a game, merely watching a looped distraction video. It put lin in the mountains ly was from, in a high alpine meadow where various creatures squeaked and sang and made all of their noises. A gray-hided bika ran past, tail twitching upwards as if avoiding some unseen predator, small round ears twitching. Life in all of its forms. The only life where he was going was that brought there, was that ky'iin needed. Maybe that was the real reason Viyar hated space.

Viyar slept, fitfully, not paying any attention to lin fellow passengers until they docked at the station. It wasn't the faint thud or the temporary lack of gravity...the shuttle did not have artgrav, given everyone was strapped in anyway...that woke lin. It was the programmed end to the VR video.

Ly took off the headset and put it back in the seat arm where it came from. Once they were docked, the stewards helped people onto the station. Most needed the help. Viyar did not. Ly had been up here just enough to have practiced the maneuver using the seat backs, and then toss oneself into the gravity gradient.

Others were less fortunate. One woman tripped and had to be helped onto the station. She developed a distinct "I meant to do that" air to her that would have made lin laugh more if ly had not been a victim linself on a prior trip. On the dock, lin glanced around. Another ly'iin, slightly shorter than lin and with the lighter hide of the northern coast. That would be the one, Viyar matching lin face with what ly knew of the people on board. The Ambassador's liaison, Erilar.

It should have been Haniyar, the ly'iin who had negotiated the treaty, then been murdered. *That* murder had needed no investigation. The people doing it had made no effort not to be caught. This was different. Poison was a coward's weapon, although ly knew better than to slip into the habit of thinking that made it a weapon used by men.

"Erilar?" ly asked.

"The same. I am going to take you to sickbay first. I suspect you will want to question the young victim before she goes into protective custody. If you're..."

"Short flight. I'm up for it."

Erilar signaled to a short man to take Viyar's luggage. The man did not seem to object, although Viyar suspected he was not a servant.

It was the modern world. Men could be diplomats, could command starships. Ly'iin could be top chefs. The world had changed and was still changing. Most thought it was for the better. But not all, and it was that not all who were, in truth the issue here. It wasn't just the influence of offworlders they feared. It was change itself.

THE CHILD WAS SITTING up in bed. No doubt this was an improvement in her condition. Viyar walked over and then knelt down next to the bed. She wasn't that young, but he still had to get on her level. She had barely hit the growth spurt that females got with puberty.

"How are you feeling?"

She pushed herself up more, although her speech was still stunted. "Better," she managed.

"Good. Don't worry too much about clarity. I'll understand you anyway. What happened?"

"She left her breakfast, so I finished it. She said it would be okay. Then I got sick." A pause. "Humans can eat *bili* berries."

"Apparently."

"Maybe they can take all the *bili* berries away with them."

Viyar laughed. "The birds can eat *bili* berries too. They would probably be angry."

"Okay."

"So, did you see anyone come into the embassy?"

"Just the guy who delivered breakfast." Her brow furrowed. "Maybe he did it."

"More likely somebody in the galley."

Ships served a lot of vat meat and reconstituted food. The station, being so close to the planet, had proper canteens. It even had restaurants. One of them was very expensive. No doubt the Ambassador had been given real food, especially as humans had slightly different dietary needs. They liked more fruit and vegetables. Including, apparently, *bili* berries.

"I wish I could...think of anything else."

"It's fine. I'm going to find out who was on duty in the kitchen." And then ly would start looking for the usual. Somebody who had a huge amount of money mysteriously appear in their bank account. Somebody who had sneaked in.

There were many possibilities, but he would bet on bribery or blackmail. Most people who worked on the station were going to be the exact opposite of isolationists.

On the other hand, some of them were, no doubt, warmongers. Some people wanted a fight, all the time, regardless of the reason for it. There were outlets, but they weren't good enough for everyone.

Ly knew ly wasn't going to get more out of the kid. "You be careful."

"They're sending me away."

"They're going to stash you someplace safe where your family can't find you." Viyar thought with a slight pang of Dhyanil. Part of lin wanted to send the girl back with him; ly thought she would be safe. But ly wasn't sure.

"I know. But I wish I knew where."

Ly couldn't help her on that. All ly could do was hope she would grow up. Next stop, the human embassy.

As ly left, ly looked back at her. She was not yet a formidable female, but she would be. For now, she was still a scared child.

"You need wait," came the voice from within the embassy. Intercom pidgin.

A very high voice, almost childlike. Then ly heard a babble of other voices. Humans weren't safe to be around ky'iin, and apparently the Ambassador had company. Ly listened, wondering if ly could learn their language. A language that was entirely verbal could be hugely useful. Of course, that thought would scare the isolationists.

A language that was not from Kyx becoming the pidgin between worlds? No, they wouldn't like that at all, but ly could see it happening. Perhaps even this language or some variant of it.

Apparently, she managed to stash her visitors, because soon the door opened. There was a green plant right inside. A *very* green plant. Ly had never seen anything so perfectly, purely green.

"Is that from your planet?" came out before proper greetings.

"Yes!"

She was smaller than most men, and ly wondered if she was small for her species. Her form was very curved, her skin very pale, and she had fur on, but only on, her head. Like ky'iin, she wore clothing; in this case a simple jumpsuit, in a soft silver color.

"I'm sorry, Ambassador. It..."

"Startled you? I can imagine, I've seen Kyxian plants." She bared her teeth.

Ly started to step back then recalled that was a sign of appeasement, not aggression.

"Sorry," she said after a moment.

"It's fine. So, proper introductions. I'm Special Investigator Viyar."

"You're here about the poisonous berries."

"I am." A pause. "It wasn't the girl, we've eliminated her."

"Good. I was worried she might have been tricked into it. I don't want her to have to live with that on top of everything else."

"So..." Ly glanced around.

She led him into a conference room. "I'm still setting everything up here."

"You need to find assistants who...I suppose I don't understand it."

"We've been both predators and prey. Recently. We're *not* exactly apex predators, as much as some would like to think we are, although we have entered the role. You are. It's like trying to talk to a tiger." She produced a tablet, angled it to face him, showed him a picture.

A large furred quadruped, orange and black striped. Ly had to admit it looked like a pretty fierce creature.

"Well..."

"I have an idea on how to fix it, but it's going to take time. In the mean time, some things they can help with. At least while the *Challenger* is here."

Like the tyrar, humans named their ships. It struck him as weird.

"They have good security, I hope."

"They do."

She didn't react with any surprise to the idea or concept that the human ship might be threatened. Which was good and bad. Good that they had thought of it. Bad that they had to.

13

THE FIRST OBSTACLE was that Meruhin wasn't in the main sickbay. The human ambassador was still extending sanctuary to her. She was in the diplomatic sector, under guard.

If Dhyanil didn't act, it was entirely possible she would vanish into witness protection after they had got everything out of her. And the person he had to talk to? The offworlder.

Or Viyar. Viyar might be willing to help. Or not. Meruhin might well have convinced them that she would be in real danger if sent home. And Dhyanil was not sure he would swear she wouldn't be.

He thought he had things under control, but where his mother was involved nothing could be certain. She was often a force of nature, one which had overwhelmed him as a child. Mothers were supposed to be scary, which had initially kept him from realizing the basic truth that she was *particularly* scary.

She was much worse than anyone else's mother. She was formidable and scary and had only become more so when he had hit puberty, when he had known for sure he would never be like her. There *were* times he wished he was female, not in the sense of actually truly wanting to be; that happened, but...no, it was more about wishing he had the advantages of being a woman.

He could not entirely trust her and there was always greater clarity on that when the two of them were apart. That in and of itself was normal.

The scent of one's father in particular did things, but the scent of one's mother could have an impact too, when she chose to stick around. His mother would never walk away from anything she thought she could control.

How did he get in touch with the human? He didn't want to. The thought of her being on the station made him shudder. The thought of the entire human ship docked with it disgusted him, made bile form in the back of his throat.

But he had to. He had to petition her for Meruhin's return. Or at least for contact with Meruhin to tell her it was okay to come home.

Was it?

He wasn't sure.

But he was not going to let her get hurt more. That was the one thing of which he was, had to be, absolutely certain.

He hesitated in the sterile corridor. The air was steady in its course, with none of the irregular patterns of weather. It smelled of cleaning fluids, but there were plants here too, breaking up the dull metal. Keeping people sane. With a sigh, Dhyanil made his way to his transient room. For right now, best to unpack. The two suitcases included equipment most would not have brought.

They also included some very nice clothes.

THE AMBASSADOR HAD two liaisons working with her, a ly'iin named Erilar and a male named Syaril. Dhyanil considered whether the latter was easier to approach, with the shared gender. He was, however, the junior, and it might look like trying to work around channels.

He sent a message to Erilar. After hesitating, he made sure it was truthful. He said he was kin to the girl, concerned about her, and gave his word he was not going to drag her back to the planet without permission.

He meant *her* permission. Technically she was far from being of age, but if she had asked for sanctuary it would violate everything he knew to deny that. Sanctuary had its roots in mainstream culture, but it had long been a coastal custom too. And apparently similar enough to a human custom...for a moment he felt kinship, a sense that perhaps they were not as far apart as he had thought.

Usually it was men who would claim it, when their women abused them. It was a protective measure, a safety outlet for the most vulnerable population. But there was nothing to say a female child couldn't. It occurred to him that maybe Meruhin had convinced her she *was* being abused.

Void, maybe Meruhin felt that way. Maybe there had been a fight he hadn't witnessed, a fight about her future, about her career. Her father was still getting used to having a teenaged girl rather than a child. He was *sure* there had been a fight.

With the message sent he donned some of the nice clothing he had brought and headed for the transient's lounge first off. That would be a place where he was unlikely to meet an offworlder, if even more unlikely to meet somebody he actually wanted to meet. Certainly, he didn't want to hang out with anyone who brownnosed offworlders, and they were likely to be a majority on the station.

The vague thought that society was splitting on the issue came to him. Well, he would just have to bring it back together. He went over to the counter and ordered a glass of ola juice. Nothing to eat right now; his stomach was still unsettled from the flight. *Certainly* no alcohol.

Did humans drink alcohol? He knew that the tyrar liked grain-based alcohol, but barely got drunk with their herbivore physiology. He suspected that wasn't true of humans. What did he bribe a human with?

Certainly not *bili* berries he thought with amusement, pouring some of the juice into his maw. He still had to get past her liaison.

THE RESPONSE CAME. A video of a lean, dark ly'iin.

A ly'iin from the coast, but from the center of the tropics, from the places where the sun burned constantly. But still coastal. It gave him a moment of hope, which he fully expected to be crushed.

"Please come to the embassy at 1400 hours." A simple message.

Meruhin was no doubt still protected in sickbay, but it seemed at least the liaison wanted to meet with him, and not merely by video. He looked down. Decided he didn't need to change clothes first. Get lunch, yes, which he did at the same lounge. It would stay down now.

He knew the effect on his stomach was mostly psychological; people did get affected by artificial gravity, but it was mostly psychosomatic. Then again, so was motion sickness in general. He ate his lunch and then walked along the promenade slowly towards the embassy. Stopping at any point of interest on the way.

He didn't want to get there early. He didn't want to look like he was in a hurry. He wanted anyone who saw him to see a ky'iin on a casual mission. There was a glen on the promenade. He heard them before seeing them. Their glassy exoskeleton clicked along the floor. Ugly, he thought. Some people thought the glen were kind of pretty. Some thought they were ugly.

He kept a wary eye on the offworlder and kept moving. The glen appeared to be doing some shopping, looking at ky'iin art. A buyer, perhaps. Or a rich tourist.

Thankfully, at least a rich tourist on the station, not on the planet. With an effort, he ignored the glen and kept walking, dodging past a clutch of young children who ran past, babbling at each other. Three. He assumed the parents hoped for one of each, although the smaller number of ly'iin made that desirable outcome hard.

He hurried past a store run by tyrar from the station's enclave. Two of them were working there, which, from what he knew of tyrar, meant they were lonely. Then he turned into the embassy area. A guard checked his biometrics. He didn't blame them. And on another occasion he might well have meant harm.

Now the only thing he meant was to get Meruhin home. Which they might still think was harm. They let him pass into a wide corridor. He walked past the tyrar embassy. Past a couple of empty spaces.

There would be more offworlders. He shuddered at the thought. He stood outside the human embassy door for a moment, letting the cameras identify him.

The door opened.

A human stood inside.

14

THE AMBASSADOR HAD SEEMED...VIYAR had no idea how to judge her. She spoke well, she had as much control over her body as any ky'iin. Certainly better than tyrar attempting to communicate. Ly still wanted to learn her language.

Now, ly stood at the entrance to the kitchen which provided food to the offworld embassies. A challenging task. When occupied, the tyrar embassy wanted stuff normally fed to livestock. The glyn ate more fruit than was typical of ky'iin and also brought some of their own food.

Then there were various ky'iin who also needed to be fed. One of the chefs had settled down at the table and was watching a video. Ly could just see it over his shoulder. It was a video of a human. Ly blinked, then realized what the human in the video was doing. Cooking. They must have asked the human ship for some recipes that could be converted to local ingredients.

Ly looked around. It wasn't quite enough to eliminate that individual as a subject. Most of the workers here, a round dozen, were male, but two were female and one ly'iin. Times needed to change more, lin thought. Cooking was still looked down on. Seen as something that you either did for a short period of time when young or relegated to men who weren't useful for anything else. Especially in areas where men had been literal property.

Finally, somebody came over to lin. "Investigator."

Clearly they'd been warned. Ly wished they hadn't been. "Chef Thiaril?"

"That's me."

"Do you have an office we can talk in?"

The man led him through the kitchen.

"It has to be a real challenge."

"The human is interesting. She *can* eat our food, but if she only eats it for too long she might start getting deficiencies. We're studying how humans eat to do our best at duplicating it, but some ingredients don't even exist in our biology."

Ly laughed. Ly couldn't help it.

"They actually...raise certain animals so they can use the secretions that feed the young as food."

That was disgusting, ly decided. "Secretions...never mind, I'll look it up."

"They make the baby food in their bodies instead of chewing it up like we do. Like the tyrar."

Ly nodded. No doubt there were technological alternatives to that.

No doubt there were people who thought it was bad for the children to use them. That had to be a universal. Arguing about the best way to raise children. Viyar would likely never raise a child, so ly stayed out of those arguments. The chef let lin into his office.

Then, once the door was closed, "I think I know who did it."

THE YOUNGER MAN stepped into the office. When he saw Viyar, not his boss, he looked like he was about to bolt. "Don't. I want to *talk* to you."

"I..."

"You aren't in the brig yet. I just want to talk." The kid was guilty as sin. He was young, young enough that while this almost certainly wasn't his *first* job, it was almost surely his second. Which meant he had probably made his career choice not long after finding out his gender.

Viyar wondered if he had given up on any other dreams. It was still very much that way. That kids had dreams and then they were funneled down.

The young man finally tilted his head. "I..."

"You tried to poison the human ambassador. Why?"

"Because they offered enough money to keep my father in...enough for him to retire on. He can't...the state pension isn't enough."

Viyar listened. "The state pension should be enough. Are you saying it isn't being properly rated?"

"Yes. You don't know what it's like. We're in the mountains. Nobody cares about us."

"I'm *from* the mountains."

The young male seemed to look at him for the first time, a slow realization dawning in his amber eyes. "Void."

"But it's been a while. If you are under financial stress, you should talk to somebody."

"I tried. Then I took this job, which helped."

"But you couldn't resist an offer of enough money not to have to worry about him any more. What about your lyka?"

"Lin's dead. And don't even ask about my mother."

Traditionalist, Viyar suspected. Or using tradition as an excuse to hate kids. Heck, some men hated kids. It was just harder to overcome the stigma.

Viyar *liked* kids. Maybe ly would break all tradition one day and adopt. Or find a man without a ly'iin sibling who would trust him enough to be a lyka.

"And siblings..."

"I'm a singleton."

"So, it really is all up to you." Viyar paused. "I have to bring you in. I don't have to involve your father. I'll make sure he gets the *full* pension."

"Thank you." A pause. "Is the...I hurt a kid."

"The kid's fine. The Ambassador wasn't even inconvenienced. I'm assuming you swapped out..."

"We discovered that humans appear to like ora berries for breakfast. They're...very similar. Humans like fruit."

Viyar made a note of that. Ora berries. If ly ever needed a small bribe for the Ambassador, ly would have to remember that. A sweetener, as it were.

Ly had already called security. But they would wait outside. "So. Tell me about the person who hired you."

THE WORLD SPUN. The station had been designed to spin and parts of it still did. Not this observation lounge, though.

This was a special observation lounge. You could see the world beneath your feet, literally. It was beautiful, blue-white, hints of red and brown through the clouds.

Viyar had no idea what to do. Ly knew what the political thing to do was. Let the chef take the fall. Blame it on some kind of isolationist idea. That would be the easiest way out. The safe thing to do.

Ly had never taken the safe course of action. Ly had to decide before ly even warned the Ambassador. Ly knew people who would blame this situation on the rise of nontraditional ideas. The chef had been hired by a councilor. A ky'iin councilor, thankfully, not a tyrar representative...that would have made things much more complicated. But still, the councilor for Norfra had tried to have an inconvenient alien killed.

You didn't accuse a councilor of attempted murder without proof, and the cook's word was not proof. You didn't investigate one without far more solid evidence than the word of a man who was probably trying to save his own hide. Yet it was not in lin nature *not* to investigate. Thus, here. Not many people came here. It was disconcerting to most. Heck, it was disconcerting to lin. This room was a kind of folly, or perhaps something that had seemed like a good idea when it was first designed. The obvious flaw of everyone getting vertigo had perhaps not been seen.

Or perhaps it had and it had been meant as some kind of hazing ritual, some way of separating out the children. It made for a place few people would go.A place ly could pace at lin leisure. Then lin heard footsteps on the floor. Ly turned. Two people had entered. A young man, and the human Ambassador.

She did not seem bothered by the floor. No, she was, ly realized. She was merely dealing with it better than most by stoically keeping her eyes fixed on lin rather than looking down.

"Somebody with absolutely no fear made this."

Viyar laughed. "Somebody who thought it would be funny to watch people deal with it has always seemed more likely to me."

"Did you..."

"I found the person who tried to poison you. He was being bribed."

She nodded, clearly unsurprised. "And the person who hired him?"

"I'm still working on that." Ly couldn't say anything out loud, dared not mention lin suspicions. Maybe on the planet in a hunting preserve with a camera jammer up. Or in some human language, but ly didn't speak them yet.

"Thank you," she said, finally. Then she bravely looked down. "Quite a view if you don't think about the fact that you're standing on transparent metal with vacuum on the other side."

"I've never been able to not think about that," ly admitted.

"If you need to think about something else, I would love to chat about how the ky'iin justice system works...and how the human ones do."

"The justice system works...patchily. It's a hodgepodge," ly admitted. "Different traditions."

"Same where I come from, but we have some basic principles. Like trial by jury."

Ly didn't know that last word. So, of course, ly asked.

15

HE HADN'T EXPECTED THIS. He froze like a child threatened by a predator.

Now he was close enough to see details, her maw was small, slightly open. It exposed flat teeth with only vestigial fangs. Above it, like the tyrar, she had a pair of breathing holes, that were contained within a profusion. Her skin was a light peach color and her head fur was brown and fell to about her shoulders, neatly trimmed.

"You would be Dhyanil?"

"Yes."

She stepped back, letting him come in. She seemed to be alone initially, then he made note of the relatively young woman sitting in a corner watching them. A bodyguard. A ky'iin bodyguard because untrained humans couldn't be trusted around ky'iin. Or some factor he didn't understand.

"I'm Suza McRae. You're a relative of Meruhin's."

"Distantly." He was never going to be able to pronounce that name. The second sound was giving him a headache already.

Her head dipped in an odd gesture, a human gesture. Intentional, he thought, given the control she showed over her body. She did not have the sharp edges of a glyn, she didn't lean away from him the way a tyrar would.

She was more ky'iin than the other offworlders. It didn't set him at ease. No, it was worse, and he thought he understood the edges of why the two species had so much difficulty communicating. He wanted to hunt her and run from her. At the same time.

"Please, come all the way in."

He did so, a little warily.

"I'm not averse to hearing your side of the story."

"She ran away," Dhyanil said. "You might not know this, but puberty is difficult for girls, and they can't...use the drugs adults use until..."

Suza lifted a hand. "Adolescence. Hormones everywhere."

That surprised a laugh out of him. "Yes, and girls have it worse. There's only so much we can do, and usually we make arrangements to let them get it out of their system."

The human tilted her head, regarding him. Her eyes were blue.

A color not found in ky'iin nature, that. Ky'iin eyes were amber, gray, brown or red. Never *blue*.

"But she ran before you could send her off to..."

"Where we are, there's a hunting reserve that can always use a little bit of extra help and where she can run off as much as she wants safely. But she..." Dhyanil paused. How did he even explain this? "She wanted things other than what her father wanted for her. He wants her to stay on the coast. She wants to..."

"She wants to fly on an exploration ship, she told me."

Dhyanil tried to control his shudder. It was rude, but it came out anyway. "And that's...not what our family does. But maybe it's best to just let her go."

"I...think it might well be.

THE HUMAN HADN'T EXACTLY TURNED him to her point of view. He had already been leaning towards it.

But he knew what they were now. Master manipulators. All she had to do was talk and look at you with those unnatural eyes and it triggered something. Dhyanil was fascinated and scared.

Once he left the embassy, he went straight to one of the promenade bars. It was mostly station workers. He ordered the strongest drink they had. Humans.

As he waited for his drink, he was torn between two thoughts. The first was that maybe, just maybe it was better to be on their side. The second was how did you control them? He found a third thought. This was *one* human, and an exceptional one. One that lacked xenophobia, for starters. And diplomats were always manipulators. It was part of their *job* to be manipulators and to manipulate each other until everyone was the same degree of unhappy.

Perhaps they were harmless and it was only her he had to worry about. He did want to know more about them. Need to know more about them. They were more like the tyrar physiologically, except for being omnivores. That he knew. They were typically slightly smaller than ky'iin, but still bipeds. That he knew. But what else did he know about them? They had sent a female ambassador, or at least they were using the pronouns for a woman.

She was probably female like the tyrar women, carrying her young in her body, not laying eggs to hand over to a man to raise. But what did that mean? He took his drink and downed it in one smooth motion. It didn't affect him right away, though. He wished it did. Part of him wished for sleep right now, to dream about a safer world.

Somebody came up behind him. "Dhyanil?"

He turned. "Hyerin?"

It was her, larger than life...she was one of the largest females he knew, one of the largest ky'iin he knew. Her eyes were a reassuring dark red, nothing like the human's unnatural blue.

"In the flesh."

"How do you even fit on the space station?" he quipped.

"With difficulty! You getting another of those?"

He considered the matter. "Eventually."

"Running to the bottom of a bottle or celebrating something."

He had to consider that answer. Eventually, he responded with the only thing he could.

"I have no idea."

LATER, Dhyanil made his way back to his quarters. He was going to regret the hit to both his wallet and his morning, but getting blind drunk had seemed like such a good idea. Collapsing into bed, it was starting to seem like much less of a good idea. He managed to get some water down before he fell into an uneasy sleep that was more like passing out.

In the morning, he was definitely regretting the previous night. He ordered a hangover remedy from medical, wincing at the elevated cost. They were trying to discourage drunkenness, no doubt. He swallowed it down with water and soon began to feel better. Doing anything this morning, though, felt very much out of the question. He wished that he could change that, but he couldn't.

He had nobody to blame for this other than himself. Instead of trying to do anything of importance, he let himself sink back into bed. What else could he do? He was a dumb man, he decided, proving old stereotypes about men and impulse control (never mind that a hormonal female had worse) true. He deserved what he was getting, in other words.

Once the headache had cleared enough, he left his tiny quarters and went to the observation lounge. He looked at the planet below, his home. The world he wanted to protect and preserve. To keep the way It was for future generations. It mattered so, so much. A beautiful world. Perhaps the human felt the same about her home. Perhaps they were not enemies but allies, both seeking to protect and preserve their people.

He turned that idea over in his mind for a moment and decided he was too sober and too hungover to pursue it further. Footsteps came up behind him. For some reason, he tensed. Perhaps there was something about the approach. He turned slowly. A female form, larger than him, not as large as some. There was something about her that just radiated dominance and sheer, raw sexuality, as if she was in rut and would remain that way forever..

She was using pheromones on him. His headache started to come back with a vengeance.

"Dhyanil."

"The same. What do you want?"

"Oh, only your help with something." She showed her teeth. "You and I, we *are* on the same side."

Honeyed and powerful at the same time. She spoke the words of a woman who's every intent was to dominate a man, to take him, sexually and in every way. He could not entirely help but respond.

16

HUMANS, Viyar decided, were actually quite smart creatures. Not just in the technological sense, which ly had known. They had starflight, after all, and that spoke to intelligence.

No, they had interesting ideas and they definitely had myoran. Of course, ly had come to the conclusion a while back that arguments about myoran were excuses. Mountain people didn't have it. Coastal people didn't have it. Then islanders. Then offworlders in general. Then specific kinds of offworlders.

Ly decided it was something needed to even build a society. You had to have altruism, you had to care for others. An anthropologist had once told him that the sign of myoran was a broken bone which had healed. He had had a point, although animals without myoran sometimes managed to keep each other alive. Still...

Myoran was simply about supporting others and letting them support you. The ambassador had spoken of ideas of policing that bothered him, that were about large men...human men were larger than women...dominating people and beating them up. She placed it in a past they had moved beyond, but it still bothered him. Different people, different mistakes. And some of the same ones. She hadn't been sure whether the ky'iin had myoran to start with either.

Maybe it was time to start working from the assumption that those you met *did* have it. Reverse everything. Make it so you assumed that at least a basic level of civilization existed on the worlds you went to. Then there could be a Council of Worlds. Treaties. Trade. An exchange of knowledge.

There were purely aquatic creatures with myoran on her world. What did that mean for elsewhere? The atmosphere of a gas giant? A world with no land? Could there be sentient beings on an ice world? Had the extinct my'iin had myoran? The stars suddenly appeared to be burgeoning with life, and the thought excited lin, made lin heart beat faster. Ly decided ly liked these humans. They had a strength to them, and an adaptability. They might well be the ones who led the quest further outward.

No, not led. Guided.

Ly shook lin head and steered lin thoughts back to where they belonged. Ly had caught a poisoner, but ly did not know who had given the order. Faint dread flowed into lin. What might happen next? Nothing good, ly feared. Nothing good at all.

Ly could not leave the station until ly was sure who was trying to kill the ambassador. Yet ly knew one isolationist on the station ly would swear had nothing to do with it. Perhaps ly could use that.

Ly's first attempt to find Dhyanil failed. Ly did find Erilar, the Ambassador's liaison.

At least until the humans had a full contingent here. Ly had no idea what would happen with that. It would take time to train them, to find the ones who could handle ky'iin. Erilar led lin into one of the side rooms, pushed out a chair. Poured min, the smell of it making Viyar almost feel as if ly was back on planet.

"What did you think of her?" Erilar asked.

"Brave," Viyar mused. "Intelligent."

"Supposedly she's not wired quite the same way as other humans, rather like Nyx Syndrome."

Kids with Nyx Syndrome were often very smart, but they definitely didn't think quite like other ky'iin. "Which helps her look us in the eye without wanting to run or shoot us."

"Apparently."

Ly nodded. "Huh. If it's similar, then..."

"I wouldn't pick somebody with Nyx as an ambassador. I *would* pick them to run the engine room on a starship."

Viyar laughed. "Definitely."

People with Nyx Syndrome were known for being incredibly meticulous and pretty much never getting bored.

"But she was apparently only supposed to be a translator. Now, she's what they have."

And by the time they had somebody else, Viyar thought, the human, who's name ly couldn't pronounce, would be a fixture, accepted by both sides. Ly glanced around the room. The ambassador had hung pictures. That was a sign that she intended to stay. Pictures of a red, barren world, not their homeworld but a world she appeared to love.

Ly wondered if she wanted the job. Ly couldn't read human body language. Had she been ky'iin ly would have said yes, but under her controlled words there was definitely something alien an unfamiliar. "So, let's keep her alive."

"I'm assuming the isolationists."

Viyar jerked lin head. "As am I. I have a contact who might help. He doesn't seem to be involved in the plot, but might know who is. Except I can't find him."

Erilar lifted lin hands. "A man."

"A very *smart* man. The dangerous kind. The ones that are raised in a traditional household, like it, but use the fact that they aren't as large and powerful as their weapon."

Ly thought of the human ambassador. Human women were smaller. Was she another one who used her small size and intelligence as a weapon? And had ly missed it because it wasn't what ly expected from a woman?

"What would you try next?" Erilar asked.

"Hrm. A well-placed bomb, perhaps."

You didn't go into open conflict with a target until you had to. That wasn't the ky'iin way. You shot from the shadows or you used poison or you blew things up. You didn't tussle in the streets. Men tended to resort to poison and women to bullets, but the principles were the same.

"But they aren't going to poison her again. Not unless..." Erilar tailed off. "I'm not an Investigator, but it's not entirely impossible somebody on the human ship might work with them."

Viyar hesitated. For a long moment. "No," ly finally said. "It's not."

VIYAR DID NOT like Erilar's thought. The liaison left to discuss it with the ambassador.

Which meant lin was alone. Lin sat, running a finger, claws retracted, around the edge of lin now empty glass. A co-conspirator amongst the humans. Somebody who had no more desire to hang out with ky'iin than isolationist ky'iin had to hang out with offworlders. And the way humans reacted to ky'iin seemed to him to make this oh, so much more likely.

Deep breath.

Ly needed to understand the humans more, but ly was not sure ly could corner the Ambassador again. She had entertained lin once, tiny, delicate but no, definitely not frail. This was a being who had survived more than one attempt on her life.

This was a being who had developed that particular kind of toughness that came with surviving more than one attempt on her life. She had been, from what ly had heard, blown up, beaten up, had a drone decoy of her killed. And now fed poison which had only not got her because human nervous systems worked differently.

Tyrar were targeted too. But it was...harder to target tyrar. There was no such thing as a lone tyrar, they were herd people, they moved in groups. The human was alone. Although likely not entirely. Surely she was spending time with her own people from the ship. If there was a human co conspirator they might easily be able to gain access. Ly wished ly had asked how *humans* handled assassinations. They might well have a different attitude towards the matter. They might well not do them at all. The glyn claimed that killing somebody was never a solution.

Ly had always sensed layers of violence under that, layers upon layers of a past that the glen spoke but little of. They were very different. Void, glen didn't even have *brains*. Humans did. Tyrar did. Brains were something which developed through evolution.

Chemistry, though? That was different. Was there anything which would affect a human and not harm the ky'iin with her? Ly needed to talk to that ship, but humans could not talk to ky'iin except through the ambassador.

Wait. There was somebody on that ship, perhaps, who wasn't human. Somebody ly could talk to without any problems. The aquatic. Could that be a window into what was going on over there?

It was worth a try.

17

THE FEMALE TOOK Dhyanil to what he realized with dawning horror was a ship. Not a starship, just an in-system ship which took scientists out to the ice worlds.

He could not...

"Don't worry, we're just going somewhere the station doesn't have surveillance," she said, as if reading his mind, as if smelling his fear.

Likely she was doing the latter. Maybe it wasn't pheromones. Maybe she had legitimately gone off her suppressors so she could use the hormones of rut to give her an edge. Some women did that.

It was dangerous for her. But even more dangerous for him. He was not going with her. He planted his feet in the corridor.

She sighed, "If I have to pick you up..."

"We aren't out of station surveillance yet."

She growled. A deep, meaningful growl, one pregnant with both danger and lust. He tried to plant his feet further, but found that they followed her anyway. She was going to hurt him, but she wasn't going to kill him. Her instincts would keep her from that, if nothing else. And he did have to find out what she wanted. Onto the ship. Larger than the shuttle, and configured for cargo.

A supply ship. The door closed and his heart rate went up again.

"So. Dhyanil of White Fish," she said, disambiguating him from any other Dhyanils without, it seemed, knowing his clan name.

Or caring about it. It wasn't, he supposed, any of her business. "What do you want? I'm a little old to tend your eggs."

She laughed. "A little, although no doubt the hatchlings would be quite intelligent."

He took that as a compliment. "Again. What do you want?"

He was terrified of her. She was everything a traditional female once was. He was amazed she wasn't wearing mating paint, the blue and white streaks that in some traditional places still warned everyone of the approach of a female in full rut. That would have been noticed, he thought wryly.

"Your help. With something I am sure you agree is desirable."

"My help with what?" He had a suspicion he knew the answer. Her scent washed over him, but he was starting to recover his senses properly.

"How would you like to make the humans go away for good?"

He would like that, he thought, very much indeed.

SHE RELEASED him like throwing back a fish that was too small. He went back to his quarters, breathing hard. He wasn't sure what to do. Yes, making the humans go away for good appealed, but...

He wasn't sure he could do or be involved in what she had in mind. Yet he was too afraid to go to the Special Investigator. He thought he was anyway. A female on the edge of rut was hard to say no to. That was how they had kept males subservient in so many places, in so many ways. Then they had found ways to suppress rut, got males and females working together without ly'iin to bridge them. The entire world had changed at that time. Changed in ways he rather thought nobody could have predicted.

And abruptly he was glad. Glad of progress. Glad of change. But not too much change. Balance.

He thought about the humans, who were definitely not a source of balance and myoran. They were too different, too alien. It wasn't the same thing, not at all. She hadn't forced herself on him.

He was too old. If he'd been younger would she have resisted? Would she have left him with a clutch to tend, regardless of his opinions? In those days men did not have opinions. Men had duties and tasks and pleasures, but not opinions. Now some men commanded starships.

His head spun. He locked himself in his room, his tiny room which felt like a coffin like a trap and when he got back downstairs he was going hunting. He was going hunting naked, the old way, catch a meal with only his speed and strength and claws. He was going to remind himself what it meant to be ky'iin.

What did humans do to remind themselves what it meant to be human?

He would tell the investigator. He was torn between these two goals. Between those two duties. He had an opinion. He would, he had to, find a third path.

HOURS LATER, Dhyanil was no closer to the third path.

Well, no, he knew what one possible third path was. He just had no idea how to get to it. He had to get to Meruhin.

Involving the child? If she wasn't already up to her neck in the quicksand he would never have considered it.

If she was a few years older. He shuddered. Yet another tradition he was happy to leave on the dust bin of history. He could not put Meruhin up against her.

But he could use Meruhin as an excuse to get his butt off the space station and back to Kyx, wash his hands of the entire thing. Cowardly? Absolutely, but in this case he was pretty sure that being a coward was the best option. Walking away. Not ever having to face her again.

He wished, for a moment, that he was a member of some species that didn't go into these hormonal fluxes. Because he badly wanted to face her again. To be rejected by her again. To push her until she accepted him. Which meant he had to make very, very sure he was never in a room with her again.

What she wanted to do was too much. He wanted the humans to go away for good. She wanted to *destroy* them. It wouldn't work, of course. There was no way it would work. There was no way anyone on Kyx had the knowledge to make it work. But she was going to try and she was going to get arrested and then fed to the humans for whatever they called justice.

With Dhyanil right next to her. If he turned her in, her people would kill him. If he claimed sanctuary anywhere, he would never see his family or White Fish again.

Dhyanil hated humans and offworlders. Right now he hated that female more, with a passion that was dangerously close to lust. He closed his eyes. There were things he could take that would dampen *his* hormones and help him think straight. He didn't want to take them. He wanted to ride the storm and come through it on the other side a better ky'iin. He knew people who believed in that. Women who would ride out rut alone in the desert.

Would it make him a better ky'iin? Or would it simply make him a fool?

18

VIDEO CALLS WERE the only way to do this. Viyar never liked them. Ly missed scent cues.

Ly wondered how the species that communicated entirely verbally even managed. They could talk without visuals at all, but surely that had to cost them something. Some connection. Perhaps that was why they used video anyway, to maintain more...to see each other's faces.

It still could not substitute for face to face.

The aquatic was a slender creature floating in a tank. He was an air-breather, no gills, but otherwise entirely adapted to the water. Grey skin, light as a coastal ky'iin, Large eyes.

His name was Iterk. The thin lines of cybernetic implants traced through his skin. The kind of thing pilots had to improve reflexes.

The advantage of a pilot who naturally thought in three directions hit him like a ton of bricks. No wonder the humans had done so well fighting ky'iin, despite not having been in space for as long. They'd employed the aquatics. Allied with them. Used their evolutionary advantages the way one might use a hunting lyrk's.

"Hello," Viyar said. Supposedly the aquatic knew some ky'iin, although of course he could not communicate back, having no hands.

"I know you can't speak my language or I yours, but I wanted to say hello and promise that we're going to find out who poisoned Susha."

Ideally before they did worse. Ly knew ly was mangling the ambassador's name, the soft hissing sound simply did not exist in his language. It did in some minority ky'iin languages and no doubt people who spoke them from a young age would have something of an advantage. Some of the island and arctic peoples. But not those from the mountains.

A string of whistles and words came from the being in the tank. Ly would have to learn that language, too. But ly didn't need to know it to know for sure that this Iterk was as intelligent as ly was. To make that connection. Ly should just call the ambassador, have her translate, but somehow ly wanted the barrier right now.

The sense of reaching across isolation and distance to make something wonderful. That was what they could do if the people on all sides would get out of the way. If people would get out of their own way. Ly suspected, though, that something terrible was going to happen first. They had already had a war.

They had already had all that had happened on the tyrar homeworld. Now it was coming home to Kyx, because of course it was. It should.

It needed to. There were deeper issues, issues that flowed back to biology and custom and tradition and to all of the things which hooked together. To language barriers and communication issues and aggression and the need to hunt and whatever it was tyrar and humans and glen felt.

"Thank you," he said to the aquatic.

Another whistle followed. Ly would talk to him with a translator.

Ly hesitated. "Protect your ship," ly said finally. The *Challenger,* as they named it, was the obvious next target.

Especially, he thought, if the isolationists believed they could start the war up again. He wasn't convinced they couldn't.

VIYAR WISHED machine translation was more of a thing. Maybe they could develop it now.

Maybe somebody else, even the humans, had it down, at least between known languages.

Who knew?

Ly certainly didn't. For right now, lin concern was the girl, Meruhin.

Her relative wanted to take her home with him, but ly rather thought that on that point at least, Dhyanil could be won over.

Ly found the man in one of the lounges, picking at a bowl of stew. He looked, Viyar decided, absolutely terrible.

"Are you alright?"

Dhyanil jumped out of his chair. "I'm fine," he tried to say, but there was no truth or sincerity behind it. Clearly, he was very, very much not fine.

"I wanted to talk to you about Meruhin," was what Viyar actually said, but ly shifted the nuances. An offer to talk privately hung under what was openly being said.

There was hesitation. "At this point I think we should worry more about what's safe for her."

"Agreed. Shall we go talk to *her* about it?"

Ly saw the man relax visibly. Something was definitely going on. Ly needed to find out what. Ly turned and left the room, the man scurrying behind him.

Ly consciously slowed; Dhyanil was both shorter and older, no sense making him labor to keep up. Once they got past a couple of doors, ly spoke again. "I can tell something is going on."

Dhyanil vibrated. There was no other word for it. Clearly he both wanted to say something and couldn't. He was under some form of duress, ly decided. Some form of coercion, and ly would have to be careful. "We'll worry about it later. Meruhin."

"Her father wants her to come home. Finish school. Work the boats."

"I doubt that's what she wants."

"She wants to join the exploration forces."

"And her family...including you...don't want her to."

For a moment, Dhyanil was in that same vibrating freeze. "No. We don't."

"So, this is more than just a girl feeling her hormones." There was an actual family conflict here. "She told us her entire family is involved in the isolationist movement, albeit without details, and that she wants out."

"I know." Dhyanil let out a breath. He seemed calmer now. "If we haul her back, she'll just leave again the moment she's of age."

His voice showed traces of frustration and disappointment.

"And her father will never agree to her going to the academy. So she'll just leave the second she's of age..."

"...and not have the grades she needs to get in. They leave school early on the coast. We *need* the labor."

"Maybe we need to start..." Viyar tailed off. No, this person would not be receptive to automating the boats, to what he would no doubt see as killing the coast's traditions.

"The people who would agree to that don't stay." Dhyanil tilted his head. "Can I talk to her? I promise I won't try to tie her up and put her on a shuttle."

Viyar hesitated. "Of course you can."

Ly resolved to put surveillance on it, though. Perhaps the man would say something to the girl that he wouldn't say to Viyar.

Somebody had a hold on him, and Viyar never liked to see that. Never.

MERUHIN AGREED to meet with Dhyanil alone, accepting his promise for now.

Pretty soon she'd hit her growth spurt and be bigger anyway. It would be *very* hard for her father to control her then. That part of it wasn't lin concern. Somebody who would stow away to the station deserved what she wanted, if it was still what she wanted in a few years.

Ly had an idea on how to achieve it if ly could keep her away from the traditionalists. Ly would have to talk to the ambassador again. Of course, that might just be that ly was looking for an excuse. Ly was pretty sure she was manipulating lin, consciously or otherwise.

For now, though, ly had to work out who was harassing Dhyanil. If it was Meruhin's family then that should be easy enough to deal with, but ly knew well that it could be something worse. Leaving the secure hospital ly headed towards station security. Ly needed access to surveillance tapes.

Station security were mostly used to keeping drunks from thinking they could breathe vacuum and the like. The office was fairly open, on the promenade. Ly slipped in behind a father who had lost one of his kids. The other kid was still with him looking mulish.

Ly suspected some kind of game that had perhaps gone a tiny bit too far. Ly hesitated, but then a woman signaled lin into the back office. Busted, ly thought wryly.

"What do you need, Investigator?"

"I need surveillance on a specific individual." Ly didn't bother flashing lin badge, they already had lin identified.

"Who is?"

Ly pulled out lin pocket terminal to show her a picture of Dhyanil. "He is *not* wanted for a crime. I suspect somebody may be putting heat on him."

She scowled. "Got it. I'll see what I can find for you."

"Make sure he doesn't find out."

The poor man was nervous enough; if he found out Viyar was trying to help him he might panic.

"Of course. Did you find out anything..."

"We know who poisoned the Ambassador, but not yet all of the threads it leads to. Stay alert."

She was more used to drunks and lost kids, and barely had a facility to hold anyone; people who caused trouble on the station generally found themselves on the next shuttle back to Kyx.

But she *did* have all of the station's surveillance cameras and right now that was what Viyar needed.

Ly remembered what Suza had said about policing and the human past. Ly was glad ly hadn't lived in that place and time, although no doubt it had seemed normal to them. Normal until they were called on it.

"Thank you," ly added.

"I'll call you when I have something."

Ly left quietly. The family were gone, along with the desk sergeant. Ly knew they would find the kid. Sy was probably just playing hide and seek.

19

MERUHIN WAS SITTING IN A CHAIR. She stood as he entered. She looked to be fully recovered from the poisoning, her hide had recovered its usual dull metallic shine. "I'm not going home."

Dhyanil hesitated. Considered her. "My mother sent me to haul you back by the ear." He tapped one of his own.

"Of course she did. But I'm not going. I claimed sanctuary."

"Technically, minors can't claim sanctuary."

She looked down. Tapped the floor with her left toes.

"But apparently the humans didn't know that. Smart move."

She looked up.

"I'm *proud* of you, Meruhin, even if I wish you'd directed your smarts some other way. Right now, though, I want you safely off this station."

Before anything else happened.

"He'll ground me for life and take me out of school."

"No. He won't." Dhyanil took a deep breath. "You've convinced me of one thing. You need to be in school. If I convince your dad to let you stay in school, will you come home?"

"I'll think about it."

She sounded very mature in that moment. "We can worry about what you *do* after school later, but you're too smart for the boats."

He knew that was true. But he would also say whatever it took to get her to come with him.

"He still has the only say, though."

"That's true. But I think I can handle him."

"They offered me protection. A boarding school."

"My mother will have *my* ears if I come back without you." He wasn't entirely serious. He knew that boarding school was the best idea, but he had to make this token effort. Otherwise, his mother *would* be impossible.

"Your mother is *old*."

That much was true. Dhyanil was too old to attract females. His mother was much older, too old to breed, but she hadn't lost her size or much of her strength. "Watch what you say. You'll be old one day too, and you'll be glad if you're as fit as she is."

Meruhin laughed. "I know. That's what makes her so scary. She *doesn't* get old."

Dhyanil, who had known his mother for, well, rather longer, "Oh, she does. Imagine what she was like when she was young?"

Meruhin shuddered. "I don't want to."

Dhyanil suspected Meruhin would be every inch as formidable. "Look. What matters to me the most is getting you off the station. I'll handle my mother."

"What's going to happen?" she asked, softly.

"I don't know yet. Something."

"Somebody's going to try and blow up the humans."

"Oh, they'll almost certainly try. And get caught. I'm worried about what else they might blow up, deliberately or otherwise."

Always the concern.Collateral damage.

And if somebody decided destroying the human ship was the right way to solve the problem? That would be bad. But not as bad as what he knew was being planned...

THE AMBASSADOR'S LIAISON, Erilar, waited outside. Dhyanil did not want to see him; the plains bred ly'ir shone nearly black and towered over him.

"She doesn't want to go home. I'm going to be in trouble for not bringing her."

"Massive family drama."

"My mother. And before you do the math for how old she is...it hasn't made her that much less scary."

Erilar laughed. "Some people get scarier with age. So..."

"So I'm going to need somebody to cover for me when I go home empty-handed. Would you mind backing up that the human wouldn't let her go or..."

Erilar considered. "I'll come up with a good story."

"I'm..." Dhyanil paused. "I'm sure Meruhin can pass the exams for the Frost Academy." He paused. "I don't want her to, but I know what will happen if we don't give her the chance. She'll just run away, come up with a fake name, and do it anyway. So..."

"You think so?" The liaison's body language brightened. "I thought she was smart."

"Too smart to spend her life on a fishing boat," Dhyanil admitted, reluctantly. "Maybe she'll decide to come back as a doctor or something, but I doubt I'll see her again."

The question was whether it changed anything? It didn't.

Meruhin might well grow up to be his enemy. Not in the sense that they would ever directly harm each other, no, but...

But she wanted to reach for the stars and he wanted to, what? Build a wall. Maybe it was too late.

"Thank you for being reasonable."

"I just don't want her to run away again and get hurt. I know she named me as a potential problem."

"You *are* a potential problem. Which is why we figured we'd let you talk to her so you could go back to the planet."

It was Dhyanil's turn to laugh. "Back where I belong."

Something was niggling at him, though. Did he tell this ly'iin there was a real danger?

When he tried, the memory of the scary female came into his mind again. She hovered in his consciousness. He had to do something about this. He couldn't let her rule his life, not when he didn't even know her. Stupid hormones.

He envied the ly'iin, who had always existed to not have those hormones. Without them, he suspected, society would not have functioned. The religious claimed ly'iin were a gift from the gods to allow ky'iin to work together and build. Given most animals only had males and females, they had a point, but it was more likely that the existence of ly'iin had made ky'iin what they were.

He wasn't an anthropologist to know the real truth of it. Or a biologist. But he did know that without the ly'iin, things would never work. Offworlders didn't have ly'iin. With that thought in his brain, he fled rather than telling Erilar what was going on. Glancing over his shoulder to see the liaison watching after him.

He did not like the look on lin face.

BACK IN HIS COFFIN-LIKE QUARTERS, Dhyanil considered what to do.

He had no reason to stay once they had a story to satisfy Meruhin's father as to why he had failed to drag her back by her ear. But there was the woman. He expected to hear from her soon, sooner if she got wind of his impending departure. He expected to hear what they wanted him to do now. And he wasn't going to do it. It was easy, he thought, to make that determination now, with only the memory of her to haunt him.

Face to face, he knew he would cave. Which meant he needed to plan for this, but how?

He didn't really know anyone on the station, and he certainly didn't know any *women* who were currently on the station well enough to involve them. If he involved Erilar he was probably setting himself up to be killed, and these people wouldn't hesitate.

They might even just shoot him or push him out an airlock. True, they weren't planning on just shooting the humans. But if he pushed them into desperation; and that was harder to evade than more subtle and honorable methods. You didn't treat beings with myoran as prey.

If pushed enough they might, and he didn't want to be hunted. Nobody did. But at the same time, an attempt like that which *failed* would take things out of his hands. Station security could not ignore it.

He was too much of a coward to risk his life that way. Far too much of a coward, and quite willing to admit it. So, what was his plan? Claim sanctuary with somebody?

He wasn't sure who had the authority and he understood why Meruhin had chosen the human. The human not only wouldn't have known she was a minor, but also emphatically had the authority. Who else constituted a representative of a foreign power from White Fish's perspective?

Almost nobody anymore. You couldn't claim sanctuary because of the World Council. And when the offworders became part of it, that avenue would be closed, too. The other option disturbed him more, but he could see the rails that led him towards it. First, though, he had to find somebody willing to provide him with certain pharmaceuticals. He hated the idea, but he had no choice.

20

VIYAR WAS NOT LIKING what was happening on the station. It smelled. Ly was not sure what, exactly, it smelled of. But it definitely smelled. Rotten fish, ly decided, eventually. There was a kind of fish that would rot from the inside, so it still looked good until you tried to eat it. A great metaphor for a situation where everything seemed normal until it wasn't.

The surveillance footage had come in and it told its own story. For the most part, Dhyanil had engaged in normal on-station activities while trying to get permission to visit the girl who had claimed sanctuary.

He had gotten blind drunk once, but only once, and most people Viyar knew had done that at least once. There was one suspicious point. He had followed a female, identified as Kysrehin, onto a freighter. Then left alone less than an hour later, shaking.

She had pulled some kind of coercion or intimidation on him. It might be biological manipulation. With the right pheromones, a woman could get a man to do whatever she said; whether from natural cycle or from artificial enhancement. The latter were illegal without a prescription, but illegal did not necessarily mean rare.

Ly contemplated checking to see if anyone had ordered *those* from the station pharmacy. It probably wouldn't help. If she had any sense she would have brought them with her. It could also have been physical threats, as uncouth as those were, or threats made against the male's family. It didn't really matter *how* this Kysrehin was doing it.

Ly pulled up *her* file. A dockworker, poorly educated, hired for her muscle. That didn't fit. Amateur, ly thought wryly. This was such an obviously fake file it was either incompetence *or* meant as a distraction. Maybe she wanted lin to waste time looking for the hacker who had put her in the system. Maybe she just assumed nobody would look twice at her. Maybe she wanted to be found.

Kysrehin. Kysre.

Kysre meant the kind of vengeance you take when the person you are mad with is just prey to you. A very specific word.

Not a word you would name a child. Unless it was a dialect of kythre, which meant a kind of pink flower and was absolutely a word you would name a child. Ly thought not. Ly thought that this was a red herring to distract lin. Treat people like prey. Ly frowned.

Ly had to get out of the man what was going on. In the meantime, to satisfy curiosity if nothing else, ly put in a subpoena for hormones other than cycle suppressants that the pharmacy had sold in the last month. It probably wouldn't go anywhere. Ly had to try.

WHILE WAITING ON THE REQUEST, ly got a call.

Erilar, the ambassador's liaison, wanted to talk to lin. The taller ly'ir came to lin quarters, ducking a little in the door.

"What do you need?"

"More what I can offer you. I got the representative of the girl's family to agree not to take her back, but he's afraid that he'll..."

"Dhyanil, right?" Lin tone turned serious.

"Yes."

"Somebody's coercing him. Could be connected."

If the falsely named Kysrehin was another member of the family or of the isolationist cell that Merehin had told them all about, then it was all neat and tidy and all ly had to do was find *her* and convince her to stop.

It was all connected to Iluhin's death, too. She had gone too far and not been able to live with her own actions. Dhyanil bore some responsibility for that.

Ly rather thought he knew that.

"Could be," Erilar said, coming the rest of the way into the room, making the verb to be part of that smooth motion. "But we can't be sure."

"No, we can't." Ly's shoulders dipped. "I'm checking into potential biological coercion, but if it's a family matter it could be any number of things."

Erilar shuddered. "We're never going to get them to stop using sex to manipulate each other, are we?"

Viyar couldn't help but laugh. "Not if we want to keep having hatchlings to teach."

"No." Erilar's laugh was weaker. "Well, there *are* artificial ways of doing that."

And the way things were going they'd come up with a way for ly'iin to have biological offspring.

Viyar rather thought that was going too far, although very few ly knew would actually want it, and most of those were the veri, those who's mind did not match their body.

For them, perhaps, it would be a good thing. "There are, but we know they won't give up the natural ways. I mean, come on, some guys won't use an incubator and claim that it messes with the natural bond between father and offspring."

"Who knows, maybe they're at least somewhat right. So, who's doing the coercion?"

"A woman under an obviously false name and identity."

"Ah, so we have grounds to throw her off the station."

"When the time is right."

Civilians often thought that you moved as soon as you could. In a case like this, ly felt it wiser to leave her in place for a little bit.

And get some protection on Dhyanil, whether he wanted it or not.

AFTER ERILAR LEFT, giving Viyar more to think about, but also hope this would turn out to be simply family drama, the results came back.

As he had expected, nobody had purchased cycle inducers or artificial pheromones recently. At all recently. The station wasn't generally a place you wanted to produce a clutch; most workers would take on planet leave to breed and then bring the hatchlings back, or not, once they could walk some.

There had been a couple of purchases of gelone suppressors, including one just that day. Ly peered. Gelone suppressors were used to dampen the *male* libido. Generally that was a treatment for a medical condition or taken by men who worked in certain types of medicine. You didn't need raging hormones while trying to treat a cycling woman who had broken her leg, after all.

One of the purchasers was indeed somebody who worked in sickbay. The other was a registered transient. Ly unpeeled the layers. Dhyanil had got himself gelone suppressors.

Which told lin everything ly needed to know. Gelone suppressors were the best way a man had to fight back against biological coercion. By dampening his libido they reduced the need and desire to do whatever the woman said in the hope of getting to mate. They wouldn't do anything about intimidation. But it told lin everything, including exactly what crime was being committed here.

Was Dhyanil enough of a traditionalist not to consider it a crime? Possible. He'd also fathered a clutch and no doubt had other matings which had failed. Most men had. So. Kysrehin, whatever her real name was, was using biological coercion on a man and while it didn't seem likely she had raped him, the possibility was rather more on the table than it had been.

Erilar was right. The ly'iin would never get men or women to grow up about sex. They *could*, they just didn't always want to. And it was hard for a woman to resist being able to lead a man around by his gonads. Viyar understood that.

Hard did not mean it shouldn't be done, though. Ly spent a moment being grateful for being ly'iin, then contemplated the matter once more. Ly had to find this Kysrehin, but now ly knew she was dangerous; and that ly couldn't take any men *or* women with lin.

Well, no. Ly could take women if ly was sure they were taking their suppressants properly. Ly didn't want to risk it. So, ly needed to make a plan. It occurred to lin that one day offworlders would be perfect assistance in these kinds of things; they surely wouldn't be affected by ky'iin pheromones. Tyrar certainly weren't and glen weren't even based on quite the same biology. It seemed unlikely that humans would be either.

For now, though, ly needed ly'iin. Ly needed several big, strong, intimidating ly'iin.

21

DHYANIL EYED the pill and the glass, then tossed the pill down his maw. He hadn't taken a libido suppressor in years; at his age, his lbido had started to tail off.

His mother, of course, was past natural cycling, although he knew she used pheromones to manipulate sometimes.

Hopefully it would be enough that he could look this female in the eyes. She was calling herself Kysrehin. He was sure that wasn't her real name. She hated humans. It was personal, he realized slowly. Kysre was an extreme form of vengeance and while she planned honorable means, it was only because of the numbers.

Maybe what she really wanted to do was tear them apart one at a time. Possibly eat them, too. He rather thought humans would taste bad, plus you didn't eat things with myoran.

He shook his head. If you got angry enough you might.Anger and rut. She was either letting herself cycle to use the anger that came when a female went through rut without mating or, worse, using cycle inducers to guarantee it.

It wasn't pheromones. He was sure of that. He wasn't leaving his quarters until the suppressor had a chance to kick in. He wished he'd expressed as a ly'iin. No.

He loved his children too much for that. Sometimes he wished he'd fathered more than one clutch. He loved children. Probably why he was letting Meruhin go. Because he loved her. Because he didn't want her to hate him. She was probably still going to hate him, not to mention everything he stood for.

The surge of anger was sudden, but it was an unfortunate side effect of the suppressors. Meant they were kicking in. Meant he might be able to face her now, but it was best to wait a day, take one more dose first. He settled in. He knew he would be pressured into leaving. But he had to stay if he was going to find out what he needed to know. And he had to convince Kythrehin he was right where she wanted him, right in her pocket, desperate to mate with her, desperate for her eggs.

Dhyanil had always been a decent actor. This was going to be harder than any play he had performed in in school.

"It's simple. An engineered virus."

Dhyanil listened with growing anger. He was an isolationist, not... a monster.

She was talking about genocide. The humans first. Then if that worked, the tyrar, the glen. But the humans? She'd found out about the human homeworld. It would be a ky'iin world, after they were gone. They would be gone with their infrastructure intact, with everything they had built just sitting there for ky'iin to take over.

He hated her with a passion he had never felt before. Hated her for thinking he would ever want to be a part of this. For thinking anyone would. For even coming up with the idea in the first place.

"So, the idea is..."

"We can't get it into the Ambassador's food, thanks to whoever tried to poison her."

That was a revelation. He had assumed Kysrehin was behind that, or it was some kind of test run. She wasn't.

"We have to get it into the air system on their ship."

And pray the incubation period was long enough. "They'll just quarantine the ship," he found himself saying.

Poking holes in her plan might be what he was here for, but he definitely didn't want to actually spend his time doing it. He might actually help her kill all of those...he stopped on the word in his mind. But no, he had to find a hole in her plan. Then drive a truck through it.

"You're right. We need a carrier."

Somebody who was infected and asymptomatic. He shuddered. He didn't say they couldn't go around abducting humans. He didn't say it because he was hoping she would try, without him, and get caught. That would solve all of his problems. No, it wouldn't. She hadn't let him know who any of her other accomplices were. He suspected she was keeping a harem. She would probably actually end up mating with one of them, without even thinking about it. He felt sorry for the kids if so. He hoped if she did then the way she was messing with her hormones would cause a failed mating.

Void, he hoped it would cause a dud mating, he was angry enough with her to...but then if she was controlling the male by his hormones, it wasn't really *his* fault. He thought several unpleasant words involving mating.

"Dhyanil?"

"Just thinking about how we might find one of those."

"The humans don't keep live animals on their ship, do they?"

"Not as far as I know. Somebody could try to find out."

A virus harmless to a food animal would work, if they could get hold of a food animal. If they could be sure it wouldn't be eaten.

"I know somebody who might well be able to do that. Good thought."

He hadn't said anything. He was just being her sounding board. And he'd already improved her plan. This was not going the way he had hoped. Not at all.

HIS MOTHER WAS on the video call.

"They won't release her to me. They might release her to Luranil, but I doubt it."

She swore in ways she never would have around him when he was a child. It had taken him years to learn that his mother was a potty maw. "You tried. Are you coming home?"

"I have a major opportunity here. So not yet."

He couldn't tell her; likely he was being monitored. And he had no idea how she would react. No, he did. She would be entirely in favor of genocide. He was lucky in many ways to have been raised by his much more sensible father.

"Make it soon. Things are..." She tailed off.

"This isn't something that's going to repeat."

"Neither is what I need you for."

There was something underlying there, a sense of having limited time, a sense of it running out. He didn't like it. But he had to see this through. Or did he? He *wanted* to see this through and no woman was going to tell him he couldn't. Not even his mother. "As soon as I wrap this up. I promise."

She hung up on him.

He glared at the screen for a long moment. She was manipulating him to come home. He wasn't going to fall for it. He was going to see this through even if it made him feel cold deep within to think of talking to the woman who called herself Kysrehin again. He wondered what her real name was. Where she was from. Why she hated the humans with such a deep, personal...

She hated the Ambassador particularly, too, so he wondered about the poisoning again. No, she'd been mad about that. But there might be other ways to infect the Ambassador as a test case. It would be too public, surely. They wouldn't, couldn't do that. Then he had an idea, but no idea how he was going to make that idea happen. None whatsoever.

And then the entire station shook. A peculiar sound flowed through the air and through the walls and floor, not one he had ever heard before. He knew the rules. He stayed put, checking the emergency locker in the room. Whatever had just happened didn't appear to be leading to any alarms. Probably a screw up on the docking level. The station had rung like a bell. Yet, it couldn't be a coincidence. He needed to find out what happened. Just in case.

22

KYSREHIN. Ly was still trying to find out who she was. Ly was working in lin quarters, which was not ideal, but space station space was at a premium.

Quarters did not have high priority, although ly cynically thought that might be because people staying in their quarters didn't spend money.

Ly was probably even right.

The station shook. A shudder that went through all of it, a faint bell-like note. Ly knew enough to know that something had hit the hull, likely something fairly large.

The drill was to stay in your quarters. Ly was *not* staying in lin quarters. Ly could override the door. But where had it happened?

Ly tilted lin head and wished lin had more knowledge about ships and stations. Had the station been fired on? The human ship was in dock, but they weren't popular. The docks. That was the most likely place. Ly slipped out of lin quarters. There wasn't an atmosphere alarm, but ly grabbed the oxygen kit from under lin bunk anyway. Just in case.

People were, it seemed, following the rules. The only ky'iin ly saw were two men scurrying down a ladder. After a moment, ly followed them, albeit while letting them get a good distance ahead of lin. Following them would likely take lin to the problem.

A quick drop down to the docks. The chaos seemed to be focused on one of the freighter docks. Nowhere near the diplomatic docks, thank the Void.

"What happened?" ly asked the nearest person who didn't seem to be doing anything.

"Freighter malfunction," she said, a little shortly. "Or somebody tried to do a manual dock and messed up."

So, nothing ly needed to worry about. No foul play, just stupidity at worst, technical problems at best. "Anyone hurt?"

"Not physically." She pointed to an adolescent boy who was kind of leaning against the wall and shaking. "Somebody got a scare."

"Kids that age scare easy."

"Especially boys."

Ly refused to agree with her. Ly knew far too many very tough males who would never be reduced to shaking in public. Of course, it was also possible he had gotten a bit of sensory overload from the noise. It couldn't have been quiet down here if ly had heard it in lin quarters. Ly wasn't needed here. Except that this was a perfect distraction. It had even worked on Viyar.

———

"Sabotage," the head of station security said, grimly. "That freighter was meant to do damage."

Viyar sighed. "I'll see what I can shake out, but there's only one of me."

"I'm not asking you to investigate, just keep your eyes open," she said, after a long moment. "I know you have other priorities."

"I think it was a distraction. We just need to work out what from."

A highly successful distraction. Nobody hurt, attention drawn to the wrong place. Viyar felt like a rookie. How had ly been so stupid as to go investigate the obvious incident when ly should have gone the other way to see what was really happening? Was ly losing lin edge?

"It got us all if so."

That made lin feel slightly better, even if she was only station security. "It was loud."

"They knew exactly what to do to make it loud. I warned the humans, they're checking their ship and dock."

"Thank you." That was one less thing he needed to do. "What about the tyrar and glen?"

"Same thing with them, but they didn't have to deal with an attempted poisoning this week."

It didn't flow together as the same people. This was too loud. People who would do this were more likely to opt for explosives. Fantastic. The last thing ly needed was for there to be multiple operators on the station tripping over each other. That was how innocent bystanders and kids got hurt.

Ly should get Meruhin off the station sooner rather than later. Now that her cousin had relinquished claim, it was only a matter of getting her and the Ambassador to agree. And the Ambassador knew so little about the options ly was fairly sure it was going to be up to the kid.

Multiple operators. "This doesn't flow. I'm going to keep poking around." Inwardly, ly sighed. Ly was *not* a spacer type. Ly did not want to stay on the station for weeks.

Ly was going to be on the station for weeks. "I don't suppose," ly added wistfully, "That you have any office space I can use."

"Not that isn't shared."

"It was worth a try." For right now ly was going to get lunch and not think about it, that often being the best way to work out a solution.

Ly thought wistfully of a hunting trip. Or, perhaps, a fishing trip. Fishing was more relaxing. Hunting was better for your instincts. After this ly was going to need, ly reckoned, both. But for right now ly had a fishing trip of a different kind to work up.

THE OFFWORLDERS HAD ENCOUNTERED nothing unusual. Viyar turned lin attention to the other side of the freight docks.

A freighter had docked there about thirty minutes before the crash.

Orbital windows were such that there was often a cluster of incoming and outgoing ships. The freighter which had hit the station had been coming from the scientific outpost on Velyx. The one which had come in just before was an interstellar from the tyrar homeworld.

An interstellar was likely to be carrying rather stranger supplies. The one from Velyx had been mostly empty; the outpost there was not self-sufficient and imported basic foodstuffs and material for replicating clothing. The interstellar, on the other hand, had likely been quite full of stuff. Surveillance cameras showed dockworkers of all genders assisting the robots in moving pallets of goods from the freighter to a dockside warehouse.

Now the reverse process would be going on. The crew, meanwhile, would be enjoying some liberty on the station. Freighter crew were rough people, the spiritual descendants of marine sailors and before that of the caravans that had criss-crossed Kyx. What might have been on this freighter that it was worth a distraction to smuggle on board? From the timing, it had to be incoming cargo not outgoing. Everything would be inspected, both to make sure it matched the manifest and to ensure there was no contraband. Which generally meant chemicals, drugs, or biologicals. From the interstellar, biologicals were a real concern. The things that had happened when ky'iin had blithely thought they could plant their gardens on Tyranis. That lesson had been learned, but of course the tyrar remembered primarily that it had been learned on their backs.

They had no reason to forgive the ky'iin, but yet they were still, if not allies, then at least uncertain neighbors. And allied with the humans who linked them together. The humans were the ly'iin of the Council of Worlds, he understood suddenly. The ones who formed a bridge as ly'iin had once formed a bridge between males and females.

Who made the difference between barbarism and civilization. The glen were too alien. Ky'iin were predators. Tyrar were prey. Humans, ly suddenly understood, were *both*. And that was what the bridge needed to be. Biologicals, then. He pulled up the interstellar's route. It had come from Tyranis. If anything odd had come from Tyranis he would bet it was engineered, not natural. That blighted world, though, did produce some odd hybrids between different evolutions. Plants and animals that mingled two worlds. Sometimes only they could survive what that world had become. Monsters, the tyrar called them.

Ly had never quite understood why. Ly looked at their manifest. Oh no. Ly was not seeing what ly thought ly was seeing.

23

WHAT HAD HAPPENED HAD BEEN a stupid accident, a freighter hitting the docks. The alarm caused was out of all proportion and the bar Dhyanil went to to get a stiff drink was crowded with others doing the same thing.

There was even a glyn in the bar, drinking something purple that it pulled through its mandible like a straw. He could see it go down. Even offworlders could get shaken up. He sat as far from the glyn as he could, keeping one eye on it. He knew he shouldn't use the neuter inanimate pronoun for them; except that glen honestly didn't mind *what* pronoun you used for them. Their language, after all, had no gender and he suspected they had had no concept of such before meeting other races. Nothing on their world had sexes.

He downed the drink in one swallow, basically just tossing it into his maw and considered a second. The incident had reminded him that it was possible for one well-placed bomb, or well-placed accident, to kill everyone on this station. Then he smelled her, and instantly became quite remarkably sober, as if her scent interfered with the action of the alcohol.

She came up behind him. "We have the first thing we need," she whispered in his ear, leaning over him loverlike.

He felt his body respond to that. "Then why not...uh...just grab a drink."

Despite the suppressors she had him flustered. It was the gesture. It reminded him of the mother of his children, years ago. Of his own mother. Of the feeling he had of running out of time, but if he didn't do something to sabotage Kysrehin's efforts, then millions would die.

He hoped it wouldn't matter. He hoped her plan was too flawed.

"Mmm....good idea." She signaled the barkeep. "Pour me one of whatever he was having."

The harried barkeep did so. As she reached for her drink he was able to worm slightly away from her, but he had to act as if she had had a full effect on him.

If she worked out she didn't have him under control, bad things were going to happen. Probably bad things involving airlocks. Or something in his drink. He wished he could put something in *her* drink. Not to kill her, but to make her miserable. To make her leave him alone.

Except then he wouldn't know what was going on, he wouldn't know the plan. In the dim bar, he shifted his body language to look receptive and waited for what else she had to say.

HE COULDN'T DO what she asked. She had failed to realize something.

He no longer had access to Meruhin, and definitely did not have access to the humans. Finding out the information she wanted was, thus, no easier for him than it was to her. Blatantly lie? Even with the drugs that was going to be very hard to do. Get himself thrown off the station? Or claim he *had* been thrown off? That was the easiest way to walk away.

He didn't want to walk away. Not any more. He wanted to stop her. Was it time, thus, to go to the Special Investigator? He thought not.

She'd asked him to find out what he could about the human's schedule, when she might leave the embassy empty, and then gone to oversee the storage of what they needed. Which he only knew in vague terms. She was smart enough to keep knowledge compartmentalized.

He needed backup he could absolutely trust. Obviously, that wasn't Viyar. It had to be a ly'iin. All of his friends were on the planet.

He felt abruptly alone and vulnerable and he found his steps taking him along the promenade. The crowds could give him the illusion of safety, but they seemed thin and scanty.

He would be better on the planet, in Capital or Martown or any of the other big cities. Or back home on the pier with a rod and reel. It *was* time to walk away. His mother needed him, or claimed she did. He couldn't. Maybe he was still under Kysrehin's spell. Somebody bumped into him. He growled a "Watch where you're going" after them. Another man.

There was something in his pocket that hadn't been there before. Somebody else enlisting him in a scheme? If so, he was getting off this station right now. He was completely and utterly done with all of this. He was going to quit. He wasn't going to be an activist any more. He got to the side, checked his pocket. It was a memory stone. He ran his fingers over It, reading the tally on it, the old way of communicating such things.

Or a code. It could well be a code they thought he knew, or it could be a way of saying he had backup after all. Only people on the coast used this type of memory stone. Somebody on the station was on his side after all. The problem was that he had no idea who they were. None, and he was not going to be able to find out.

Yet, it made him feel bizarrely better and more comfortable. Safer. Now he just had to work out what the stone meant.

THE MEMORY STONE sat on the foldout desk in his quarters. If you could call it a desk.

In the light, it was streaked with blue, which meant it was a family record. He had a relative on the station who didn't want him to know. Or it was from his mother. Another attempt to get him to come back. Saying things she couldn't or didn't want to say through a link which might be monitored.

It was a tally of deaths. His mother was dying. And of course too proud to say it where an enemy might hear. He felt an odd, cold chill go through him. She had always seemed immortal, but of course she was old. Very old.

It was her time. And she needed him. And billions of people were going to die. What did he do? He felt his heart split down the middle. He was a bad son. But she was only his mother, not his father. He did not owe her anything, by tradition.

By tradition the humans were insects, because in that tradition only ky'iiin could have myoran and anything without myoran was an animal. He wanted another drink, but he needed to keep his head clear. And he needed to resolve this quickly then get out and go home.

It was a time limit, that was all. A time limit before he would have to throw himself on Viyar's mercy and hope he had enough information to purchase his freedom. The room felt very small right now. The memory stone felt very large. But the courier who had brought it was likely still on the station.

He didn't have a stone and a knife. He had access to the next best thing. He could print a fake memory stone, and somehow get it to the courier. It would tell her he was doing what he felt needed to be done.

But he would have to lie to her and hope she never found out. Hope she died thinking he had done his best to destroy the offworlders. Not save them.

His heart fell into little pieces and became glass that lay on the ground where he could step in it. He was not who he thought he was, and there was no way for him to be anything else. He had no integrity, no purpose. He went back to the bar.

He got very, very drunk indeed.

24

VIYAR WAS WORRIED. Ly had no proof, nothing to act on yet. But ly was pretty sure that somebody had smuggled *verians* onto the station.

Verians were an insect that carried a virus lethal to tyrar. It was not lethal to ky'iin unless they had a compromised immune system. Release them in the tyrar embassy's air flow and there was no risk of harming anyone but the tyrar.

Well, and possibly the human. Nobody know what verian fever would do to her. Ly would have to talk to the doctors on the station, but for right now ly had to warn the tyrar contingent. With the caveat that ly could be wrong. There could be another reason why the ship was carrying a certain mushroom; it was considered a delicacy by some when turned into a sauce.

Void, maybe they were hoping the humans would have a taste for it. It was also the only food on which *verian* larvae would feed. And it had been brought on behind anyone's back and, furthermore, buried in the manifest. Lying would have got them caught if inspected. Flying under the radar combined with the distraction?

No, this was bad, and ly knew it. Ly headed for the embassy level. There were tyrar and glen embassies, plus the currently-lone human.

There was room for more. There was a rumor about another race that the humans had found, but they were not yet starfaring.

Their homeworld was under a threat that nobody could resolve, so they would *have* to become so. They would be here too, before long.

Ly rather thought that if this continued they would have to build an entire second station to house the embassies and whatever council formed. That might not be a terrible idea. Ly stopped outside the tyrar embassy, waiting to be recognized. The door opened, and ly stepped inside.

The wet fur smell of the tyrar hit lin right away; ly knew ly would stop noticing after a few minutes, but it was a smell that was at once disturbing and unfortunately reminiscent of prey animals. Tyrar *were* prey.

One of them detached herself (most likely) from the group and came over to lin. "Special Investigator," she rumbled after tapping the frequency transponder that would translate her voice to a pitch he could hear.

They still kept it deep. The slight latency after she moved her lips was also a little disturbing.

"I'm afraid there's a potential threat."

She nodded. "As always."

Ly thought of some of the things tyrar had done to ky'iin. They had reason. Things were being fixed now, slowly, but the initial relationship between the species had been one of disturbing exploitation. One of destruction and pain. "I stress that this isn't confirmed, but there might be *verians* on the station."

"I'll double check with the tech types that our air system is isolated."

"Don't accept any deliveries from anyone you don't trust for a while. I'll get to the bottom of it."

Which was station security's job, not lin. Ly was starting to think ly was the only competent person on the station.

Ly might not even be wrong.

AFTER WARNING THE TYRAR, lin hesitated at the human's door. Ly wanted to warn her. Or at least talk to her.

It was unlikely verian fever would impact humans. Virii generally didn't cross ecosystems well, although this one certainly *did* to a degree. But they'd already had one ill-thought-out poisoning attempt.

Ly stopped outside the door. It took a bit longer for her to answer, but when she did the reason was readily explained. Her head fur was wet. She must have been bathing. A faintly floral scent wafted off her, perhaps that of some bathing oil or soap.

"Can I come in?" ly asked.

"Second." She ducked back in, then a moment later called, "Come."

Ly had *not* caught her ready for visitors and ly felt sorry. "I'm sorry. I should have..."

"No, it's not your fault it took me forever to get started this morning." Her teeth showed for a moment.

"I've had those mornings too. So, here's the thing. It's probably not aimed at you, but it's possible somebody smuggled a disease-causing insect onto the station."

She sighed. "What do they look like?"

"They're tiny. They can get through the air system. They're from Tyranis, the tyrar homeworld, and they're only a worry to tyrar as far as we know. They can't bite glen, and ky'iin may get it, but very mildly. The virus just isn't programmed to affect us."

"But you don't know about humans." She nodded. "What are the symptoms?"

"Fever and headache, in ky'iin. In tyrar...it progresses to paralysis and death if not treated. And sometimes even *with* treatment."

She used a word he didn't understand. It sounded oddly technical. Then, "Thank you."

"It might not affect you at all."

"But it's not going to kill ky'iin."

"Not unless somebody has a major immune system compromise."

She nodded. "A biological weapon."

"*Or* it's possible they're just trying to sell mushrooms. If somebody tries to sell you mushrooms, let me know."

She made a startled sound. "Mushrooms?"

"The insects lay their larvae in them. But they cook down into a quite tasty sauce. It's just..."

"...that the person bringing them here sneaked them onto the station." She started to pace.

Ly looked around. She had spent some time decorating the room. On the wall were a few pictures, and he turned to look at one which showed a desert world. No, past a desert world; from the color and complete lack of vegetation, ly suspected it was a dead world. The ground was littered with rocks, and in the distance was the entrance to some kind of canyon.

Ly turned, "Where is that?"

"It's a bit outside Bradbury City, Mars. Where I'm from."

"Not your species' homeworld." She was a *colonist*?

"No. That's Earth. Mars is a terrestrial planet that's not technically habitable, but with the right technology you can live there."

Ly tilted lin head. "I guess I assumed..."

"That I wasn't from a colony?" A pause. "I was picked for my...abilities."

"You're good at languages." It wasn't even a guess. She had to be very good. "I'd like to talk to the dolphin."

"I'll translate. Iterk said you already video called him out of curiosity. He was curious too."

"It makes me wonder what other species have myoran that we don't know about."

She paused, then, "Me too."

Viyar got a sample of the verian fever virus sent to the human ship for analysis. They knew how to handle potentially dangerous diseases. From what she had hinted before ly left there was quite the list. Back in lin quarters ly also requested videos about the history of Mars. Ly was curious now.

Ly discovered that it was the fourth planet in their system, one out from their homeworld, but too small to have sustained a magnetic field and atmosphere long enough to develop complex life. It seemed there had been simple life forms once. Now it was a dead world to which they had brought life. Not like the ice worlds. But with that technology...there was no similar world in the Kyx system, or they would have colonized it.

It was something they could learn from the humans. Colonizing a world without a magnetosphere wasn't something the ky'iin had ever attempted. The tyrar had a similar world in their system. Somebody should tell them about this. Ly reminded linself ly was not a diplomat and should not interfere. But they could learn to colonize it, or they could sell it to the humans in return for something else useful.

Ly saw the patterns starting to form. And who would be the true center of it? Ideally no one. Lin terminal flickered with an incoming message.

The message was anonymized. Lin could see the body language of the person on the other end well enough to recognize what they were saying, and from their build ly was sure it was a male. Other than that. Ly watched it three times, body language wilting a little with each one. Then ly sent a simple response.

So, ly was almost certainly right. These people at least thought verian fever would harm humans. But if they intended to infect the human homeworld, then they would need to release something there.

The mushrooms. Humans might *well* have a taste for them, and if they were preserved in the right way the larvae would survive. Then they might well breed on the human homeworld.

But not on Mars. The domes would, surely, control vermin well. Which meant that even if they succeeded they would fail. Well, except for starting the war they no doubt wanted. Or did they?

Ly didn't know enough and while ly suspected the identity of the person sending the anonymous tip, ly was going to respect his anonymity. It would benefit nobody if *anyone* went out of an airlock. Except perhaps the person behind this.

25

ANOTHER MORNING OF REGRETS, and of fear that he was turning into an addict. Running away into a bottle was something he should definitely stop doing, but he wasn't sure what other escape route he had. Wasn't that how addiction started?

It started when you were trapped and it was treated by getting out of the trap. Nothing else would work in the long term. You had to solve the problem. His problem was Kysrehin, and he should run away back to the planet.

Instead, he took a hangover remedy and tried to put himself in her shoes. What did she need? She needed a virus that would affect humans but not ky'iin. She probably would not care if it affected tyrar, glyn, or anyone else. It wouldn't affect glyn, likely. They didn't have the same genetics.

She didn't have access to the human homeworld for any kind of starter disease. She did have access to various ky'iin colonies and Tyranis.

Tyranis was a mess, but that only meant there were more interesting diseases there. All kinds of interesting diseases with all kinds of vectors. He shuddered. Yet another reason why it was better for *everyone* if offworlders stayed separate. If the ky'iin had never come to Tyranis, then it would still be a beautiful world.

Dhyanil shook his head. It was their fault. And then he understood. The philosophical difference between him and Kysrehin.

She wanted to protect ky'iin from offworlders, from inferior influences and beings of doubtful myoran. For him, it was about protecting *everyone*. Ky'iin, tyrar, humans. It was about how different species inherently could not and should not work together. He sent a quick, cryptic message to somebody on planet who might be able to help. Then he turned his attention to what the public databanks could tell him. He couldn't escape the Tyranis thought.

An interstellar in from Tyranis. It carried, he was sure, a nasty package indeed. Or he was completely wrong and it was all being done in some lab on planet. They couldn't test it. If he was a scientist, he could stop this very easily, without anyone getting hurt. Or killed. He was going to get killed. He was sure of that. Or he was going to end up in protection somewhere, never to go home to White Fish.

And it was his own fault. That was enough to make him want more alcohol. He managed not to go there.

This time.

THERE WAS somebody outside his door.

Dhyanil sighed. "Come in."

Station security. Two *burly* women, clearly chosen to intimidate.

"Am I under arrest?" he asked. Of course, if he was then they would most likely solve his immediate problem by the simple method of putting him on the next shuttle back to Kyx. The shuttle he badly wanted to be on.

"We need to talk."

"Then talk."

The door closed behind them. The transient room was too small for three people, and these were not small people. It was likely to have any desired effect. He thought of just telling them everything.

"Your cousin is missing."

"Merehin?" he squeaked.

"She didn't make it to the shuttle she was supposed to take. Protective custody was breached. You don't know anything about that, right?"

He shook his head. "I don't." He couldn't and wouldn't vouch for the rest of the family. But he had not grabbed her.

One of the women turned to the other. "He still stinks of alcohol."

"What of it? I might have had one too many last night."

"Which is a good thing," she said, turning back. "When did you *start* drinking?"

"About the nineteenth hour."

"Which means he was either already blind drunk or well on the way there when she was snatched," the other said. "Which bar?" she added, turning back to him.

He gave the name. He wasn't going back there. He'd probably been permanently cut off.

"Okay. Doesn't mean you aren't involved."

"I would never hurt her."

"But dragging her back to her dad, that you would do."

"That was the plan. She's now bigger than I am." He hoped the joke would achieve something.

It did get laughter. Then, he added. "Please tell me when you find her. Tell me she's safe."

As they turned to leave one of them said, "Of course."

He let his heart rate return to normal. It took a while. It wasn't alcohol he needed. It was answers. It was to know she was safe.

And to know for sure Kysrehin did not have her. Because he could not be sure. He could not be sure she had not been taken to use as leverage.

Or she could have run away again. Void, maybe she'd stowed away on an interstellar this time. Maybe she hadn't trusted them not to take her back to White Fish.

His headache was back.

This time, it was not the booze.

HE IGNORED KYSREHIN. He ignored the prospect of billions of dead humans; not that he thought they would pull it off.

Dhyanil cared about one thing right now and only one. Finding Meruhin.

The interstellar had just left. They were standing off while they searched the ship for stowaways. He half hoped they would find her there. He would then help them put her on a shuttle, dang it. He would escort her down to the planet if they let him.

He did not want to let her out of his sight again. He felt for the people she had got away from. She would make a fine adult one day. If she didn't get herself killed. And that was assuming she had run. What if she *had* been kidnapped? She was already bigger than him, but that wasn't exactly hard, and she was young, inexperienced and definitely smaller than any adult female.

She could have easily been taken by force, but he suspected if she had been taken it had been by guile. There were so many things that she could be lured with. That was usually how you grabbed a kid anyway. He *prowled* the promenade. People, even women, avoided him and his body language. He was too obviously on the hunt.

Which might get him stopped by station security again, but he did not care. Meruhin was his responsibility. Getting her safely to school was his task. He knew he should return her home. It was a waste of time to even try. He knew and accepted that now. It wasn't hard to accept it, given the circumstances. She was going to soar.

If she was still alive.

"Sir?" somebody asked. A single syllable, quite understandable.

He turned. He'd seen this man with Kysrehin. Small station.

"Oh, it's you," he said.

He growled, "If Kysrehin or *any* of you lay one finger on her every deal is off."

"I think you had better come with me."

They had her and they were going to use her for something, and whatever it was he wouldn't like it. The acrid smell of the space station strengthened for a moment. He snarled, then he followed the other man. He had no choice. He had had choices, but now they had been stripped away from him. Kysrehin wouldn't kill him. She needed him.

The real question was, what did she need him for that was this important? The man led him to a transient hotel, not the one he was staying in. Not that it mattered; they were all the same, except for the signs outside, the numbers assigned to them. Or was something else going on?

26

VIYAR WAS ABOUT to give up.

Well, no. Ly was constitutionally incapable of giving up. But every day something got added to this case, only making it worse. It was a tangled mess. All the threads pulled together just nicely enough that ly couldn't ignore any of them, but not so nicely that ly could solve it. The girl was missing. Ly couldn't find the mushrooms.

And they had just caught another man trying to put something in the tyrar embassy's air supply. From talking to the tyrar, it would have been harmless to them, just hugely irritating. Ly would have called it a prank if it wasn't for everything else going on. The humans had been warned. The human response to being warned was, "If they try that with us, we have the chemical composition of skunk in our databanks on the ship." Ly wasn't sure what skunk was. Ly was pretty sure ly did not *want* to know what skunk was, except that humans would consider it appropriate retaliation for bad smells.

It might be time, ly thought, to bring Dhyanil in again, but he was neither in his quarters nor in any public part of the station. He had an alibi for the girl's disappearance by virtue of being blind drunk at the time. The man had a problem. Of course, if he *had* taken her and dragged her home, there would not be a case; as a related adult acting on behalf of her father he had every legal right to do so. The fact that he hadn't was probably bad for the kid, but ly was more concerned about other dangers.

The isolationists wouldn't kill a kid. Ly had to assume they had enough myoran for that. If she was a few years older, though... A few years older and bigger and stronger. Children were prey at so many levels. Small, weak, and naive. Maybe that was why people felt protective of the human. She was child-sized. Ly found linself outside the embassy. Ly needed to lay it all out with somebody and why not the ultimate outsider. Ly had talked to her earlier on video.

The door opened. "Will you help me with something?" she asked.

"Gladly, if you'll be a sounding board for me."

She made the rattling sound that passed for human laughter. "Of course."

No doubt she had realized and understood that to ky'iin she was a potentially-useful outside viewpoint. Maybe that was why offworlders were valuable. Ly understood the point of view of the isolationists. Ly understood that not everyone would see their value. As ly came all the way in, ly realized there was another human in the room.

Viyar kind of stood frozen. So did the other human. They were lean, lighter in color than Suza, with black headfur that had been cropped much shorter. Very light, almost unhealthy looking, although perhaps that wasn't a fair comparison. Who knew what was healthy for a human? They carried themselves in a way that made him think, for a moment, that they were ly'iin. Humans had no ly'iin and their women acted more like men and vice versa. But he couldn't entirely shake the vibe.

"It's fine. You'll be a good test." She turned and rattled something off in her own language.

The other human responded. Their vocalizations were quick and rapid and slightly tonal. Nothing like ky'iin speech. An advantage, ly realized. A major evolutionary advantage the ky'iin had skipped. The disadvantage was that you couldn't communicate anything if the other person couldn't hear. Ly did not think it evened out.

The second human, who wore a jumpsuit with a word on it, likely the name of their ship, turned to face him, but he could see the distress in their...no, her...eyes. Definitely a female with the extra curves. In the human language, she stammered out, "Hi."

A greeting.

He stood very still, not wanting to scare her further.

"I'm Tiffany Bailey," she said, finally.

He understood a name."Viyar," he greeted. Just the personal name. Humans used their clan names in such informal contexts.

She nodded, brushed back her head fur, and then couldn't stand it any more. She fled the room.

Suza watched her go, then turned back to Viyar.

"We're trying a drug which blunts the human reaction to ky'iin, hoping that will allow for desensitization. We're also trying some video desensitization I came up with." There was no bragging in her tone or her body language.

Just a simple statement of fact. No, there *was* bragging, but it was the kind of healthy acknowledgment of one's own capabilities that everyone should have.

"I don't mind being a test," ly said finally. "Especially if your liaisons..."

"They're kind of busy," she admitted. "So, you wanted a sounding board?"

"I need an outsider. You're more of an outsider than anyone on this station." She didn't even come out much. Or perhaps ly had simply not seen her.

"So...does this have to do with stink bombs?"

Ly laughed briefly. "Not directly. The fact is...we have some very strong elements here for isolationism. And they fall into two broad groups."

She nodded. "One of them is the offworlders aren't really sentient crowd. I know *all* about them." Her face made an odd expression. "They tried to kill me more than once while I was negotiating peace."

"And the other is the people who feel that any contact between species is dangerous to both. That we will contaminate each other and lose touch with who we are."

"We have both groups back where I come from," she mused. "We *think* we screened them off the *Challenger*." She paused.

"I hope you did, I'm having enough difficulty with ours without human isolationists allying with them."

Not with the first group, ly meant. But there had to be sympathy with the second.

"Maybe we should set up colony worlds for those people. Offer them land and infrastructure. Tell them they can be..." A pause. "A control group, or something. We already have people on Earth who isolate from the rest of society."

"Of course you do. We have some people in the mountains who still want to follow their old ways. They're the only patriarchal society on Kyx."

"I suppose there had to be one somewhere," Suza mused. "Is there a society in which the ly'iin are in charge?"

"All of them and none." Ly laughed. "I suppose you have had more contact with ly'iin."

"I have. No offense but I'm trying to fix that. I'm aware that you believe having ly'iin is vital to civilization."

"You seem to manage."

"Maybe in different ways. We don't experience rut, so...maybe that's why we don't need you. Although to be fair, we have those who don't consider themselves male or female either, and some societies have expelled them, but others have valued them." She glanced at the door the other human went through.

"That was one of your ly'iin?"

"Not in a biological sense, but...yes. Something like. And very different. I don't know if she would be flattered or insulted." She paused. "Some of those who don't align as men or women still use the same pronouns, some don't. She considers herself to be something not quite a woman."

Ly couldn't help but laugh. "You are more like us than we thought."

"And less," Suza said simply. "It's always going to be both more and less."

ALWAYS BOTH MORE AND LESS. Ly thought about that for a long moment. She had turned away from him, was looking at the picture of the colony world she had grown up on.

Ly waited for her to turn back. "You probably don't have to worry about stink bombs."

"If they try anything like that they will learn about getting into prank wars with humans. I *meant* that."

"But we do have to worry about other stuff. How long is your ship staying here?"

"Until we have a full diplomatic delegation, which is in the works," she said. "They don't want to leave me without *any* backup."

"I understand that."

She seemed remarkably unconcerned with it, though. Was she brave? Did she simply not see the ky'iin as dangerous?

Or, more likely, ly was just unable to read her underlying body language. Viyar did not, after all, know humans. Ly struggled with tyrar, despite longer experience.

Ly didn't even try with glen.

"It probably won't be too long. We have some potential candidates who are resistant and then we can start working on desensitization. No more accidental shooting."

"No, no more deliberate shooting for no good reason. Never say no more accidents."

She rattled again. "Ky'iin have that superstition too, I remember."

Something else they had in common. Or perhaps all species with language. It was logical to fear that speaking something made it true. Quite, quite logical.

Ly understood that. "We certainly do. Even people who have long since given up on religion."

"I think it's about sentience itself and the way we see patterns. We might see different patterns, but without pattern recognition things are hopeless. You probably can't even survive."

There was an enthusiasm to her. Ly tried to work out what her body language meant, what her scent meant. Her scent, mingled with a faint floral one. Multiple faint floral ones. From the plants she had put in here, the green plants. One of them now had pink blooms on it. That had to be at least one of the scents.

Then the station shook again.

"Void."

"That's not good."

"I doubt this is another freighter accident."

No, it was something else. Ly was not sure what. The embassy was as good a place as any other to wait to find out.

27

A CONFERENCE ROOM in the motel, the kind of place travelers rented by the hour for meetings they weren't comfortable having in public. The air scrubbers were slightly wheezy, like an old female snoring as she slept. The place smelled. This was most definitely the low rent district of the station and was no place Dhyanil wanted to be.

"We have your...cousin."

"She's not involved in this," Dhyanil said.

The man set a box of suppressors on the table. "You won't let us control you, we needed more leverage."

"Void forsake you," Dhyanil swore, snarling. "She's a child."

"She was old enough to put herself in this situation."

Perhaps there was a point to that argument, but Dhyanil was not going to blame Meruhin for this. Well, maybe a little. It *wouldn't* have happened if she'd stayed safe at home. Yet, she certainly hadn't intended anything. He fell silent, listening to the snoring wheeze for what felt like a very long moment indeed.

"What do you want me to do?"

"Go back to Kyx. Bring us Professor Garil from the University of Northspire."

Whether he wanted to come or not was the undertone. "I don't think I can..."

"You're a clever man. You'll think of something."

He would think of something indeed. It was going to involve Kysrehin, this guy, and airlocks. He was going to tear them apart. He was angry enough not to care about honor and ethics, but until he had a plan he had to play along.

"Prove that you have her."

"I sent a video to your account. Run along now."

He didn't quite run, but if ky'iin had not long since lost their tails, that appendage would be firmly between his legs. He should have gone to Viyar right away, or to station security. Now they had a hostage. A hostage who could not, quite, be trusted to rescue herself. He wished she could be. In a few years he wouldn't want to take her on.

He had to find her and get her out, except that if he didn't get on the next shuttle to the planet...

...and as pointed out, Dhyanil was a very clever ky'iin. They'd think of this, they'd check for it, but it was the only hope he had. That and the hope that they would not really be willing to harm a child.

IT WASN'T GOING to be hard to find somebody willing to be him in order to get down to the planet. No, that part was going to be easy. Find a stranded worker, or somebody with a family emergency and not quite enough money for a trip downstairs. Doing it without them knowing when it was the obvious dodge? That part was going to be hard, and he went over and over it in his mind.

He couldn't let them send him after this professor, although it would...maybe he could enlist him in this. He was a professor of virology. They were going to coerce him into helping them kill all the humans, if they couldn't persuade him. He couldn't do any of this. He couldn't even move for a moment, caught in a freeze state where there was nothing but fear and anger and frustration.

There was a word for it in the mountain language. He couldn't dredge it from the depths of his mind right now.

It didn't matter. He even considered an ancient and very final out, for half a second. It would solve everything. Then he considered it some more.

He would not kill himself. If he did they would simply find somebody else; the only thing it might do, maybe, was save Meruhin. At least he could trust her not to go over to them. He was sure and certain that she would never do that. She would try and escape.

A child, but one who was on the verge of becoming an adult. He went back to the issue of what would happen if he was dead. He wouldn't be able to get any more information. Why was he so determined to save them? He had no reason for it.

No reason other than not wanting to be tarred with their brush, to be part of taking things to their extreme. The humans going away benefited him. The tyrar going away benefited him. He was packing. He certainly couldn't stay in this room. Disappearing on the station? He tried every way in his mind. It couldn't be done.

It could be done, there was one way to do it, but his mind shied from it. Besides, they hadn't been able to protect her. They wouldn't be able to protect him. But if he was dead...

It was not despair, it was rational consideration.

He knew he could no longer try to achieve this on his own. And then the station shook. Rung like a bell. Again.

He finished packing, then hesitated. He had brought too much. If his stuff was discovered here, then everyone would know something was up. He hesitated too long. The door opened. It was station security.

"Packing, I see."

"I'm getting myself out of your hide," he informed them.

"You're coming with us."

With a sigh, he followed. He seemed to be spending his life being taken places by different people. He was never going to actually get to go anywhere of his own choice again. He followed mutely.

"Keep it casual," one of them said. "Try not to look like you're under arrest."

Which, of course, he was. He absolutely was under arrest. They just...

...didn't want him blamed for whatever had happened, but wanted him off the board. It was *that* kind of a situation. He was escorted to the security offices.

"I am *trying* to get off your station."

"So are a lot of people. Somebody decided to make that harder."

"They blew up the shuttle."

The fact that he was packing probably made for an alibi of sorts. He was clearly intending to leave. But...

"Somebody blew up the shuttle. We think their timer malfunctioned."

He was meant to be on that shuttle. But that had to be a coincidence, surely. They needed him alive. Unless somebody else had in mind killing him.

It *was* a neat solution to the problem he presented. "I didn't do it and I doubt I was the target."

"We're confident on the former," the chief said, finally, shooing the others out of the room. "Not so much on the latter. Start talking."

"Somebody tried to recruit me into a plot."

"And you said no, and they're mad about it."

A pause. "I couldn't say no. She used pheromones on me." This wasn't the person he wanted to tell.

Her face said it all. Utter disgust.

"It's a plot against the human ship. I believe they're going to try and sneak something nasty on board when it leaves." Then he swallowed. "And they took my cousin."

"To make extra sure you'd do what they said."

"I...want to talk to the Special Investigator."

"I'll see if ly wants to talk to you."

She left him there. The door wasn't locked. He could walk out. She was counting on the fact that he had, at this point, way too much sense to do so.

28

"THERE WAS A BOMB," station security informed lin.

"Did you already..."

"We brought in a couple of people, but both had either...alibis or explanations. One of them wants to talk to you."

"Are they a flight risk?"

"Absolutely."

Viyar laughed. "I'll come over." Ly didn't want to have whoever it was dragged to lin office. And a cooperative witness who could turn into a flight risk at the drop of a hat was something to be a little bit concerned about. Ly didn't ask who it was. Ly was pretty sure ly already knew.

The station was a bit subdued, but only a bit. Truth was that attacks like this were far too common; they were how too many people expressed their politics. What had been blown up was the shuttle in dock. The planetary shuttle. Viyar suspected they had intended to blow it up after it was loaded but something had gone wrong. Station security hinted at suspecting the same thing. Reaching the office, a young woman showed lin into an interrogation room.

"Why am I not surprised to see you?"

The scrawny man seemed to study lin for a moment. "Because I'm trouble?"

"Because you *are* trouble."

"They have Meruhin."

"Do you have proof of this?"

"Close enough. A video. It could be faked, but where else could she be?"

"Thankfully not on that shuttle."

Dhyanil shuddered. "We're all lucky it went off early. Was anyone killed?"

"No."

And that was a good thing. Shuttles could be replaced. Lives were, well. Gone when they were gone, and you mourned and you moved on.

"Good."

"So, *they* have Meruhin. Did *they* blow up the shuttle?"

"Given they had easier ways to kill me and were trying to put me on it, no."

Viyar elected to take that as read for now. "Who's trying to stop them?"

"I don't know." Dhyanil reached up, claws retracted, to rub his temples for a moment.

He seemed genuinely exhausted and stressed. His life had definitely taken multiple turns for the worse. "Of course, it could be some other..."

"It wasn't a very neat assassination attempt."

"I'm suspecting it wasn't an assassination attempt, but old fashioned terrorism. And if that's the case, maybe it *didn't* malfunction."

Maybe the bomber hadn't actually wanted to hurt or kill anyone, just make people scared and keep them on the station. Viyar stored that up. "So, what do they have in mind?"

Dhyanil hesitated. There was something in his eyes. "Genocide."

VERIAN FEVER. Reengineered to affect humans.

That was their plan. "I...feared something like that. There were ylari mushrooms on an interstellar that they tried to keep quiet."

Ly wasn't sure ly should tell Dhyanil everything, except Dhyanil already knew more of everything than ly did.

"That makes sense. And if they play their cards right, they could try for the tyrar too." Dhyanil looked at ly. "I swear on my father's soul, I am *not* in favor of this."

"What are you in favor of?"

"Staying apart. Not contaminating each other."

Viyar thought of Suza, the human. Who's name ly still could not pronounce. "What if it's not contamination?"

"Things will..."

Ly rested a hand on the table. "Things will *always* change. Things need to change. Doesn't mean we should let change barrel onwards without a check, but things will always change."

"I know that. I'm not one of those who wants to turn back the clock to the time when being male meant the only thing I was supposed to worry about was hatchlings."

Viyar laughed. "I didn't think you were. Those types...well..."

"Incubators and suppressors. We can't go back to that. Nobody's going to stand for it. But seriously..." The man's tone turned that way, his gestures sharpening. "Look at the tyrar homeworld."

"We aren't going to repeat that mistake."

"We don't think we are. But there's only one sure fire way to keep from repeating that mistake, and that's to *stay away from the humans*. For our sake. For their sake. Don't we make them a little crazy?"

Viyar thought of the human who had only been able to stand lin presence for a few minutes with the help of drugs. "We can work around that. We *should* work around it. Because they aren't going away."

Dhyanil thought about that. "I..."

"We live in the world as it *is*, not as we dream it."

An old mountain saying, that. "The world we dream is the one we should work for." The counter, awkward in the man's coastal accent.

"Sometimes you can't get the dream, Dhyanil. I'm not sure about them either." Ly was telling the truth. Ly liked Suza McRae but, of course, she was an ambassador. Being likable was a professional skill for her. "But we can learn from them."

"What can we learn from them?"

Ly thought of some things ly had seen. "How to colonize a world with minimal atmosphere more effectively. How different species deal with their biology."

The conflict between biology and myoran. The man unable to walk away from the rutting woman and the ly'iin standing between them. Protecting him. Protecting both of them.

Ly had been wrong. It was not the strange individual who did not quite consider herself a woman who was the human ly'iin. It was the ambassador herself.

LY FOUND OUT WHAT, exactly, Dhyanil was supposed to be doing for the genocidal maniacs.

"Do it. Go to this professor. We'll find Meruhin and tell you when she's safe."

"Should I actually bring him here or stall?" Dhyanil had asked, all willing to help.

Viyar didn't trust him, and never would, but he was not a genocidal maniac.

"We're going to give him a head's up. He'll stall *you* from what I've heard about him."

"Great. How many lectures on virology?"

"As many as it takes."

The man had returned to his quarters to finish packing. On the next shuttle, the damaged one having been taken to dry dock, he would go to the university and pretend to recruit the professor. Assuming he survived.

He seemed to know the risks he was facing, at least. He was not some child to be unaware of exactly what these people were capable of. He'd apparently considered faking his death as a way out of the situation.

Viyar owed it to him to find the girl. Ly held lin breath, though, until the shuttle was away. Had it been possible to hold it until the shuttle landed safely, ly would have. Station security had their eyes open for the girl, but Viyar knew ly couldn't rely on them. On the next shuttle would come some more suitable backup; people with experience in hostage situations. Ly hoped she could wait that long.

Stall them. It was the only answer. But ly could not be sure there was not already some serious suspicion. Ly could not be sure the girl was alive, although ly doubted they would kill her. At least not before spending a good, solid amount of time on trying to recruit her. Ly was counting on that. Fanatics were always looking for recruits. She wouldn't budge. Or she would pretend. There was some intelligence in that family, Viyar mused. Worth checking on.

Intelligence and strength of will. Dhyanil seemed a little short on the latter, but if it was true that he had had to deal with a really hot woman in rut asking him favors? There was a reason all civilized women stayed on suppressors until it was time to breed, then sequestered themselves with a chosen mate. The massive advantage: Most people now had children with mates they actually *liked*. More children had a relationship with their mothers rather than just their aunts. Families were tighter together.

But those old biological impulses weren't gone. They were just buried.

29

DHYANIL FINISHED PACKING.

Except now he had no idea where he was packing to go. Well, he was going to the University. After that? If his family got any whisper of the fact that he had betrayed the isolationists, they would disown him. Certainly his mother would. He thought of Iluhin, who had killed herself because she could not live with having accidentally killed.

He thought of the way his mother had called her weak for it. His mother was dying. He did not want her to end her life at odds with him, but there was the faintest understanding, like the distant scent of a scavenger, that she was not somebody worthy of his attention and love, not any more.

He stopped that thought. He had a ticket on the shuttle. He was going to the University, where he would pretend to spend a long time trying to convince a certain Professor to come help commit genocide. Hopefully, he could enlist the professor in this endeavor. It would be much easier if they were both working off the same script. So much easier. The downside to that was the obvious fear; that the professor would take their side. He didn't know. There were ways to find out, but those ways would also make a decent way to occupy himself while he was sitting in a shuttle. He would have a few hours at least to look over what the professor had published and see whether any of it gave a clue to Garil's politics.

Genocide was politics? He thought not. He got his luggage together. He had way overpacked. He had way underpacked. There was so much he wanted to go back to White Fish for. He was not going back to White Fish. Wherever he ended up, it would not be his small house by the beach. Where his children knew to find him if, rarely, they needed a father's wisdom.

Where he could walk on the beach any time he wanted. Where his expertise was valued by those who did not know that coast, the cliffs, the beaches. The reefs off the shore. It was home. It was lost to him for the sake of...

And he knew what he wanted. What he needed before he left. To see something of what he was giving it all up for. Ethically he was doing the right thing. But there were other urges. Biological and psychological. Ties of family and home. The likely quite natural desire to put one's own kin over others. He finished packing, and he turned to the terminal in his room.

And placed the call.

THE EMBASSY WAS FURNISHED a little oddly. There were pictures, old fashioned ones, on the walls. Those pictures showed images of a red desert of a world, a place where surely they couldn't live without assistance.

There were living plants, their leaves greener and less purple than the woods that ran inland from his home. Plants from the human homeworld.

And the human. She was child-sized, smaller than him, smaller than Meruhin. Not as small as a dwarf, but small enough to look young. To even trigger the instincts of a man to protect or a ly'iin to teach. Maybe that was a good thing.

She wore clothing over her body...blue trousers and a button-down shirt. It was not that different from what a ky'iin might wear. Clothing on bipeds was bound to meet certain functional requirements.

"Can I offer you some tea? It's harmless to ky'iin, but contains a very mild stimulant."

"How mild?" he asked suspiciously.

"Very. Unless you were planning on sleeping in the near future..."

"I'll try it." He couldn't believe he was saying these words. She poured an amber liquid into two cups, offered him one of them.

He took it carefully. The liquid was hot and he tilted a bit into his maw. The taste was...different. He was not sure whether he liked it or not.

"You..."

He took a deep breath. "I became embroiled in a plot to try and introduce a nasty disease that you would carry back to your homeworld."

"Now we know, we should be able to make sure that doesn't happen."

There was a steel to her voice. He had been warned not to see her as a Ky'iin female, but it was clear to him that she was something just as dangerous if not more so.

"One way or another?"

She dipped her head. "One way or another."

He tried the tea again. Now the edge was off the heat he could see the appeal, although he doubted he'd pay the elevated prices for an import. What was he even thinking? It was an offworld drink. He didn't want or need it. "I don't like offworlders," he said, finally.

"You aren't alone. And you don't have to."

Those were not words he had expected to hear from her. He watched her gestures, she made them smooth as a dance, looking for any sign of a lie.

"You don't have to like us," she repeated, her grey-blue eyes fixed on him. "You can avoid us, you can ignore us. And you've already proven you won't kill us."

"I might have. Not that long ago." He thought of Iluhin. She would never know the impact her death had had.

"But you won't. Some ky'iin will want to trade with us. Some won't. Same with humans."

She acted like it was okay. Like it was no big deal. Like, and this was the strangest thing, she wasn't insulted by the concept at all.

"But you like us," he said, finally.

Her lips curled back from her teeth for a moment, then quickly returned to normal. "I like your species better than I like most humans."

HER SCENT LINGERED in his nostrils. She did not smell like a woman. Or like a man. Or...or like a tyrar.

Tyrar smelled like livestock. It was easy to dismiss them as animals.

Glyn, with their heavy exoskeletons, smelled like rocks.

Humans were the most dangerous, because they could convince you they were people, they could do so quickly. She had convinced him. But then he had never been one to think the offworlders were animals. He *knew* they were dangerous. They were venomous snakes that pretended to be harmless.

He was terrified of her. He was not going to let anything happen to any of them. Because they were too dangerous to let out of ky'iin sight. He saw it now. These little people with their control and their willingness to work with and to try and understand were going to start something.

They were going to *spark* something and if the ky'iin threw them out of their system that something would grow and spread without them. They were the most dangerous beings in the universe, not because they didn't have myoran, but because it radiated from them. He shook his head as he headed to the shuttle. She was no doubt an exceptional specimen, especially as most humans *couldn't* look ky'iin in the eyes. But she could not be unique. Their leaders and diplomats could *all* be like that, divorced that bit from their biology.

He needed to meet more humans to know what to do, but he wanted to run from her. He wanted to hunt with her. He didn't have to have anything to do with them. That was almost the most frightening thing she had said. Utter confidence that they would win and pull the ky'iin into their web. Of course a diplomat would believe in working together.

This was somebody who had ended a war. This was somebody who was working alone as a sole liaison. He could not take her as typical. But he had seen those pictures. She came from a red desert world. But her homeworld was *green*, brighter green. A world, no doubt, that was lovely in its own way.

Once on the shuttle with his luggage stowed, he pulled out a standard headset, pulled up Professor Garil's work and started to read. It distracted him from reentry, from the burning fear and desire that came from understanding what the humans might be capable of.

Bringing everyone together. Those who did not come would be left behind. A small, unpleasant part of him wondered if he had done the right thing. Without them...

But he knew he had. The price would have been too high.

30

"HE CAME TO *SEE HER*?" Viyar kinda stared at Erilar.

"He asked. She said yes. We had security in the next room. They talked." A pause. "I don't know if she convinced him to stop being an isolationist or scared the wits out of him. Or both."

Viyar laughed. "She's..."

"Intense. They aren't all like that, though. Her ability to tolerate us is apparently linked to a syndrome. Most of them are louder, more gregarious and more...frivolous, from what I hear."

"But no less dangerous," Viyar said finally. "I think we need to make sure they stay *our* danger and not somebody else's."

Erilar was the one who laughed. It was a meeting of ly'iin, that quiet thing which so often ensured the future of the world. Which had once determined the fate of dynasties, when Kyx had had such things.

Viyar was glad to be ly'iin and glad to be who and what ly was.

"I have to find the girl."

Erilar shifted lin shoulders. "I know."

"You know the station better than I. I asked security, but I need multiple opinions."

"Don't ask me where to find good hiding places."

Viyar's eyes widened and then narrowed. "You..."

"Ask the station's kids."

Viyar laughed. Of course. There were children on the station, and it was a law of nature that children knew where all the good hiding places were in any situation, in any place. Where ly had grown up, it had been caves. Places where they had hid when somebody's father had been unreasonable. (Or, rather, perfectly reasonable by adult standards).

Of course, the station's children would know of any place somebody might be hidden. Because they had hidden there at least once, whether to avoid parental punishment, get away from their teachers, or just have a place to play that would be less observed.

Which meant ly needed to talk to the kids and persuade them to cough up their hiding places. "I'll do that."

"I'd help, but they won't tell me. They'll tell *you* because you're leaving."

Viyar laughed again. "I won't tell any of their fathers."

"I know you won't. They don't. They'll be much more comfortable talking to a transient. Especially if you bring bribes."

Ly would have to stop by some place on the promenade and get suitable treats.

Ly had never been a teacher. But ly could handle children. Ly thought so, anyway.

WALKING through the station corridors with a bag of treats. Viyar felt as if the kids were animals ly planned on catching. Ly *really* need to spend more time with kids. There. A small group of them, three siblings and two slightly older. Possibly two clutches from the same male, but it was unlikely these days.

Slowing down reproduction had been required for civilization. Otherwise, other things had to happen to excess offspring. Some people thought they could breed more again now they had the universe. A slightly cold thought; if these people killed all the humans, then ky'iin could have their territory. Was that the true motivation? Because ly could counter it...perhaps. It was the ly'iin job to moderate such desires, but ly would have to think of good objections.

For now, ly approached the kids. "Hey." A single verbal syllable. It got their attention; five suspicious young faces turned towards lin.

None of them had reached puberty, although the older two might be close. "There's a geki bar in it for you if you give me some information."

"What about?" said one of them, they grouped together more closely.

"I'm looking for a missing kid. You have any idea where somebody might be hiding around here?"

The suspicion grew. Ly pulled out one of the geki bars. "I won't tell your dads."

Ly presumed the plural. They shook their heads almost as one and ran off. Apparently lin manner with children was worse than ly had feared.

Ly sighed and kept walking. The promenade was not large; about as large as a main street in a small town. It had restaurants, bars, and some stores. Most things up here were printed; it was much cheaper to ship up filament than finished objects. But there was always that demand. That need for that built by ky'iin hands. Some people argued that objects also had myoran, and that printed stuff simply didn't...didn't have it. Viyar did sometimes think that a craftsman put myoran into things.

Ly saw two more children. Ly approached them, this time trying not to be scary and already pulling out the treats. This time, ly had more success.

Ly FINISHED the day with several possibilities. Now ly had to think where *ly* would put a teenager. Other than the hiding places there were, of course, the three transient hostels, but local security was checking those.

Ly would not put her there unless ly was *very* confident ly could keep her quiet and out of sight. From what ly knew of this girl, that was hard enough for her family. Strangers would never manage it. There was also the possibility of a docked ship, and ly added those to lin list next to the three places the kids had suggested. Ly couldn't get station security to storm all of these locations; there simply weren't enough of them. If things got bad enough, ly could involve the military.

They wouldn't come out for a kidnapped adolescent. Ly was, over-all, glad of that. There had been times in history... But no. Ly had to narrow things down. Which meant involving somebody else in this; not station security but people who would be able to help in more efficient ways. Folding the list, ly stuck it in a pocket and headed for the promenade.

Then down a level. The bar ly walked into would have been a dive had it been on Kyx. On the station, it was a bit cleaner than that. It was full of station workers and personnel. Tourists would not come here. Crew from the starships would not come here. Freighter crew might.

This was a place of the working class. A place where the people who kept the station working came to relax and blow off steam. A rather lively game of *chia* was going on as ly entered. Ly avoided it, not because ly didn't want to play *chia*, but because ly did and did not have the time. Instead, ly made lin way to the bar. Ly was definitely noticed.

"You..."

"I'm not investigating anyone here, at least not yet."

The barkeep relaxed slightly. "But you aren't here for a drink either."

"No," ly admitted. "I'm not. I'm here because I'm..." Ly decided the truth would be the best leverage. "We have a missing kid somewhere on the station, and she didn't run away."

The barkeep was an older male. His eyes darkened. "A kidnap case."

"I need to find her and quickly. I have some ideas for where she might be hidden."

"You want help looking."

"I want somebody to, off the books because I don't know who is involved in the conspiracy, reprogram the automated maintenance robots to keep a sensor out for her."

"I know somebody who can do that. How do you know *I* am not part of the conspiracy?"

Ly shrugged. "You don't seem the type."

And if ly did accidentally involve the wrong person, then ly could leverage that, too, into something which would progress the case. As long as they didn't know ly was coming, ly could stick with plan A.

But ly did have plan B ready to go.

31

DHYANIL STEPPED out into the cold. For a moment, he thought he was going to turn into an ice sculpture of a ky'iin.

He was a tropical creature; he really hadn't anticipated just how cold Northspire was in winter. Not many people did. Northspire was in the northern hemisphere, in the middle of the Grea continent, with no ocean currents to moderate the temperature.

It was thus known for the cold, and for ridiculous amounts of snow, even during Kyx's more stable times. Thankfully, *that* had been cleared from his route out of the airport and from the road the car started to take him on. It was cleared into piles at the side of the road, slightly dirty and off-white. Melting it all would have used far too much energy. The heated roadway was just enough to keep it from drifting *back*. The sky was clear blue and the sun reflecting from the snow caused him to pull on a pair of goggles and be glad he'd been warned to bring them. It helped.

People lived here, he reminded himself. Many people lived here by *choice*. A crazy choice it might be, but people did live here.

He wasn't actually going to freeze, and as the car warmed up he started to believe that again. It would take him to a hotel near the university, a cheap one mostly used by family and friends visiting students during the semester.

It was more than good enough for him; and after the space station it felt like a palace. The room was small, but it was still a room, not a closet. He could finally spread out.

Unpack all of his stuff all the way and pretend this was the home he feared he would never see again.

Once he had done so, he left the room, and just walked. Walked out on the surface of Kyx again. Which he hoped he would never have to leave. The sky above him, the natural air, the breeze.

All of it wrapped around him and made him feel safe. Even if he was wearing a heavy coat and still cold. The cold was worth it. His hands were freezing, though.

He headed straight for the nearest shopping center. He knew exactly what he needed.

Only then could he face what he needed to do.

ARMED WITH A HAT AND GLOVES, Dhyanil made his first assault on the university.

The campus was built for the climate here. Once you were inside, there was no need to leave again. Opportunity, yes. Need, no.

Once he was inside. He stepped into the nearest entrance, finding himself in a multi-level lobby. There were not that many people moving around; at this time of day most students would be in class.

Some argued that universities weren't needed any more, that VR learning was sufficient.

But there were things other than classes. There was the learning to work together. When he did see students, they showed the usual pattern of slightly self-segregating by gender, but it wasn't the way it once was.

There was a receptionist, an elderly woman with white patterns across her hide. Old enough to retire, no doubt, refusing to do so because she enjoyed her job. She was, thus, a somewhat intimidating figure. He had met enough of the type to know better than to think she was anything but a gatekeeper.

He had checked the directory, though. He knew this wasn't the right building, he had just wanted to get in out of the cold. To take off the hat and gloves, open the heavy coat and feel somewhat ky'iin again. He had no idea how people lived here without freezing off fingers and toes. There was a map by the receptionist's desk. He went to look at it.

"Can I help you?" she asked, leaning into his field of vision.

"I just need to find the biology building."

He was hoping she would assume he was a parent checking on his offspring. He might not look rich enough for a prestigious institution like Northspire, but maybe his kid was a scholarship case.

"Everyone's in class right now," she said. "But if you head that way and then go into the skywalk, it's signed."

He lifted his shoulders to her, and headed that way, relaxing once out of sight. The skywalk was empty except for one young man who was sitting with his back to the glass wall, reading. Possibly evading class. Possibly evading his roommate.

Dhyanil had been to college, although not Northspire. No, he had been able to afford, and wanted, only a local education.

He had had a roommate he would definitely have preferred to sit in a corridor rather than deal with and he shot the young man a sympathetic glance as he passed. He mused on how recently Northspire had even admitted men, much less on equal terms, but that was in the past. The skywalks were a maze, and they looked out on a campus buried in snow.

When spring came, no doubt there would be games. Actually, there still were. He saw a group of students throwing snow at each other and shivered. Brrr.

He was definitely not staying here one moment longer than he needed to.

THE BIOLOGY BUILDING had a faint smell to it, the climate control perhaps not completely eliminating the scent of chemicals and lab animals. Or perhaps it was all in Dhyanil's mind; the lab surely had the best filters in their systems.

Another scent drifted across his maw. The scent of a woman in heat and he hurried his pace. Somebody had gotten too drunk to take her suppressors and he did *not* want to be in the middle of that. Then he heard a yelp.

That he could not ignore. Turning, his coat actually swirling around his legs in a manner that he hoped would be intimidating but which was probably ridiculous. The woman had a man up against the wall, pushing him against it. He smelled rut and, yes, alcohol. In the middle of the day, even.

Putting on his best authoritative voice, "What's going on here?"

She just snarled at him. He might be older, but he was only a man, and thus not a threat to her in her current state. It might take a non-lethal to get her off her victim. Or several large women or ly'iin.

He hesitated for a moment. He could not take her on; she'd put him through the wall. Or, if the kid ran, turn her attention to him. He would get hurt. Not to mention the fact that his own arousal was starting to flow through him. He should have stayed on the suppressors.

But there was one very unpopular thing he *could* do if the sound-proofing of the labs and classrooms wasn't allowing this to be heard. He pulled the fire alarm. Its strident sounds flowed through the building. It *was* an emergency, after all. At least for that poor kid.

The woman did not move, but a nearby door opened and a variety of students poured out. Three of them saw the situation and stopped to deal with it.

Dhyanil snuck away. Pulling the fire alarm in the middle of winter would not make anyone popular. He might even get sued by the university.

It was worth it.

32

Ly found what ly had expected.

A hole in the sensors. Ly did not know if the robots and scanners were unable to detect the area because of a hack by these particular criminals, a malfunction, or a hack by some smuggler who had been caught and never removed it. Or, for that matter, some *current* smuggler. Either way it was now reported and would be corrected, but only after ly had investigated.

Accompanied by two burly security officers, both black-skinned plains women, in case things went bad, ly made lin way through the maintenance corridor. The kids had mentioned this as a place where they might go to hide, but adults could fit in the area readily. Always something to consider, that.

Some hiding places were suitable only for children or, perhaps, a small male.

Or, thinking about it, a human. They weren't, apparently, that much smaller than ly'iin, but they were a little. The Ambassador claimed to be a smaller specimen.

Ly believed her; she had no reason to lie about the matter.

Then ly saw the door. It was a very firmly closed door, very solid in appearance, and marked with a biohazard symbol. Ly turned to one of the burly females, "Mazehin, I have a feeling..."

She stepped forward. "Brilliant," she hissed, her anger showing in her features. "That door is not on the plans."

"It's not in the description the kids gave me. But any random civilian who wanders down here..."

"It's really good work, too," she added, admiration mingling with her obvious irritation. She seemed professionally offended that some-body had put such a good fake door in this corridor.

"Well, then. Let's crack this egg."

Ly stepped back, letting the security officers work on the door. It was, of course, locked, and a small explosion here wasn't safe. They were probably going to have to cut through it, and ly didn't want to be in their way. Instead, ly focused on aspects of the scene. The smell was station, the women, and now the welding torch. The corridor was featureless.

There was remarkably little dust on the floor, which told its own story about how this place was seeing more use than intended. No footprints. No clues except the door which wasn't supposed to be there. Which told lin that ly was in exactly the right place.

It also made ly ready to hit the deck when the door did, in fact, open.

THERE WAS an explosion from behind the door. Ly flattened linself to the ground. By the lack of yelps, the women had also managed to avoid significant damage.

Ly listened, but heard no hiss of escaping air; whoever had set the booby trap had known something of what they were doing.

This was a situation in which guns were acceptable and honorable; ly wasn't armed, but the women were. Thus, ly let them go first. Into the smoke of the room beyond. Hopefully the booby trap hadn't set off anything to harm their hostage.

Ly would not be able to look Dhyanil in the eye if the girl wasn't safe. Not that ly truly expected to ever look him in the eye again.

Ly followed the women. One of them fired at something in the smoke; again, ly hoped it wasn't the girl. That she wasn't being used as a shield. The smoke was clearing, although its acrid scent teased against the outer edges of lin maw and stung in lin eyes. Ly did *not* like smoke. But then nobody did. Well, there were certain kinds of recreational smoke in which ly may or may not have indulged linself on occasion.

As it cleared, ly saw the corridor, the back of one of the women, and what was clearly the room the kids had talked about, opening on the left side.

It was presumably a storage room that had lost utility as the station expanded, a place maintenance might have kept and perhaps still sometimes did keep tools and the like.

There were two figures in the smoke. Ly heard another shot. Low velocity bullets. Not dangerous to anyone wearing armor, which ly was. But also not dangerous to the station. All ly had to do was protect lin head.

Ly did so, ducking and moving forward. One of the women tackled the nearest of the figures to the ground, held them pinned. Ly thought her, but could neither see nor smell properly as yet. The latter might take a while.

The smoke was still clearing. As the two other figures wrestled, ly did lin best to dart past them into the room. The only thing in the room was a box. No, not the only thing. A large box, a bunk bed, and a toe sticking out from behind the box. Smart girl, he thought. Best place for her to be. Best place for her to stay.

One of the strangers broke free and came in. Ly growled, turning to face them. Her. Ly'iin generally did not fight.

Viyar was likely to present her with a highly unpleasant surprise.

SHE CLOSED ON LIN. "You should not have come here. Now we're going to have to kill you."

"I don't think so." Ly'iin were typically only slightly smaller than women, but lacked the musculature that came with the sex hormones. She was naturally stronger than lin.

Ly had to be faster. It was the only way. Not just the only way to beat her, but the only way to stay alive. Ly was prey now. There was no honor in this and there would never be any honor for her again, win or lose. She apparently didn't care. Ly twisted to the side, trying to glance at the girl. If she ran, that would be for the best. She might not be able to run. Ly did not know. Ly was avoiding extended claws, avoiding a maw that closed on lin.

Ly struck out, lin own claws shorter but no less sharp. Ly growled, the sound normally reserved for hunting as some still did; naked. Only one's self and the prey. Or, the other woman one fought over the man while the ly'iin watched and made sure it didn't go too far. This was going too far. Claws tore into hide, purplish blood dripping from both of them. Where were the security guards?

There! One of them launched herself into the room, dragged the other female from him, the two became a whirling mess of claws and teeth and fists. Ly knew what ly needed to do. Ly dived behind the box. The girl couldn't run. She had managed to get free of her bonds enough to dive behind the box, but not enough to get out.

Ly didn't have time to mess around. Rather than freeing her, ly threw her over lin shoulder and ran. Her dignity would be harmed, but ly didn't care about that. Ly ran, and behind lin ly knew death was being dealt. The first rule was to get her to safety.

The second was to get backup to the security officers, who were doing more than their jobs. Were doing work nobody should have to do. They were clear. Ly set her down and used lin claws to cut her bonds.

The first words she said were, "They all need to die." From a girl her age those were chilling words indeed.

33

"So, you hit the alarm because..." The older ly'iin glared at him through the lenses that covered lin eyes.

"There was a rape in progress." He wished he'd thought to take a photograph.

The administrator sighed. "Do you swear to it?"

"I swear to it. I was more interested in stopping it than taking pictures."

"I swear, we're going to have to start putting suppressors in the water."

So, it was happening a fair amount. Sadly, Dhyanil believed it. Young people, fighting against their instincts. Some of them would decide to let nature run its course.

Or, more likely, they were young, stupid, and thought they could control their biology. Women. "Kids," was what he actually said. "Thank you for believing me."

"Just don't do it again. Please. So, you aren't a student or a parent. Why are you here?"

"I'm writing a book and was in the area. I was hoping to talk to Garil about infectious diseases."

Hopefully when the book never materialized it would be assumed to be excessive ambition not a lie. Dhyanil had no intention of writing a novel. Writing a guidebook, that he'd thought about. But something that would require a virologist's expertise? That would be at least assumed to be fiction, and the annoying fact was that he had a vague idea. Something set during the Liroc Plague, perhaps. That had upended the world in so many ways.

"Professor Garil. You'll be hoping to talk to him or *listen* to him?"

Dhyanil laughed. "I take it listening is rather easier and more likely to, in fact, work."

"In one. His students love him, but that man can talk and breathe at the same time."

He had met the type more than once. "Can you tell him? I'm willing to meet up over food or whatever kind..."

He couldn't talk and eat at the same time, no ky'iin could do that. Tyrar could, it was one of the freaky things about them. They talked through a completely separate orifice. Humans had that going on too, but it didn't *seem* like they could do that.

He didn't want to imagine it if they could. Honestly, he didn't really want to think too much about alien eating and breathing arrangements. Who did? Well, the aliens and their doctors, he supposed.

"Watch out. He'll drag you to his favorite dive."

Dhyanil spread his hands. "That sounds like a plan I can get all the way behind."

Favorite dive? Dhyanil could think of few things better.

Knowing he would not be popular with any student or faculty who might have seen him around, Dhyanil elected to temporarily flee campus. That left him with few ideas of where to go. Finally he found a trail that led away from campus, through some woods. It had been cleared enough that in the new boots he had acquired, he could traipse along it in reasonable comfort. It was interesting. People had lived here for a long time, long enough to adapt to the cold, but with modern connectivity, those ethnic divisions were starting to come back together.

Except when they weren't. Putting suppressors in the water. Unfortunately, it couldn't actually be done because ovulation suppressors did rather bad things to ly'iin, for reasons Dhyanil had never read up on. Biology had never been his strong point. If he was going to...and he suddenly knew what his target was. The nearest public library.

He pulled out his personal computer, looked up the location, and headed that way. If he was going to talk intelligently with an infectious disease expert, he needed a refresher.

Also.

It was starting to snow.

Dhyanil had never been snowed on and was in no hurry to experience it. The snow was there, though. Falling on him from a sky that had turned this odd shade of white. It didn't feel wet. It felt surprisingly dry, flakes landing on his coat and hat. Out of curiosity, he pulled off his left glove, held out a hand. They hit as this peculiar almost dry sensation, then melted quickly to form small drops of water.

He elected not to repeat the experiment, but instead hurried down the trail further, cutting through behind some houses. The trees had no leaves on them, in winter dormancy, stark against the sky. Snow rested on the branches. It was beautiful, in its own way, but it made him want to go home even more. To escape this, all of it. To be somewhere warm.

Yet, he knew, people lived here. Down the street and onto a kind of college town main street. He knew the kind of place. There were stores, a couple of restaurants and, yes, a library. A decent-sized one, but he wasn't interested in their book archive right now. Well, perhaps he was. He was interested in their heating system and the potential to borrow faster net and a larger screen. He looked up as he stepped in, but the clouds blocked any view of the heavens and what might be up there, what might be orbiting far over his head.

Satellites, no doubt.

Maybe a ship.

It was an odd juxtaposition with the station and even with Northspire. This was a place that hadn't changed. This was a place which....might never change. It wasn't his land, it wasn't his climate, but it was the kind of place he wanted to preserve.

THE LIBRARY WAS warm enough that he stripped off hat and gloves and used a mat to get the snow off of his boots. It held older physical books, stacks that reached to a high ceiling, with sliding ladders to allow even short men to access them. It also held the network rig he had been hoping for. Library internet was *always* better than hotel internet. The question was whether his card would give him reciprocal arrangements.

He slid it into the reader and it did, with a two hour limit on the computers. That should be enough, and if it wasn't, the stacks called. The coat came off too as he got settled down. The librarian, for now, ignored him. Probably would unless he asked for help. He didn't plan on asking for help.

Basic biology, he knew. He couldn't live in the society he did without understanding the basics. He knew how to not get sick when various illnesses swept through. He knew how reproduction worked. He knew what a virus was. Skimming through all of that, thus, was quick, if very necessary work.

He needed to understand verian fever, but it was beyond the scope of *this* library in terms of the actual archives. However, they had a shared account at the university. Viruses with intermediary hosts existed on both Kyx and Tyranis. Generally, small bugs were the culprits, things that liked to bite people and drink their blood.

He could make a reasonable assumption the humans had similar problems on their homeworld. He didn't want to think about the glen. He would bet they did too, but it might not work the same way when you had an exoskeleton. He had had days when he might have wanted to borrow one.

Verian fever was a mytovirus, a common family on Tyranis. What he really needed was to understand human viruses. They had to have them. Every ecosystem did. Except, possibly, the glen.

He really wished he knew more about them. For the first time in life, curiosity was overcoming fear.

Mytoviruses generally caused blood diseases, and the very

different blood chemistry of ky'iin and tyrar was what protected ky'iin from them. So far, so good.

What was human blood chemistry? He knew that if he tried to find out it would be flagged. He was probably flagged as a potential terrorist at this point. He actually almost hoped he was. He hoped that somebody was keeping an eye on him.

The computer time was up. He had reminded himself of a few things. Hopefully he wouldn't look like an idiot when he met with the professor. He became slowly aware that somebody was watching him.

34

MERUHIN WAS IN SICKBAY, being checked over. Viyar did not envy the medics doing so; the girl was a bundle of anger and hormones.

She definitely needed to be shipped back to the planet before she got herself hurt. Or killed somebody. It was not easy for females going through puberty, and being kidnapped and humiliated was possibly enough to send her into a full blown rage. Yet, Viyar had to find out if there was more to it than that. Ly got linself checked out, establishing that ly had indeed got away with bruises and a couple of cuts. The bruise over lin ribs was enough to make lin wonder if ly had cracked them, but the scanner said no.

Ly waited until Meruhin had been checked out, and stepped cautiously into the room. "Still angry enough to kill somebody?"

She gave him a stubborn face, maw firmly closed.

"You're allowed to be angry."

Finally, she spoke, "But not act on it."

"They'll be dealt with."

"They want to commit genocide."

"We know. They were using you as leverage on your cousin."

"Dhyanil? Is he..."

"He's fine, he's pretending to play along."

"That must be sticking in his maw. Having to work with the authorities."

Those words heartened Viyar. They were the words of somebody thinking, not reacting. "Oh, it is. But..."

"Dhyanil hates offworlders. Doesn't mean he wants to kill them all."

Viyar shifted position, lifted a hand. "And you don't hate them."

"The human is actually pretty neat. She showed me lots of pictures of where she comes from and the human homeworld. They have awesome *pets*."

Viyar laughed. "You have a cery?"

"Had. It got old and died. I was going to get another one..."

Viyar idly wondered about human pets. Ly would have to ask. "The humans are interesting. And dangerous."

"That means we should be friends."

"Always make friends with the biggest bully on the playground, right?"

"Right." Her brow furrowed. "I think they might think the same thing about us."

Viyar considered that. "We might never know. Look, don't forget they have different instincts. So, what did they let slip about the plan when they didn't think you were listening?"

"Oh, they didn't do that. They tried to recruit me. I pretended to be faintly interested."

"Good girl. So, tell me what you found out?" Ly hated to grill her.

Ly had to. She might be key to stopping them. And now he could tell Dhyanil to stop stalling with the professor.

Ly was fairly sure ly would have all the names soon...

THEY WOULD BE ROUNDED up before the end of the day. Viyar celebrated with a tankard of vril in one of the station bars. It wasn't the best ly had ever had, but it was vril, it was cold, and the case was over thanks to a brave young woman.

Who was already on a shuttle heading to the Academy, where she would begin her journey. *Not* back to her family. Perhaps they would come round to her choice. No, they definitely would, eventually. Families almost always did. Especially when there was prestige involved, and if Viyar didn't miss lin guess, that one was heading for command.

Ly thought for a moment of the fact that being a woman gave her an unfair advantage. Things had improved, though. Ly was not going to go into any kind of depression about the state of the world. Ly was going to enjoy lin vril, maybe get a little bit drunk; not like that man had been drinking, but enough to break down a few inhibitions. Enough to let linself be happy for a while.

Ly looked around. This bar was mostly full of traders and transients; ky'iin in shipsuits mingled with those dressed more smartly; insurance agents, lawyers, tourists.

Ly could fit in, because *anyone* could fit in here. As things changed, ly wouldn't be surprised to see humans joining the crowd. Ly wondered if humans liked vril. Tyrar certainly did, and they had the unfair advantage of a ridiculous alcohol tolerance. A tyrar could drink as much vril as they wanted to, for they would run out of room for the liquid before they got anywhere close to drunk.

You didn't drink tyrar liquor. Except in very, very small doses and if you *wanted* to be off your head.

Ly decided that if ly was going to drink more, ly had better order some food. Lifting a hand to flag down the waitress, ly noticed three individuals entering. One woman, two men. Something about the way they were walking and moving bothered lin. Ly lowered lin hand and pushed away lin drink.

Ly could smell a bar brawl building a mile off, and this one was not that far away.

THEY CAME IN LIKE PROFESSIONALS. Not high end professionals, but definitely people who had at least some experience in starting a fight without making it too obvious. The fact that two of them were male made it more likely, not less. The two men went over to the bar, while the woman casually scanned the room. Ly reached for lin vril again, took a sip. Ly would not get so drunk off of one tankard that it would affect lin ability to deal with this.

Not drinking would look suspicious. Ly was, though, waiting on ordering food. Ly probably wouldn't get to eat it.

Were these people not on the list? Or was this just somebody after a fight. The men were ordering a pitcher of vril, the woman chose a table after a moment. A bit of tension went out of the room, but Viyar knew it to be extremely premature. This wasn't just people spoiling for a fight; and Viyar knew that somewhere on the station there was a venue for people who *were* just after a fight.

A place where they could do so safely, which would appear illicit to its patrons but actually have the sanction of the station's commander. Which everyone knew was the truth. Ly finished lin drink and stretched, keeping only one eye on the table. It happened about ten minutes in. Their conversational gestures became more dramatic, voices raised.

The table was flipped by the men towards the woman. That told lin it was staged. Ly was on lin feet in a moment, lin chair falling to the ground with another thud. Ly was not the only one. Half the room had stood. The half wearing ship suits. Some of the business types were already deciding to settle their tabs tomorrow; the barkeep was not preventing them. It was easy to track down non-payers on a space station. Or the money was just coming out of their accounts anyway.

The woman picked up one of the men and threw him. Another staged move. He landed on a table where a couple of remaining sales-people were frozen.. Had they had any sense, they would have run. The ly'iin did. The woman let her hormones get the better of her and threw a thankfully unclawed punch at the man.

It was on. Viyar sighed, rolled up lin sleeves and prepared to defend linself.

35

Dhyanil turned slowly, feeling eyes on him. He expected the librarian. It wasn't the librarian. It was a young man who was just...staring at him. As if he was an alien being. Was it the color of his shirt?

He hadn't spoken or moved much, so it wasn't his accent, which *was* no doubt strange to people here, colored as it was with his native tongue.

A language he put his effort into preserving because, well, it was worth it. Because it was part and parcel of everything. "Yes?" he said, finally.

The student continued to stare, maw slightly open. Were his pants unzipped? He stood the rest of the way up and started to walk towards him. He assumed he was a student, anyway. Reasonable assumption from the age. The student took a deep breath. Then closed his maw again.

Dhyanil decided he was not dealing with this any more. He stuck his personal computer back in his pocket, stepped around the student and stepped outside.

Instantly, he smelled smoke. Something was burning. Something on the campus was burning. Smoke rose as a thick column. With a frown, he took off running in that direction. Too late, he realized he had left his hat and gloves in the library. He would have to come back for them. Hopefully he wouldn't freeze. Hopefully bits of him wouldn't freeze off. He did manage to fasten his coat as he ran through the snow. Through the gates that marked the edge of campus.

What was on fire? It was apparently part of the biology building. Please tell him somebody hadn't done what he feared they had done. Please tell him it was an accident.

"Void," he swore.

Then he looked around. The automated fire control systems were starting to deal with the blaze. The firefighters were approaching. There was not much he could do here. Well, there was. A student had showed up with a case of bottled water. He began to distribute it to those fleeing the building. He did not, for right now, feel the cold. Only the heat coming from the building, dying down as the fire came under control. The smoke stung his eyes.

He really hoped this hadn't been any kind of attack. He wished he could be sure.

THE EXCITEMENT OVER, Dhyanil fled back to the library to retrieve his cold weather gear, shivering the entire way. He stayed there to warm up.

Nobody had been killed, at least. Or even hurt. The fire had started in a lab. It was probably just an accident, just one of those things which happened. He didn't want it to have happened.

Part of him was wondering how he could use this to get to Garil. Part of him was hating himself for thinking that, except that nobody *had* been hurt.

He didn't think it was arson. But he couldn't be sure. He stayed in the library until he was sure nothing was going to fall off from the cold, then braved the main street again. Well, not before getting a dinner recommendation from the librarian. The place served a hunter's stew which was absolutely fantastic; it wasn't like anything he would have eaten at home, but it warmed him from the inside all the way to the fingers, and he wondered if he could get the recipe. Or a similar one, anyway.

Although it would probably be *too* heating for where he was from. For where he could never go back to. His mother didn't even know where he was. His mother was dying. He stared into his stew for a long time at that thought, then realized it was going to get cold and basically poured the rest of it down his maw.

Then considered his options. There was alcohol here, and it tempted him. Then he remembered how he had felt after his last binge. He could have one. He called the waiter. "What would you say is the signature local liquor?"

"Hevi," he said.

"I'll have a shot of it. And don't sell me any more than that no matter how much I beg.

The waiter bobbed his head and left. Hopefully he would stick to the promise.

Dhyanil couldn't trust himself, especially if the booze was good. Maybe it wouldn't be. He couldn't recall what hevi was or what it was made out of. Probably, he'd never had a reason to ask.

It turned out to be red and faintly bittersweet, more to be sipped than downed. He sipped it, thanked the waiter, and then as there seemed to be no demand for the table, he relaxed. The fire. Garil. It could all wait until tomorrow.

THE NEXT DAY dawned bright and cold, which Dhyanil suspected was most days in the winter here. The sky was greenish-blue, free of clouds, and the white brilliance of the sun beat down to the point where he needed goggles to go outside. He wasn't the only one; even the natives here were apparently worried about snow blindness.

He walked back to campus. Everything here was so walkable that it reminded him of home, although he certainly saw vehicles on the road. The biology building was still closed. He stood looking at it, wondering exactly how he was going to find Garil now. Maybe this would count as stalling. He had a very good excuse for why he hadn't talked to the man yet.

For right now, he had to look for the guy, or at least make a good pretense of it. He pulled his hat down some and trudged to the nearest open building, ducking inside. It turned out to be an adjunct life sciences building. Focused on xenobiology. Because of course it was. Verian fever.

He checked the building directory. Garil's offices were in the main building, but there was a xenovirology lab here.

In the middle of the lobby was a hanging sculpture of the solar system. Further in was a similar orrery, but this one showed the home system of the tyrar. Apparently they hadn't met the glen yet when the installation was put together. Between them were walkways, leading to more labs and classrooms and skywalks. Perhaps a specialist library. He felt faintly wistful. The small college he had been to was nothing on an institution like Northspire. He had never been able to study in a place like this. Perhaps he shouldn't feel envy, but he did.

"Can I help you?" came a ly'iin voice.

"I was looking for Professor Garil, but..."

"But he's likely staying home today like anyone sane."

"I smelled the fire. What happened?"

"Lab accident. We think."

One could never be sure. "Was it Garil's lab?" he asked. "Sorry, I'm a little...concerned. I was hoping to get his help with my book."

"It *was* Garil's lab." Amber eyes were narrowed suspiciously.

Had he overplayed his hand? "Oh dear. I hope he wasn't hurt."

"He wasn't. And he didn't lose any data, knowing him. He's a stickler for backups."

Which meant if it was arson, they had utterly failed. Unless, of course, the idea was to slow him down. Or the idea was, in fact, to keep the isolationists from getting to him. Dhyanil might have an ally who thought they were enemies. That was *not* a good thought. An ally who thought they were enemies was more dangerous than an actual enemy, by any stretch of the imagination.

The cold he felt had nothing to do with the snow outside.

36

"IT WAS JUST A BAR FIGHT," Viyar explained to station security. "Except that it wasn't."

"Do you think they were targeting you?"

Lin lifted lin shoulders. "I think the girl didn't see all of them and yes, I think they were targeting me. They were professionals, but not highly-skilled ones."

"Well, I can use the fight as an excuse to deport them. None of the three worked here."

Which meant they had been brought in for the plot. "Did they work on a ship?" A sudden cold feeling was flowing through lin.

Ly had a thought, ly saw a pattern, but ly was not entirely sure what to do with said pattern. Not yet. Ly needed more pieces of the puzzle.

"...yes, they did. An interstellar."

"Please *don't* give them back to their captain just yet."

She turned to the board. "I don't think she's going to be taking them back."

"Let me guess. The ship they're from left dock."

Ly wanted to snarl at her. The ship had left dock, and ly would lay bets that the remaining conspirators were on it. They hadn't quite got everyone on the list. They had got some. Plus the three they'd left behind to take lin out in a very dishonorable way.

Dishonorable but highly deniable. Killed during a bar fight might not have been believed by lin superiors, but they would have to pretend to at least. Station security would have bought it.

She caught the edge of the not-quite-released snarl. "I..."

"Save it," ly said, finally. She would be dealt with, although ly would argue for her to keep her job. She had done good. Except on this one thing. "Save it and give me their flight plan."

"They filed one to Verx, which I did think was strange."

Verx was a science outpost in the outer system. It didn't really need an interstellar. Unless somebody was in a real hurry. Or unless they were lying.

"Where else could they go? Did they..."

"They were fully fueled. With their range, they...normally do the route between here and tyrar, with the two intermediate stops."

That wasn't, Viyar's instincts said, where they were going. No, Viyar's instincts said they had something quite else and other in mind.

Viyar did not like this. At all.

FINDING out where the ship had gone was beyond even lin jurisdiction, which ended in Kyx orbit.

Going after them? Ly would have to talk to people. To certain people. Of course, there was one way to overcome all jurisdiction issues. Ly wasn't taking *that* route unless ly had to. Ly wasn't going to risk causing a, well, incident.

Stalking out of the security office, ly prowled to the docks. Ly could do nothing there, but the anger within lin needed an outlet. As there was unlikely to be another bar brawl any time soon and there was no hunting preserve on the station, motion was all ly had to burn off that energy.

The docks were oddly quiet. Ly looked over towards the diplomatic docks. There was more movement and energy there. Tyrar? No. Glyn.

A glyn ship had docked and was discharging a trade representative who's brilliant, crystalline form was hung with ribbons. Ly watched for a while. Ly wondered how they thought; they were the most alien of aliens, not even having brains in the same way everyone else did.

Evolution on their world had taken some very different and bizarre paths. Or perhaps, when they moved further out into the galaxy, they would discover that the glen were the more common thing. That they were the exotics. Ly stood there, frozen as patterns of thought flowed over lin. The same knack that had made lin a special investigator in the first place.

Humans were not that exotic.

Viruses, now they were exotic, as alien from other forms of life as the glen. And universal across all the worlds they had encountered. Universal and sometimes able to reprogram and collect DNA from other places.

It wasn't useful for the case, but it was an odd, bizarre insight that ly should pass on to somebody. Perhaps that Garil guy Dhyanil was still pretending to court.

Ly watched the glen disappear, then turned the other way. To the working docks where the interstellar freighter had been. Ly did not even need to look up that it was the same one the suspected infection had been on.

Ly already knew.

WITH A SIGH, Viyar put in the request to track the freighter.

Not being able to do it linself added to lin frustrations. Instead, ly found linself in the diplomatic area. Part of lin wanted to talk to the glen about lin weird insight. However, as lin case was *not* over after all, ly had to save that for when it really and truly was. However long that took.

Instead, it was the human embassy ly made lin way to, standing in front of the door until recognized. There was a soft scent from within. As ly stepped inside, ly realized that it came from one of the ambassador's plants, which had rather abruptly decided to produce a plethora of red flowers. No doubt to attract some pollinator.

Poor plant was not going to be able to reproduce here, but there was no indication plants understood that. Not that they really understood plant cognition. It existed, but nobody had yet managed to actually talk to a tree, despite the claims of many mystics.

The ambassador stood up from her chair, uncoiling neatly as ly arrived. "Viyar," she greeted. "Any..."

"I wouldn't be here if I didn't have news. It's mixed. We rescued Meruhin."

She heaved a visible sigh of relief, reaching up to brush at her head fur for a moment. "Is she alright?"

"By now she'll be at the Academy, under protection. She *should* be safe."

From the dip of her head she understood why ly could make no promises. "Good. So, what's the bad news?"

"Some of the conspirators fled on a ship."

"And *you* don't have one available to chase them with and no doubt they filed a false flight plan."

"I have absolutely no doubt of that."

She shrank for a moment, but it was only a moment. "This keeps them off the *Challenger* for now, and if needed they can undock."

"What about you?"

She lifted her right hand, twisted it, "I know every risk I take."

Viyar had to stop thinking of her as a child. The size and gender kept leading lin in that direction. "I know you do."

The floral scent increased. "What kind of plant is that? It's very strong smelling."

She sniffed the air. "It isn't *that* strong..."

Oh.

Crud.

Humans were *sight* predators. They had a sense of smell. It was nothing like lin own.

Ly turned, but the human was already moving towards the environmental control panel.

Hopefully it was not too late.

37

THE STANDOFF LASTED A MOMENT LONGER, then, "What do you *really* want with Garil?"

Dhyanil could keep lying. He could tell...a different lie. The truth was not happening, the truth would be too dangerous for everyone involved.

But he could say something ly might buy. "I really am writing a book," he said, finally. "But I suppose I probably come over as..."

"Garil has groupies. You are *not* one of them."

Dhyanil laughed. Maybe that would save him. He was planning his next lie carefully, but finding the humor in lin statement was surely a step. "He does, does he?"

"He's a really quite exceptional teacher. Some of his students don't like to admit they graduated."

"Maybe I can audit a class." It would make sense for an author to do that, it would get him close to Garil.

"Just promise me you don't intend any harm to him."

"Far from it." He almost said 'the exact opposite.' "Has that been a problem?"

"Well, he's had two female students try to get him to father their eggs and he had to fight one of them off with a broom."

Dhyanil tried not to laugh. Rape was *not* a laughing matter even if the image she conjured was. "I'm not ter," he said, meaning somebody who had sexual interests in the same gender. Or in ly'iin. "He's safe from me on that front."

She made a bit of a face. "Nothing wrong with being ter, but...it doesn't matter who you are into, you shouldn't be an ass about it."

"I know what you mean."

He rather thought she *did* think there was something wrong with being ter. He'd never been tempted to try it. "And I'm not here to abduct him to work on a secret virology project."

She laughed so hard that he knew he had successfully planted a red herring. "Is that the plot of your book?"

"Nah, in my book the scientist gets abducted to try and stop the pandemic before it spreads, and they're covering it up. It's set about a hundred years ago."

"Ah, alternate history then."

"More of a period piece." Had he actually had any writing talent, he would have written the book.

Unfortunately, it really wasn't that easy. He couldn't write to save his life. Maybe he could give the idea to somebody who could.

It wouldn't be the first time. Ideas were easy.

Books, from what he'd seen, were written in the writer's own blood.

GARIL WAS PRETTY MUCH the image of an elderly professor, except that the stereotypical image was, of course, ly'iin not male.

He sat casually in an office that was so messy it was clear he knew where to find everything in it. "Writing a book, eh?"

Dhyanil closed the door behind him. "Can we talk...safely?"

The professor stood, looked at him. He was slightly taller. "In my office, yes."

"Somebody sent me here to, and I know it sounds like the plot of a book, recruit you to a genocidal project."

"Genocidal?"

"They're the kind of isolationists who think the best thing to do about offworlders is kill them." As opposed to whatever he was.

He'd never been in favor of *killing* offworlders. Not in numbers. Maybe tactically, yes. An individual here or there.

"And you are..."

"The kind of isolationist who just wants them to go away. They thought they could use me as a go between. And they have somebody in my family." Coming clean right from the start just felt right. Besides, Dhyanil was certain that this guy could smell a lie a mile off.

Any good teacher could, even if they weren't ly'iin.

"A hostage."

"So, mind pretending to go along until I hear word that she's safe?"

Garil sat down. "This has...well, *this* has not happened before. But I have had people try to get me to engineer a virus to just kill their enemies. They eventually realize it's not possible and, I suppose, go find poison instead."

"This is...they want something to kill humans."

"Ah. I can see why the isolationists would be afraid of them. Highly adaptive omnivores, I hear."

"I met one. They're scary, if you are smart enough to realize size doesn't matter."

Garil gave a faint laugh. "Not overly large, then."

"No, although their ambassador is supposed to be a small example of the species. But why do you think we *should* be scared of them?"

"Not scared in the sense that they're likely to kill all of us. But to an isolationist, a species that is more adaptable is one likely to have more...influence."

Dhyanil couldn't help but agree. "So..."

"I have a better idea than just playing along until they have your kid out...is it your kid?"

"Cousin. I only have one clutch and they're adults."

"You mated young, then."

Dhyanil took that as the compliment it was. He did not ask about any offspring Garil had.

No doubt they had some somewhere. He might not be ter, but Garil had no doubt been handsome in his youth as well as smart.

NEXT STEP.

Dhyanil and Garil probably needed to be seen in public together. Garil arranged for Dhyanil to audit a freshman class that he felt would be within the understanding of, well, a tour guide.

Then he booked them dinner. The place was a dive, but it was a college town dive. That is to say, the food was cheap and plentiful. A couple of students were loudly playing electronic trivia. Garil headed for a table in the corner. "The vril here is excellent." Dhyanil decided that would be helpful for keeping him to vril and not anything stronger. "And the food?"

"Get the ground patties, with whatever fixings you want. This isn't a fancy place, but trust me."

"I'm in your hands."

A waiter showed up shortly. Dhyanil let Garil order the vril, and then picked the ground patties with, pretty much, everything on them. That was about when he realized how little lunch he had actually had. Well, he could always order more food.

The vril came first, and Tylanil sipped at it. "So, how can viruses affect things from different evolutions?"

"Sometimes they can, sometimes they can't. But basically there are only so many proteins that have the right kind of complexity to code life. The genetics of a ky'iin, a tyrar, and even a glyn aren't *that* far apart."

"The glyn..."

"They're still alive. More so than a virus, anyway. A virus is a piece of biological computer code looking for something to run on."

Dhyanil liked that analogy. "So..."

"So...as long as there's some protein overlap, there can be some replication, but it's generally not as efficient. Sometimes, though, it's worse."

Dhyanil shuddered. "Wasn't there..."

"The blight on tyrar was bacterial, not viral. Bacteria for the most part just kind of...eat you. But it *was* a particularly bad example of something from one ecosystem doing a number on something from another. Fungi could be worse, though." A pause. "Fungi would have been much harder to stop." The plague hadn't even been the worst thing to happen on Tyranis. Far from it. A blip in the ongoing ecological crisis.

He took a drag from his vril. "Meaning what they intend..."

"Oh, it's not remotely possible. Look, no matter how alien a virus is, there's going to be enough degrees of resistance and immune response to slow it down enough for anyone remotely smart to stop it. A hundred years ago, sure, but assuming your aliens have the same medical tech we do..."

Dhyanil relaxed some. He glanced around. No, nobody was listening. "Okay, that's good. Means that I can ramp up the drama with scientists on both sides trying to solve it before anyone else dies."

Garil grinned. "Exactly." Then their food arrived and they both focused on eating for a while.

Dhyanil just hoped Garil was right.

38

VIYAR WOKE UP WITH A HEADACHE. Ly was lying on the floor of the embassy, but somebody had put a folded jacket under his head.

"How long was I out?" he asked as he sat up.

"Not long. I'm guessing that was another thing which is toxic to ky'iin and not humans." The ambassador stood over lin, her face rueful.

"I don't know. The scent wasn't familiar."

"And I didn't smell it at all. It was definitely meant for me." Her nose wrinkled.

Had to be something offworld or something new. "I thought it was your flowers."

She didn't offer lin a hand up; at her size ly would have pulled her down with him rather than the reverse.

Ly elected to stay where ly was for now. Getting up might seem smart, but it also might have come with a wave of dizziness. "I don't think it was meant to be fatal."

She nodded. "Which means..."

"...that any moment now..."

And the door opened.

Ly hit the deck again and she landed next to lin.

It took them a moment to get in. Ly heard footsteps.

She whispered "Pretend."

A word that could be pronounced without gestures. Ly suddenly saw the massive advantage of an entirely spoken language. You could whisper. And ly got her message right away. Smart woman.

Pretend to be unconscious and maybe the kidnappers would let something slip. Ly heard their voices. Ly couldn't catch everything without looking, but the gist was there. They were discussing whether to take lin. Hopefully all of this was being recorded. Surely there were hidden cameras in here. Probably two or three sets of them. Ly stayed still. Lin head was still swimming, or ly would have tried to knock them down. Then they tried to pick lin up. Ly thought of struggling, then had a better idea. Ly went as limp as possible, making linself utter dead weight.

Stall them. They must have blocked security's access somehow.

And then ly heard a shout. And another one. Ly was dropped roughly to the floor. Ly managed not to oof. Ly heard the sounds of a fight. Ly still stayed down, just in case.

Then, "You okay?"

Ly rolled over and looked up into the face of the ambassador's liaison, Erilar.

Erilar offered lin a hand and ly took it.

The fight was over and the good guys had apparently won. For now.

"So, somebody put a distillation of kyealar in the air system. It's a tyrar plant."

Viyar's head hurt. Verian fever. Tyrar plants. The interstellar. At this rate...

"Somebody tell the tyrar about this. Maybe they can help."

Erilar nodded. "Laril here is going to take you to sickbay to be checked over. There shouldn't be any lingering effects..."

"Best to check." The male offered a steadying hand, which Viyar took gratefully. "The human seems to be immune."

"Her people will check her over, just in case, but yes. And this is the second time..."

"No, it's not," Viyar said. "The first time was an assassination attempt. *This* was an abduction attempt."

Erilar blinked twice.

"They weren't trying to kill us and from what I could gather without being able to see, they were discussing whether to bring me or leave me."

The ambassador stepped into the room. "They were, I checked the recordings. And they said leave, not kill. They were considering whether they could get far enough away before you raised the alarm."

Meaning they didn't want to actually hurt anyone. "From the way they were starting to manhandle me, I think they'd decided."

"They wanted you along for the ride, yes."

"Did they say *anything* which indicates what they were after? Do we have any of them in custody."

"One, but I had to knock him out," Erilar said ruefully. "They already took him to sickbay."

The others must have run. "When he wakes up and is coherent, I want some time with him," Viyar said, finally. There was a snarl behind it.

Ly was *distinctly* unamused. On the other hand... "We've got everyone wanting a piece of the ambassador."

"Or," she said, "They wanted a test subject."

Ly heart dropped in lin chest. "Of course they did. Without their virology expert, though..."

"Their..."

"They were trying to recruit a guy. I suborned the person they sent to recruit him. He's stalling.'"

"Maybe they found somebody else. Or maybe..."

Viyar didn't like where lin mind was going and ly suspected that she was heading in the same direction.

"Don't leave her alone," he said, before accepting assistance to medbay.

Hopefully the prisoner would be awake soon.

Ly had some words for him.

VIYAR HATED MEDBAYS, DOCTORS' clinics, and hospitals. Part of it was, of course, the smell.

Part of it was that lin doctor as a child had had, let's just say, a truly lousy bedside manner. Ly had never quite gotten over the way lin had been treated.

Once ly had been checked out, ly headed to somewhere *else* to wait for the prisoner to wake up. The ambassador was presumably under solid protection, and ly was sure they would also search the embassy for any other nasty surprises. A test subject.

Ly hoped she was wrong. An abduction attempt on a diplomat most often meant somebody being overly traditional. They'd done that to end the war. Grabbed the first human who had tried to communicate in a ky'iin language, held her until she knew it fluently. The humans had apparently not been too amused by this. It wasn't the way they did things.

Viyar had no idea how they did things. Ly did know the ambassador was very intelligent and could see patterns very well. Maybe all sentient species saw patterns. You had to see the pattern of your prey or of a predator to survive. Humans were both.

Ly waited in a kind of alcove, where a woman in a suit was working away with a portable computer. They studiously ignored each other. Ly did glance over, to see what glyphs were on the screen. Just numbers, and ly was better with patterns and people than with numbers.

Ly looked away, and studied the pattern of people moving in the corridors. Something felt a little bit surreal, although that might be the aftereffect of being knocked out with tyrar flowers.

Did these people think humans were more like tyrar than they were like ky'iin? Of course they did. Tyrar had two sexes. Humans had two sexes. That probably meant very little in the evolutionary sense. No, it meant less than little, to those who really understood what ly'iin where and *why* ky'iin had three sexes. Both species were live bearers, which might well mean more. But...

These people thought they could commit biological genocide, but they were clueless. Part of lin thought, with amusement, that ly might not need to stop them after all. So far, they did not seem to be much of a threat. But why had they moved without securing Garil? There were several possible answers to that. None of them were good.

39

GARIL, Dhyanil decided, was a good person. Neither an isolationist nor wanting to rush into learning from the offworlders. Balanced. But there was something in his body language that seemed just a little bit off. Dhyanil shrugged it away.

He had the guy's agreement to make it look for all the world as if he was being courted, seduced in a non-sexual way. Pulled into this. Spiraled in and trapped. But it wouldn't actually happen. Dhyanil was not going to *let* it happen. And Garil said that the bonus to hanging out with another guy was that it might keep the groupies a bit further away.

Dhyanil never wanted to be somebody who attracted groupies. Thankfully, he never would be. Of course, what would he be after this? His career, his value to society, came from local knowledge. It would take him years to develop that somewhere else; years, and then he would be old. He would never see his mother again. She didn't even know where he was or, at this point, who he was. He might not see his grandchildren. All of that led him to a bar, but he didn't go in. He stood outside, looking at the people within, snow starting to fall out of the dark sky.

If he went in, he knew what would happen. He was not going to let that happen again, but he had no true idea of how to stop it. Unless he could... He needed help. No, he had managed to stop at one shot, at one glass of vril. He could handle this alcohol thing on his own, he was sure of it. Absolutely and utterly sure of it, which meant he probably couldn't.

Tucking gloved hands in the pockets of his coat, he walked back to his hotel room instead. He could watch a show and go to bed. He was not sure what he could do anymore. He could plan out his new life, on the assumption he would have one. For some reason, it was the human's face who floated in his vision, her odd pale pink-beige coloring.

Some of them were brown. They were a warm color, warmer than ky'iin. And they were dangerous and they were the enemy, but they were also something else. They were the *other* and he was no longer sure how he felt about that and perhaps never would be sure again.

DHYANIL COULDN'T HANG out with Garil all the time. In the morning, he audited the class recommended to him.

He learned a lot about how viruses worked that he didn't know. He learned about protein sheaths and protein spikes and the difference between an isolate and a strain. None of it was practically useful, but it was *interesting* and he wondered how he had never studied science. Because from where he was standing, it wasn't useful or important. Well, no. Certain *kinds* of science mattered in White Fish. How many fish you could catch. How large they could be before you kept them. Water temperature, water nutrients.

Those things mattered in White Fish. Viruses only mattered when somebody got sick and the doctor had to work out which medicine to give them. They mattered even more when it was some new virus and there *was* no medicine except what fathers had done for generations to help sick hatchlings get better. That happened. It would always happen. Universal vaccines were a pipedream.

Now he understood why. But why had he never learned this stuff for the fun of it? Because he had never known it could be fun. Garil made it fun, made it dark and exciting and entertaining.

The ky'iin was brilliant. A teacher like that would bring so many kids into science, and Dhyanil headed to get lunch with it all still spinning around in his head. What kind of protein sheath did verian fever have?

He didn't need to know, but he *wanted* to know. Garil had awakened something in him he had not had for years, perhaps had never really had at all. Straight up intellectual curiosity. The desire to know for the sake of knowing. He was too old and not smart enough to belong in a place like this but as he left campus in favor of a diner, he wished that was not true. He wished he could at least manage smart enough; nobody could turn back time, not even in hyperspace. Nobody could change the past, because there needed to be that perception of time or minds could not exist. Where had he heard that?

Part of some speech, somebody trying to explain esoteric temporal physics in words ordinary people could understand. Dhyanil would never be *that* smart.

He entered the diner and ordered a soup lunch. It was soup weather. Winter here was always going to be soup weather, especially for those not used to the depths of the snow. He would never be that smart, but he wanted, suddenly, to be...not smarter than he was, but more aware, more engaged. As he tucked into his soup, his personal computer beeped for his attention.

He finished his soup in record time and fled to the only privacy he had; his room. Viyar had given him a device that could detect bugs and it showed that none were present. That was one good thing, perhaps the only good thing.

The computer showed Viyar on the screen. "Are you in a private place?"

"Why do you think I didn't respond right away? I was getting lunch."

"Tell me you went to the Soup Bowl."

Dhyanil laughed. "I did." He didn't ask how Viyar knew about the place; surely he'd been here at some point.

The most prestigious university on this continent was bound to attract attention. "So, what's going on?"

"They have their virus, or at least a prototype. Garil's a red herring."

Dhyanil's shoulders slumped and his arms drooped. "Of course he is. There's no way they'd have trusted me with anything important."

"Keep things up a little bit longer. Meruhin's safe."

"That's what really matters to me. No offense."

No, it wasn't all that mattered, but there was a part of him who did indeed care more about his cousin than about humans. Part of him didn't.

"None taken. Family is important." Viyar studied him for a long moment. Silent. Still.

It would have been very intimidating face to face. Over vid, he found himself wandering. He broke the silence before he drifted into rude levels of daydreaming. "Garil is a fantastic teacher. I audited one of his classes."

"Did he make you want to take up virology?"

"Make me want to *and* remind me I'm not smart enough."

Dhyanil was glad he was a red herring, though. But he hoped Viyar would work out what expert or experts they *were* using.

"You never know."

"I'm too old to change," Dhyanil insisted with stubbornness in his voice he did not truly feel. He was too old to change. He had no choice. So, what was the path of least resistance?

"Nobody is ever too old to change," Viyar said, wryly. "Trust me. I've seen wizened grandfathers make *remarkable* changes in their lives. And you're a long way from a wizened grandfather."

"I dunno, I'm starting to see wrinkles." His hide definitely did not have the metallic flush of youth to it any more and was, indeed, creased in a few places.

Viyar laughed. "For now, keep doing what you're doing. When this is over..."

"I'll work out what to do when this is over when it's over."

Or perhaps he would now. He had, after all, nothing else to do for the rest of the day...

40

Garil was a red herring. Ly was sure of that now. Or Garil was already working with them and Dhyanil was going to be...ly really hoped ly was wrong.

Ly really wished ly had had that thought *before* talking to him. Ly did not want to call him back until ly was more certain. Ly wanted a drink. Just one. But not vril, either. Ly wanted a *stiff* drink. Some cases were like that.

Some cases were worse. This one had yet to involve any mutilated bodies or, and ly shuddered, smashed eggs. That kind of thing was generally dealt with more locally. And the last smashed egg case had turned out to involve a major need for a psychiatrist.

Ly still shuddered at the memory.

Ly could not get a stiff drink. Not until ly knew what was going on. Station security were doing their best. They were, though, primarily trained to escort people to the docks and find missing hatchlings. They needed to be trained for more intrigue, but there had always been Special Investigators for that. Ly contemplated backup. It would look bad to call in another investigator, but ly was not sure ly had the choice.

Aha. That. Yes. Ly made a recording, sent it off, and felt rather better. Hopefully that wouldn't be needed, it was for lin worst case scenario. Then ly considered. The tyrar and the interstellar. The tyrar could *not* be involved in this. They had to know that if somebody found out a way to wipe out an entire sentient species...

In fact, if anything, he would expect the tyrar to ally with humans against ky'iin. Humans had not exploited and wrecked Tyranis. Ky'iin had done that. Perhaps only because they had got their first, but if ly was a tyrar ly would be more inclined to trust humans. They'd always been a little bit more inclined to trust glyn.

Ly didn't blame them. There was shame in what had happened on Tyranis. Shame and lessons that should have been learned already, here on Kyx, when cultures came up against each other and clashed over resources.

The tyrar had had to learn the ways of their oppressors, turn them back, then demand equality not everyone wanted to give to prey. The humans had already learned those lessons.

Ly wondered why. Then ly went back to staring at lin computer as if it would give up the secrets of the case right then and there.

"So, we got a look at who put the device in the embassy air system."

Ly nodded. "But do we know who it was?"

"Male. That's all we know."

Which made sense. You hired a man to crawl around in tight spaces when you could. Really shady people might have hired a child. At least they hadn't done that.

"Face covered, then."

"Wearing a pressure suit helmet."

Easy to get on a space station, sufficient to fool most facial recognition. "Send me the footage and I'll see if we can do anything with it."

Maybe their computers could tease out a face through the visor.

"I don't think that will help. It was mirrored."

"So, professionals."

They hadn't realized that their toxin wouldn't work on humans, but they had taken all the other needed steps. Whoever that person was they were probably already on the...

...ship which had left.

Was that *also* a red herring? Yes, it had to be. Or it had gone to get something.

They had tried the abduction after the interstellar had left. "Send it me anyway. And get me the dock manifest, schedule, and flight plans."

There almost had to be a second ship. The interstellar would move bulk stuff. It was expensive to operate in system, though. Unless you were in a real hurry and were planning a short hop. Most freighter grade pilots weren't great at short hops, but they could have hired a veteran. Somebody with neural implants.

But for moving people around the system? No. Unless, of course, they wanted lin to think that way.

"Got it."

"I'll be in my office. I hope."

At this point, ly was fairly sure ly was a target. The kidnappers had not wanted to kill lin. They probably wouldn't try to do that.

But ly was going to have to be quite, quite careful if ly didn't want to wake up in a hold or something. All they had to do was stick lin on a ship and fly around in circles for a while. It had happened before. Not to lin, but to other investigators in the past. Ly made it back to lin office with no such incidents, unless ly counted being slammed into by a teenaged male in a hurry to go somewhere or other.

Kids.

Ly closed the door, double checked all the safety gear was present, locked it and settled down. Ly was not safe here; ly was not safe anywhere on the station, most especially a place ly was known to go and had already told somebody ly was. This was, of course, the point.

FORTUNATELY OR UNFORTUNATELY, nobody took the bait. Viyar managed to get through all of the work ly had in mind. Then ly considered.

Ly could get food without leaving, but as nobody was taking the bait, perhaps ly was going to be better off around others.

Others would only get hurt if they were involved. Ly wanted to throw something. *That* was what ly needed to do. Ly all but exploded out of lin office. Stalked down the promenade. Nobody ran into lin this time.

The station recreation area wasn't going to give lin everything ly could get on a planet. It was going to give ly enough. Ly looked around, and then headed for the weights. Lifting would help, it would clear lin head. Ly had *not* gotten enough exercise lately. That was a big part of lin problem. Ly couldn't use the bench without a spotter, but claimed a couple of free weights and started to go through lin routine. Sweat began to form on lin hide, glistening. This was exactly what ly needed, and ly made a very firm mental note not to ever let it happen again, no matter where ly went. Never sit around not exercising. Ever.

Ly finished with the weights and then took a lap around the room. The station was big enough to have a pursuit track, albeit a fairly tight one. Ly ran. Ly pretended it was the last part of a chase. It was not. Ly would hunt soon enough, but that was one thing no station or ship or empty world could supply. Virtual reality could help, but it wasn't the same thing. Ly wondered what it was other species needed. Ly realized somebody was running alongside lin. Then they...no, she...cut lin off, forcing lin to slow, turning to face lin.

It was rude, but not violent. "What do you want?"

"Just to talk, Special Investigator. I promise."

"If it's not about my case I don't want to hear it," ly found linself snapping, claws starting to poke out from lin fingertips.

Ly really didn't. Ly didn't want to have to worry about anything but the case.

"Oh, but it *is* about your so-called case. Which is over. Or soon will be."

"If you're here to gloat, I don't care about that either."

"We will have the human soon enough, and we'll know whether it works."

"It won't work. It can't work."

"That's what they say, but it *will* work."

Then she turned and ran off. Gloating? Or trying to rattle lin. Ly would not let them do that. But ly did worry. What if they *had* found something that would work?

41

AVOIDING the snow without locking himself in his hotel room was proving to be hard.

People here apparently "hibernated" all winter. There was an indoor swimming pool, but the idea of swimming in a pool? Instead, he went out to one of the lakes. Some people were out skating. He had no idea how to skate, and wasn't about to try without at least some formal instruction.

Keeping his hands in his pockets, he watched the skaters. The sky was clear. He glanced up and saw small lights, satellites. It wasn't possible to exist in the world anymore without space technology. The computer in his pocket ran off of it. Was he a hypocrite?

All of the technology was ky'iin. The glyn had yet to trade any of theirs, although he suspected they would. The tyrar had been in the steam age when the ky'iin had found them and exploited them. That was why people were more afraid of humans. But this was all *their* technology, nobody else's.

He looked out at the skaters again. Part of him wanted to join them. Most of him knew better. He was just a figure standing by the lake. Anonymous. Nobody here could know who he was. And after this, he hoped nobody would ever know who he was. He couldn't go home. He would have to find somewhere new.

He didn't want fame; he'd seen the edges of it now. He'd been threatened with sexual assault, all but abducted, coopted, because people knew he was an isolationist.

It did not occur to him, quite yet, to just stop being an isolationist. But after this, he rather thought he was done with activism or anything resembling it. He was going to...find a job somewhere quiet and disappear.

The sky was starting to cloud in. This was a student town. He needed to find entertainment that didn't involve alcohol. Fortunately, he had an idea of where to look. He sought shelter in a building by the skaters, pulled out his computer and started investigating.

There was a student concert that evening. It was in a bar, but he was sure he could avoid getting blind drunk again if there was something to listen to, something to focus on other than that.

He made a note of the address, then fled back to the warmth of his hotel room. It might not be good music. But it offered music, food, and a chance to forget all that was going on.

THE BAR WAS FAR ENOUGH AWAY that Dhyanil elected to call for a car, riding to the other side of campus. Once he stepped inside, he felt...out of place. Everyone here seemed to be a student.

He was sure there were faculty here, but he couldn't see any. He felt old, and he felt unhappy and wistful. But there was nothing better to do. He pushed through the crowd and claimed a place at a table. A waiter swung by. He ordered vril, and then studied the menu.

The band was warming up, he could hear faint notes over the noise of a crowd that would, no doubt, quiet once the music started. A couple of students sat down on the other side of the table. They didn't ask his permission and he didn't expect them to; this place was too small for niceties like that. They ignored the old man. He would have ignored the old man too at their age, so he couldn't exactly criticize them for what was a very reasonable decision. Of course they would think he was boring.

A third joined them, but that one peered at him, then pushed his chair back so he could talk. "Hey, what brings you? Tell me you aren't a talent scout...most of us are here for the food!"

Dhyanil laughed. "What's good on the menu, then?"

"Everything. Try the cari stew."

He would take that under advisement. "I'll try that."

"So, what are you, then?"

"I'm researching for a book. If it ever gets written."

"You and half the students here."

Dhyanil lifted his hands. "I know, I know."

"What's your day job? Anything interesting?"

"I'm..." A pause. "Between jobs. I was doing personalized travel itinerary development in the southern coast and isles, but I'm kind of...looking for something new."

The kid laughed in his face. "Writing a book isn't it."

He shrugged. "I can live off of basic if I have to." And he could, but he didn't want to. Very few people did.

Having a job and a purpose, after all, mattered. The waiter arrived. He took the kid's advice and ordered the stew.

Then he settled down to listen to the band. They were every bit as bad as he had been warned, but somehow it didn't matter. It came with an earnestness, an authenticity that meant something. That made this art, not something which could just as easily have been developed by an AI.

He appreciated that.

He envied them.

THE CONCERT WENT LATE, but not too late. Dhyanil was tipsy, but not drunk. He felt good about that as he made his way back to his hotel room.

He'd enjoyed himself without crossing the line into harming himself, which was honestly all he really cared about. And there had been a weird sense of relief about admitting he was between jobs. Because it wasn't the tour guide job he meant. He wasn't going to be an activist anymore. He was going to be something else; he didn't know what yet, but something that wasn't about getting people younger than him to commit acts of vandalism to make his point.

That had led to this. It had led to Iluhin's death. But it had also led to the idea that ky'iin were better than offworlders, not just different and separate. It had led to...he could see, in his vaguely drunken state how his thinking led to their thinking. How did he get what *he* wanted?

He wanted a world where ky'iin ways were preserved. Where tyrar discomfort with hunting didn't lead to pressure to shut down the preserves (Sure, shut down any that remained on tyrar. That was different).

Where he could be sure that his descendants would know who they were, would know history. Would know what they had shed and why. He stumbled a bit. The snow was uneven. There was a color in it, some kind of dye that had apparently caused partial melting and then refreezing...

...and he hit the ice and slammed into the ground. The wind was knocked out of him.

He lay there for a moment, really hoping nobody had seen that. Tricky snow! Of which he now had a maw full. He spat it out as he tried to get up, but the world spun around him.

Had it been the ice? Had it been something else? Had he hit his head when he went down?

Something was going on. Something in his vril? In the stew? In the air? Maybe it was just the cold, cold could do weird things to people.

Heat could do weirder things.

He tried again, and fell into a heap in the snow, his coat falling around him. The light faded out before he could try to move again, moving becoming something he no longer felt like doing until everything flowed away and out into silence.

And darkness.

42

"Void!" Viyar swore with feeling. Taking creation's name in vain was something lin grandfather would have taken lin to task for.

Viyar did not really believe in any kind of deity. But ly still seldom swore.

Now was one of those exceptions. Dhyanil was missing, likely snatched by...somebody. Ly thought ly had found the ship they were going to put the ambassador on; a yacht of uncertain ownership. They only *thought* they had good fake papers on it. Ly could order it seized. Ly was choosing not to, waiting for them to make another attempt. Of course, ly had made sure station security was taking appropriate steps to ensure any attempt would fail.

Maybe that wasn't the right approach, but ly could not ask a foreign dignitary to act as bait. That was exactly the kind of thing which would start another war. Ly had no idea what ly would do if she volunteered. She struck lin as the type to do that. Whatever else you said about humans, they did not lack in courage. Or the ability to act as individuals.

Tyrar couldn't do that. They were evolved from herd animals and were anxious if not in a group. Ly wondered what that was like. Maybe ly saw it as worse than it was, as more confining... Instead of ordering it seized, or swearing until ly had run out of swear words (which would not take long, although he knew people who could easily fill an afternoon that way), ly stalked out of lin office.

Ly walked out onto the promenade, looking. Hunting. Prowling. People avoided lin, whether they were tourists in nice clothes or station workers in their practical overalls. Ly was looking mostly for the woman who had cornered lin in the gym. Facial recognition had no match on her, which meant she had not come onto the station by normal means. Perhaps on the yacht?

Ly knew full well that rich people, or those perceived as rich people, could still get something of what they wanted by being, well. Rich. Showing up in a yacht like that was enough on its own to get one perceived as rich. Despite all society's efforts, people could still get rich.

Or she had sneaked on as crew. She had not come through the port and she was not recorded as a station resident or transient. Which might have been their mistake; it was easy to think that somebody who wasn't in the local system was the best to send as muscle. Easy to think, but not necessarily the right choice. She could not get *out* through the shuttle port before ly tracked her down, as somebody there legitimately might have.

She could hide on a ship, of course. The yacht had yet to file an outgoing flight plan, but ly was sure they were ready to go the second they had...

...and a shrill scream echoed through the promenade. Ly turned towards it and broke into a run.

THE SCREAM CAME from a prepubescent child backing away from the collapsed form of a tyrar.

A *lone* tyrar. That was not just bad, it was terrible. Tyrar could literally die if alone for too long, or so lin had been told. It was perhaps an exaggeration, but... The tyrar on the station moved in a cluster. If only one of them was out here, something bad was happening.

Ly knelt next to the fallen offworlder. They (ly had never worked out how to determine tyrar gender) were still breathing, raggedly.

The breathing of exhaustion. They looked up at him, and their mouth opened, their nose working. They said nothing. Or they didn't have a frequency transponder active. Viyar could not speak tyrar, few ky'iin could manage it even *with* a transponder.

It was easier to speak the ky'iin language for creatures with a nose they spoke through, than the reverse. The tyrar finally seemed to realize they were not being heard. They struggled towards a button on their belt.

Viyar pressed it for them and their rumbling speech became audible. "Child," Viyar said, pulling back. "Run to medbay. Tell them I need a xenologist."

Sy ran in what ly was fairly sure was the right direction, small feet making a surprising amount of noise on the decking. The tyrar had a medic with them. But given the state of this one, and their solitude, Ly was afraid of what ly might find in the tyrar quarters. Ly got the tyrar into a sitting position.

They did not seem injured. Merely panicked, glancing around with an anxiety Viyar could not understand. Maybe somebody who worked with working beasts would. Ly could not. The tyrar was alone, surrounded by predators, and apparently unable to speak a ky'iin tongue.

Or they had forgotten how, reverted to their native language under stress. Ky'iin who spoke more than one language did that. Tyrar probably did too. Their eyes began to focus on lin. Their breathing became steadier. Sweat matted their cream fur, light colored for a tyrar. They were in a terrible state, and ly wished ly could do something about it.

Finally, they managed a few words and gestures, "They betrayed us."

Who betrayed who? Ly needed to know, but there was no way ly could press a being in such distress. Not ky'iin, or at least not ky'iin as a whole, or this one would be running from lin. Or trying to.

Ly tried to be gentle, tried to be non-threatening, knew that no matter how hard ly tried ly still *smelled* like a predator.

"Who betrayed you?"

"The herd. The herd betrayed..."

A conflict within the tyrar delegation, then. In some ways not lin business. Except that all of this did circle back to tyrar. Why?

STATION SECURITY WENT to the tyrar embassy. The lone tyrar was in medbay, with a xenologist looking her over.

The consensus was that there was nothing physically wrong with her, just stress and anxiety. Viyar could not blame her for experiencing *those*.

Betrayed us. That was all ly had gotten out of her, and ly did not want to try and question her further right away. Instead, ly went to the embassy.

Verian fever was tyrar. *Both* of the things used to try and poison the ambassador were tyrar. They'd tried to kill her then changed their mind?

But why would the *tyrar* be involved in this? There was something going on here that ly didn't know about. Something ly had missed because all of lin focus was on ky'iin isolationists. Who would cheerfully use, abuse, and exploit tyrar. Maybe *they* were the ones who betrayed the herd, but the implication was an internal betrayal.

Ly glanced further down the hall to the human embassy. The tyrar door stood open. There was a vague, faint smell from within that was distinctly prey-like. Tyrar sweat? No, tyrar *blood*. Blood which had been mostly cleaned up. "There was a fight in here." The security female within turned, and lifted a hand. "There certainly was."

"Any bodies?" ly asked first.

"No. If anyone died they were already taken away. From the amount of blood I suspect that everyone here left alive, though."

Tyrar could hold a lot of blood in their bulky bodies. Ly understood the point right away. The suite had two sleeping chambers; calling them bedrooms would have implied the existence of a bed. They were full of cushions and, of course, shed fur. The kitchen had a faint grassy small, probably because of the bales of hay stacked in the pantry.

Ly had seen tyrar eat in restaurants, but apparently what vegetarian food was available on the station did not quite satisfy their high need for fiber. There was neither hide nor hair of a tyrar. The computer system had been shut down and locked. Ly could not hack it linself and even if ly could, dared not do so without permission.

Ly would have to put in a request.

"There *was* a struggle, though. Blood patterns here and look at the fur."

The tufts of fur caught on the door. Somebody had been dragged off. Somebody else had escaped and looked for help. Ly owed it to them to give them that help.

And it would, ly was sure, be part of the case that not so long ago ly had thought close to over.

43

Dhyanil came round tied up. Of course he did.

He'd been kidnapped. Which meant they didn't intend to kill him, unless they had no honor at all. He supposed he could not assume they had honor. But most likely, whoever had drugged him...because that was now obvious...wanted him alive for whatever reason.

"Awake?" He managed to move to see the speaker; of course, they wouldn't let him not, but with his hands tied it was hard to respond.

A tall but very slender woman. She ran her hand along her knife. "If I free your hands, will you promise not to try to run."

"No, but I will promise not to try to run until you've said what you intend to say."

She gave a short laugh and cut the ropes.

He rubbed his wrist. "I guess that's good enough. You *could* just have asked."

"Ah, but then you might have been seen cooperating with us, and I don't know which side would treat you worse. The isolationists, or the cops."

"I'm an isolationist," he said, automatically.

"No, you're a conservative who *thinks* he's an isolationist. I've watched all of your videos."

"Not true. The genocidal maniacs aren't isolationists. You can't isolate from something which you've destroyed."

He realized what was happening a moment later and couldn't help but laugh. "So, what are you?"

"Your enemy," she said casually but cheerfully. "Hopefully, though, for the most part we can fight with words as our weapons."

"A progressive who thinks offworlders..."

"I think offworlders have things to teach us and vice versa."

"And what about what we taught the tyrar?"

"Our worst mistake. The fact that most of them are even still willing to talk to us is a miracle."

It amazed him too. That the tyrar hadn't all become isolationists. Tyrar isolationists could be his allies. Or could have been.

"So. What do you want?"

"Garil's not what you think he is."

"It's fine, I'm pretending to recruit him to the genocidal plan. Except apparently they don't need him."

"Hard to need what they already have."

He understood in a moment. The red herring wasn't Garil. This was all a cover so that if they got caught, he would escape to continue his work. "You burned his lab."

"We made sure nobody was there. We thought it would slow him down, but..."

"...but they're ready to make their move on the humans. Who are they working with?"

"You can't..."

"I have a high security line to a Special Investigator. I can...get information to him without it being known."

"So, you would..."

"I don't know that I care any more," he said, finally, looking away from her for a moment. "But yes, I would ally with the craziest of progressives to prevent genocide. Besides, they involved a child."

"There is no honor in them."

He thought about that. Then decided that he agreed.

SHE UNTIED him the rest of the way, now it was clear (or she thought it was) that he was not going to punch her. Or run until the time was right. She'd let him go, eventually. "So, Garil has been working on understanding *how* viruses from one ecosystem infect another."

"He talked about that with me."

"Which is useful for both protection and weaponization. That's the way it is."

"Science," he mock-grumbled. "Not something I have ever really understood."

"Takes a few years of study to *really* understand it. In any case, he's been under watch for a while because of that."

"How do we know he's *not* just trying to protect us from something worse than verian fever?"

"We didn't. Until now." A pause. "You might have to just trust me on some of this."

Dhyanil tilted his head.

"Because you *aren't* a scientist. It's all in his latest results."

"*Is* he studying verian fever?"

"No, he's been studying a related disease that might mutate to affect certain breeds of lifestock."

"A tyrar disease."

"Yes. And he's been in heavy talks with the tyrar about it."

"Why would the tyrar ally with..."

No, he knew why the tyrar would ally with ky'iin isolationists. He would do it himself. Maybe they didn't know. Or maybe they didn't think they would be next. Or...an even darker thought. A bioweapon from tyrar against humans would be no harder than one from tyrar against ky'iin.

"We don't know, but they sent a bunch of stuff, including some quite dangerous samples. Verian fever doesn't make ky'iin *that* sick, but there are other tyrar viruses which can. And vice versa."

Dhyanil lifted a hand to his throat as she spoke the words that his mind had started to form.

"Exactly."

"So, you think that...this communication with the tyrar?"

"We intercepted it. They speak pretty well, although we can't be 100% sure about some word choices."

"Better than my tyrar," Dhyanil quipped.

"Hah. Yes."

Not that that was fair as ky'iin couldn't pronounce their languages at all. "So, they're working...why do the tyrar want to destroy the humans?"

"We don't know. If you find out..."

"I'll let you know. Just don't kidnap me again."

"We were worried about your reputation."

Dhyanil laughed. "I'm already on the outs with the people I care about." There was a bitterness to it.

Would he see his mother again? He was not entirely sure.

It mattered, it had to matter, but stopping genocide mattered more.

It had to. And that meant...

Her words about being a conservative thinking he was an isolationist crossed his mind.

"Then perhaps I'll see you again."

"With less snow in my maw next time."

She laughed and everything was, oddly, alright.

THE NEXT MEETING with Garil was tense. Dhyanil did not, of course, know whether to believe the progressives. Who admitted that they had blown up the professor's lab.

But the most important thing was to give no clue of any of this *to* the professor. He knocked on the door of his office, after the students had gone. It was still untidy, but some things were in subtly different places. Clearly, Garil had a system, and he could probably find anything in here *unless* some well-meaning person tidied it up.

"So, anything from your isolationist friends?"

"Nothing."

"Sure they haven't hung you out to dry?"

"It's you they want. They're giving me space to get you." It was a good test *not* to tell him Meruhin was safe. Let him think that

Dhyanil was still being blackmailed. Watch to see if his attitude changed.

"Or they found somebody else."

That would be something Garil would want the world to believe if he was guilty; but also something he might want to be true if he was innocent. Dhyanil was *not* a trained detective. He couldn't read people's thoughts in the edges of their words the way some Special Investigators reputedly could.

After meeting Viyar, he was inclined to believe it. The human scared him in a similar way. She focused on him so peculiarly, but without ever meeting his eyes. Or perhaps he had just never met an offworlder who might be inclined to prey on *him* before.

"I suppose. You'd think they'd call me back, unless this is a red herring to distract people from their actual candidate."

"It could be. But while I'm here...can you explain to me that thing about protein locks?"

"Okay. Viruses have various ways of getting into cells, and they often involve shapes in the protein envelope that are quite specific. That's what antibodies look for."

Dhyanil tilted his head.

"A protein lock is is the connection between a virus and a cell that causes viruses to infect *specific* cells. Some viruses will infect almost any kind of cell, but a lot of them have preferences."

"Okay."

"It's not a term everyone uses, of course. But when you're talking about xenoinfection, weird stuff can happen. Sometimes they can't invade any cells. But also, there's a tyrar disease that's a lung disease in tyrar, but a blood disease in ky'iin."

"Makes sense. You should get the humans to send you some of *their* data." Dhyanil paused. "Hopefully there isn't a human disease that could wipe us all out."

"I hope not. But it's unlikely. Nine times out of ten xenoinfection is milder, unlike zoonotic infection *within* the same ecosystem. *That* is how plagues start."

Dhyanil didn't want to think about a plague.

That night, he had nightmares about one.

44

THE TYRAR DELEGATION had their own yacht for if they wanted to leave. It was still docked.

Like all tyrar vessels, it was a little on the large side. Tyrar tended to be larger than other sentients and their need for company discouraged *small* ships. In fact, they built some of the largest ships in the universe. This was, well. A yacht, but it was easily twice the size of a typical ky'iin ship of the same type. It was interstellar capable, although probably not with that much range.

Station security was searching it for lin; ly could trust them with this kind of simple task. Backup was going to be needed. Ly hated calling for it, but ly couldn't finish this alone. There was now too much ground to cover, too many moving pieces.

Dhyanil had been snatched from the street, then released unharmed. Ly would have to find out from him what was going on with that. Ly also thought they might need to bring in Garil.

Heck, maybe they should bring in every expert that could potentially do this, call it protective custody, watch to see who freaked out. Ly *hated* those kinds of tactics. Rounding up the usual suspects had once been a way peacekeepers enforced not the peace but the hierarchy.

Round up people who had too much or too little skin pigmentation, or who spoke the wrong language. Round up offworlders, of course. Although very few came down to the planet.

Almost everyone had learned from what had happened on Tyranis.

Hopefully the humans would learn too, before they made a similar mistake. Eventually, no doubt, there would be offworlders as citizens on Kyx, but they had to be sure. They had the privilege of being sure.

Unlike their victims.

Ly stepped onto the tyrar ship, aware that this was a breach of diplomatic protocol, but a needed one. The surviving tyrar had sent to her homeworld for help. They would be here soon, and they would smell lin presence. The survivor had given lin permission, but ly was still likely to be yelled at by tyrar, a sometimes physically painful experience. But it would be worth it if ly could find something. The ship smelled of prey.

Ly headed for the bridge. Off of it there would be some kind of office. Somebody in the delegation was the nominal captain of this vessel. Or rather the leader-by-consensus. Tyrar hierarchies were oddly flexible, shifting as situations varied.

Ly stepped into the office.

Ly stared.

THE OFFICE HAD CLEARLY BEEN OCCUPIED, NOT a long time ago but recently.

Perhaps they had left clues. Perhaps they had left red herrings. Ly casually picked the lock on the desk and started to go through the drawers. Tyrar wrote things down on paper, and that was most of what was in here. Ly could not read, like most ky'iin.

Ly would need a tyrar or a diplomat to translate. Ly pocketed a small book. Everything else was just kind of...debris. The book was the only thing that could possibly have been important enough to lock up like this. On the desk was assorted debris which no doubt wouldn't be there when the ship was in space.

Or, yeah. There was a gravity net spooled to one side of the desk, which would hold everything down. Pictures of the tyrar homeworld. Some star-shaped squishy thing, the purpose of which ly was really not sure of. Tyrar were weird.

Ly found nothing else of interest. Ly would get the book copied and return it, then translate the copy. When the tyrar's backup got here, they would at least not know ly had looked at it. Or, depending, ly could work with them on anything the contents might reveal. Ly moved away from the office, heading for the airlock. Viyar trusted security to find anything else. Then ly stopped, and headed to the cargo hold. The yacht's hold would presumably only carry supplies and diplomatic property. A ship like this was not used to carry cargo.

"Investigator, I'm glad you came."

Ly studied the woman, who seemed barely more than a child. "What did you find?"

"We're not sure. It wouldn't ever be...even now we're..."

"You know I'm taking responsibility for breaking the rules. If the tyrar are going to yell at anyone in infrasound, it will be me."

And if ly was forced to retire, ly had a backup plan for that. Twenty years ago, ly would have been much more worried about that prospect. Ly followed her into the cargo bay. There was a fridge tied to the wall.

"We opened it. It's got...science stuff in it."

"Keep it closed!" Ly snapped. Then ly took a deep breath. "Who was in the room when you opened it? Everyone who was in the room needs to quarantine and be checked."

That probably included lin now. But ly had some things to do first.

IT WAS NOT hard to get hold of the kind of protective gear ly needed. With it in place and the hold empty, ly opened the fridge. It was just a fridge. But in it was, indeed, science stuff. Specifically, vials of what looked like tyrar blood as well as vials of clear fluid.

Could be tyrar medical supplies, but if so why were they on the ship not in the embassy? Ly took pictures of everything, intent on sharing them with the tyrar survivor.

If it was innocent, ly could relax. If it wasn't, ly should still be checked over. Just in case. What harmed ky'iin but not tyrar? And what about the verian fever?

Ly needed a scientist. Ly needed, to be specific, a xenologist ly could absolutely trust. Abruptly ly knew exactly where to find one. There was only one source of scientific knowledge that ly could be absolutely certain was not part of the conspiracy. But did they have the experience? Ly closed the fridge and headed for medbay to be checked out. What was in it? Ly needed to know. Ly didn't want to know. Medbay put lin in a quarantine room while waiting for the results.

From that room, ly made two calls. The first was to the person ly hoped could find lin an expert. The second was to Dhyanil. The isolationist could not be trusted, but ly knew exactly *how* and *why* he couldn't be trusted. That made him more trustworthy than anyone on the station. Ly rather thought the male's activist days were over, in any case. He was seriously spooked. In fact, when the male finally answered the call, ly could see the signs of stress in his face and body.

"Is this secure?" he asked.

"As secure as it can be made. You in a locked room?"

"Locked, and I used the sweeper you made me. So, I got abducted by people who think Garil is already part of the conspiracy. That's who set fire to his lab."

"So, these people..."

"Wanted me to look and see if I could find more evidence, I guess. They think we're on the same side."

Grimly, "We are." A pause. "Every sane being is going to have to be on our side soon enough. I can't say everything yet, but..."

"But the virus is close to deployment."

"I don't know that. I do know that this mess involves more people than we thought. I think it's time for you to disappear."

"No." Dhyanil took a deep breath. "Not unless there's absolutely nothing I can do."

"Are you willing to risk your life?"

"Yes."

That was not the answer Viyar had expected. It was, though, an answer that changed what might happen next.

45

DHYANIL'S REST WAS INTERRUPTED. Strange dreams flowed through him, dreams that superstition would say came from the heart of the Void. Or, in more animist circles, from whatever spirits and messengers lived in this cold place. There were times when he leaned towards the latter.

A creator deity made no sense, but perversity in inanimate objects he could absolutely get behind. He woke with scratchy eyes and headed to a small diner he had found to break his fast.

They had very good sausages. Dhyanil was not normally a fan of sausages, but these had interesting and varied herbs in them, a sharp and bitter taste that was unfamiliar and perhaps acquired, except he was having no difficulty doing so. They probably shipped well, he thought as he sat there, surrounded by people who's worst problems were their next exam or their issues with their professors. That wistfulness was back. He was not too old to get a degree, but he was not smart enough to be here, to be anywhere close to here.

He did not belong here. He belonged on the beach; but he didn't belong there either any more. Probably why he was getting anxiety dreams. Finishing his sausage, he drank down his glass of keri juice. Inferior keri juice. Shipped too far, preserved too long. It was the middle of winter, perhaps he should eschew juice for now. Something hot would have been better, but he had wanted his keri juice.

There was better on the space station. He stood up and left, ignoring the chattering students. Snatches of conversation reached him, a word here and there. Nothing he could use. Had he heard the name Garil, he would have reacted. Maybe it was time to stop this pretense. What if Garil was working with the bad guys? What if he wasn't? Both options were almost equally scary. He preferred the first.

Hat and gloves on, and he was out in air so crisp and cold that he felt it dry his maw when he tried to breathe. The buzz of the diner died away behind him. He glanced up at the sky.

Beep.

Beep.

What the heck was beeping? Not his computer. Not any of the nearby vehicles. He turned around slowly. Then he did what you generally did when you heard unplaceable beeps.

He ran like beings from the Void were after him.

THE EXPLOSION HAPPENED as he ran around the corner. Thank the Void he had chosen the right direction. Car bomb. Couldn't possibly be aimed at him.

Slowly, he walked back towards the scene, trying to see what was going on. It was *probably* just a regular murder attempt. As if anything could be regular about that.

He approached cautiously. The scent that drifted on the air puckered his maw. It was the scent of cordite and burned plastic. It was not the scent of burned flesh and bone. There had been nobody in the car. A timer based off of somebody's usual habits, then.

He turned and walked away before the peacekeepers could find him to ask him what he saw. Which was, of course, nothing. That beep, beep haunted him all the way to campus, though. Once there, he took the very first entrance to the network of buildings, tunnels, and skywalks that he could find.

Tugged off his hat and gloves. Let his heart rate finally return to normal, or at least to normal for him. He didn't need any more excitement. Through the mess of tunnels towards the biology building and Garil's temporary lab (his permanent one was still being cleaned up and repaired).

It was not where he wanted to go. It was where he needed to go.

He needed, he realized, to know if the affable professor he was getting to know was secretly a supervillain capable of trying to kill millions. Then something hit him, a thought came up through his mind and he stopped so suddenly a student nearly ran into him. The bombing, not aimed at him, not hitting anyone.

What *would* be aimed at him? The progressives had abducted him, but they had treated him with honor. But the people he was in real danger from were messing around with viruses.

Were messing around with *diseases*. The symptoms of verian fever in Ky'iin were mild. He knew what they were. Coughing, a bit of a temperature, minor body aches. Not dissimilar from a bad cold.

In tyrar, the worst outcome was pneumonia and death. Now he was going to keep coughing. But... You didn't use disease against somebody, because you never knew to whom it might spread. In theory Garil cared about who it might spread to. But Dhyanil decided to be very careful what he ate or drank around the man.

Just in case. He still hoped they were all wrong.

WITH THAT RESOLVE IN PLACE, he went to a lounge near Garil's office. Garil was overseeing his post grads in some kind of lab work. Dhyanil wanted to know the nature of it, but couldn't come up with the words to ask; and if it was anything shady, Garil would just lie. Or he would not involve the post grads and do it on his own in the middle of the night or something.

Dhyanil would definitely do it on his own in the middle of the night, covered by some kind of fake project code. Of course, the professor kept his office locked.

The lounge was another matter. It had posters on the walls that showed pictures of cells and the like. Not over his head, but outside his normal interest. He had always taken only enough interest in his body to feel he could look after it properly.

He had always cared about viruses only as things his doctor told him he had. Or that he suspected he had, but it wasn't worth seeking medical aid. He was surprised he hadn't caught anything on this trip, or maybe he had and it would incubate for a while to show up at the least convenient time. A couple of students came in, chatting animatedly.

They were so wrapped up in each other that Dhyanil was able to eavesdrop quite nicely, and he was perfectly comfortable doing so. He probably shouldn't be, but he was.

"I'm not comfortable with that," one of them was saying. She was a woman, but extremely short, shorter than some men he knew.

"Gleyin."

"No. I'm *not comfortable* with that or with him."

"He's the best..."

"I don't care. I don't like him. He won't respect me."

"He's just old-fashioned."

The afore-named Gleyin turned to glare at her companion. Something was a bit off about the way she moved. "My grandmother is more progressive."

Were they talking about...

"Garil's perfectly *progressive*. He's not a conservative twat."

They *were* talking about Garil!

"No, he's not. Oh, he gives good lip service, but I've *heard* some of the things he says to other faculty when he thinks we're not there. He's pretending to keep students." This could be really important. Dhyanil didn't move, not wanting to bring any attention to his presence. They were ignoring him as some old fogey.

"He's a good teacher."

"Who secretly hates all of us. Of *course* he seems like a good teacher to you. He *likes* you."

Did he say something?

"Gleyin..."

"He can't even get my name right."

Oh.

It was about *that*. She was short, she was...she was ble, and some people didn't respect that.

Dhyanil managed to keep any reaction to himself. He wasn't sure how he felt about such things, although he fancied himself as better than those who wouldn't even use the right suffix.

It wasn't relevant. But he made a mental note of it nonetheless. It was certainly a chink in Garil's armor.

46

VIYAR HAD ASKED Dhyanil to keep an eye on Garil, for now, and find out what he could. The easiest answer was that the professor was the one responsible. The hardest answer was that he was a red herring, or involved against his will.

Viyar headed over to the human embassy. Ly wanted to check on the ambassador. Maybe even pick her brains a little. She was smart, and he was appreciating the way that she thought differently. There was clearly no intelligence difference here; and it was easier to see that there wasn't when dealing with them as equals.

Part of what had gone wrong with the tyrar was that people had mistaken their tendency to run rather than fight for lack of intelligence, their quiet passivity (until pushed too far). They were, after all, prey, and who wanted to admit prey were their equals? The door opened, and she showed her teeth to lin.

Ly wasn't bothered by that any more; it was amazing how fast one could adjust to alien gestures.

"Please, come in."

Ly did so.

"So, any updates..." She let her hands fall.

"We are currently trying to work out if the person they sent somebody to recruit is already working for them or is a red herring."

She made the sharp sound of human laughter. "I have no idea how two such disparate cultures could share the same saying."

"You mean..."

"We use the same phrase, although for us it doesn't mean a poisonous kind of fish and, of course, the kind of fish is equivalent rather than translated."

Ly couldn't help but laugh. "Are you okay?"

"I'm holding up. We're working on getting me some help, but we're having to test a lot of people to find one able to deal with the ky'iin. Your people are helping me with desensitization tapes, though."

"Good. We need to have more protection on you. When is your ship leaving?"

"Soon," she said a little sadly.

"Because I could use your help. Or rather the ship's help."

"What with?"

"We found some stuff. It might be dangerous to humans, but any lab on the station..."

"...could be observed. Is this disease stuff?"

"Honestly, we don't know."

The risk was real. Ly could be introducing the very infectious agent they were working with to the humans.

At the same time, allies needed to trust each other.

"We can probably do it, but I think we'd like...some kind of identification first."

"I would *never* intentionally put anything that might kill humans on your ship."

She laughed again. "You wouldn't. Many ky'iin would, and vice versa. We have a long way to go."

Ly knew that. But the ship was a resource ly could perhaps use. If ly was careful.

OF COURSE, Viyar was not going to be allowed on the ship. The Ambassador was now talking via vidscreen with somebody while ly stayed slightly out of view.

Listening carefully.

Ly was hoping that somebody would produce a language learning course for the primary human languages (there were two primary and, of course, hundreds of others) soon.

When they did, ly was going to take it. Ly was not sure which of those languages was being spoken right now, but ly could listen to the rhythm of it at least.

Try to pick up on emotions held only in tone and the length of vowels.

It had to be a lot easier for them to lie.

She finally finished speaking. "We'll take a look, but you have to let us take our own biocontrol precautions."

"Of course!"

Ly was not going to argue with that. "We have to assume that whatever is in that fridge is dangerous."

"But not as dangerous as those who made it think it is." She showed her teeth to him. "We've had people try this kind of thing before. It never works."

"Still...I hesitated to ask on this, because I didn't know about the safety. I'm not a scientist."

"Neither am I," she admitted. "I'm a linguist."

Ly tilted lin head. "You were not trained as a diplomat?"

"No, but I like to think I've learned well on the job." Again, the teeth.

Flat omnivore teeth, small canines. "I think you have done very well. And learning the language probably *was* more important..."

In the middle of a war. Abducted by aliens. Ly tried to imagine linself in that situation.

Ly couldn't.

Of course, the humans should technically have reciprocated, but they hadn't known to do so. Forgivable.

"Were you always a detective?" she asked.

"Pretty much. We used to train people from the peacekeeping

forces, but we realized the skills were far too different for that to make sense. About at the time we realized that locking people up for crimes..."

She shuddered. "Yeah, we used to do that too. Still do in some very narrow cases, but..."

"Oh, some people need to be taken out of society for their own good and that of everyone else, but there was a time when we thought it would work as punishment. So, no. I got a degree in this at Northspire."

She nodded. "I never got a formal degree. Mars isn't big on formal degrees, especially not for..."

She tailed off.

Ly decided ly didn't want to know what she hadn't said.

RETREATING FROM THE EMBASSY, back to the more normal-smelling corridors of the station, Viyar wondered when ly would get back to the planet.

Viyar wondered *if* ly would get back to the planet. There was this feeling of a shift in the air. Something bad or good was going to happen. Ly headed for the docks where the yacht was. It was taking no less than three burly females to maneuver the fridge, the entire thing, onto a cart to be moved to the *Challenger*.

Ly watched that process for a moment. They were wearing protection. Ly had, of course, not been infected by anything. Whatever was in there was well enough sealed that simply opening the door shouldn't cause issues, but they couldn't be too careful with it.

Ly had an idea. It was a dangerous, foolish, and stupid idea, but it was an idea, and ly was precious short of those. Ly headed back onto the yacht and began checking out hiding places. It was something from an old movie, but hiding and eavesdropping? It was the only idea ly had for finding the rest of this crew. Give them their yacht back.

Put an identical fridge where the first one had been, so hopefully they wouldn't notice right away. Station security was already taking care of that.

Not that ly thought they wouldn't know. More likely they would try to get their fridge back.

Ly had handed the book over to somebody trained to read tyrar script; an odd thing for the ky'iin, who's written language was limited to tallies, pictorial glyphs, and oddities like memory stones.

The humans had written language too. Ly wondered if that would prove a disadvantage. Ly wondered if it meant that the ky'iin would have to start to read and write in order to keep up with offworlders. The traditionalists and isolationists would *hate* that idea.

The fridge was gone.

Ly left the ship again, watching from across the dock. Ly was dressed simply, if they did not know who ly was they might mistake lin for a dockworker. Ly'iin did manual labor sometimes.

Being ly'iin, after all, didn't make you *smarter*. It just gave you fewer biological distractions to deal with, which was definitely an advantage.

But not smarter, no; look at somebody like Garil. Modern medicine also helped reduce those biological distractions to something more bearable, too.

No tyrar.

Then the station rang like a bell.

47

Garil seemed as affable as ever. Of course, Dhyanil wasn't going to bring up what the students said. It wasn't relevant. Also, while eavesdropping was something he was comfortable with, sharing what he had heard was not. Not with Garil. No, not with anyone.

"So, what did you want to learn today?"

Dhyanil considered the question. Garil seemed to genuinely enjoy helping him get his biology knowledge up to something resembling that of a solid hobbyist. Which was, of course, as far as he wanted to go. If he did go back to school to learn something new, it wouldn't be biology. Garil made it fascinating, but it was Garil, not the subject.

"Hrm. How about something about how vaccines work?"

Garil launched into an explanation about how vaccines were basically fire drills for your immune system. Dhyanil listened and made notes, but most of his attention was on how the professor talked.

He was trying to reconcile it with how he had treated that student. It looked more and more like he had a blind spot about certain things. Sometimes somebody's mind didn't match their body. It was rare. It happened. Some people found it hard to deal with, for reasons Dhyanil would never understand. It didn't connect at all to Garil being secretly a supervillain. It was just a little prejudice.

No, it wasn't just a little prejudice to those affected by it.

Garil finally stopped to breathe.

"So, vaccines are very virus-specific?"

"Yes and no. Sometimes they'll help with a closely-related virus. And there's also evidence that getting vaccinated every now and then strengthens your immune system. There's even evidence that it can reduce the activation of endogenous viral genetics."

"Of *what?*" Dhyanil asked. He wasn't sure he wanted that translated from Scientist to Regular Guy, but he really had no idea.

"So, our genome contains strands of inactivated virus. It gets copied in and if it doesn't cause problems, it can stick around and stick around. Then something turns those genes back on and bad stuff happens."

"What kind of bad stuff?"

"Degenerative conditions. Mysterious allergies because your immune system has no idea what it's doing. Bad stuff."

He thought about that for a long moment. Even in isolation, things would stick around. The influence of offworlders could last generations and then abruptly wake up. It was too late to stop them. But it might not be too late to make better use of what they offered.

"ARE THEY WORTH ANYTHING?" Garil asked. "Your thoughts."

Dhyanil glanced around the cluttered office, the images. Was that a memory pole? It was. The video media.

"I was thinking about viruses and culture, and how things that "infect" a culture can also get..."

"...permanently included. The difference is that the genome makes mistakes. Cultures generally only keep around stuff that's useful."

It was so close to his thought that Dhyanil found himself going along with it. "Which means that maybe we don't have to worry so much about offworld influence. If we can keep only what's useful."

"The issue, I suppose, is what it replaces."

Garil was, of course, not *that* progressive, Dhyanil mused. "We've already replaced plenty of things. I mean, we don't get carried off by random women and left with eggs anymore."

He laughed. "Oh, some people still do. But I think they *want* to be."

Dhyanil considered that. "I suppose if she's hot enough."

Garil's turn to laugh. "I've got students that if I was thirty years younger."

"Don't go robbing any nests, now," Dhyanil felt emboldened to tease.

Not that he was entirely wrong. There were some quite nice young ladies around. Who needed nice *young* males to brood their eggs. But a guy could look.

"Oh, believe me, I would never distract them from their studies."

Dhyanil was tempted to mention the cute, short woman he'd met, that he was pretty sure was male-bodied, but he decided not to push that particular issue. No, he was *definitely* not pushing the issue.

Then the lights went out. Just like that. No flicker first, just gone.

"Shelter?" Dhyanil asked, abruptly limited to only certain parts of speech. Ky'iin did not move around in darkness.

He was already starting to feel tired, to feel relaxed, as if the darkness was a blanket wrapping around him. Warm and comforting. It was a natural reaction, but he fought it off. He was no child to be put in darkness to calm him down. Somebody had put them in darkness. He heard something, and then he tried to focus.

The window? There was one, but it was blocked. He could, though, see a tiny bit of light. He seized on that light, pulled it towards him. Light, day, wakefulness, life. Then he dived towards the door, tried to open it. It was locked.

"Sorry," came a voice.

Garil's voice.

Whatever was going on here he seemed to be in on it.

The door stayed closed for what felt like a very long time.

THE DOOR FINALLY OPENED, and hands that might as well have been steel wrapped around Dhyanil's arms.

Garil's apology did the exact opposite of helping. They threw a hood over his head and, once more, he had to fight to keep from feeling like a hatchling, safe in his father's arms. He was dragged into some kind of vehicle. The hood stayed on. He heard nothing, nothing except the faint whine of the electric motor and then the rattle of the road.

They must have cut a lot of power, perhaps to the building, to pull this off unnoticed. Garil had apologized. That could mean so many things and none of them were good. He needed to escape. He was a middle-aged tour guide. He was not going to be escaping this time. Before, he had been allowed to leave.

He found himself hoping that Viyar had tagged him at some point, or that the progressives had while he was out. That somebody had a trace on him which he could be followed by. Which he could... He was unfond of that thought, he didn't want to be traced. But if he was, rescue might come.

The vehicle went along a smooth road. From the sounds, it was going fast. Part of him insisted, of course, that he might as well sleep. He might as well just rest and then when he got to his destination he'd find out what they wanted of him. He fought it for as long as he could, but the darkness and the motion of the vehicle were just too comforting.

Sleep came, and this time it did not contain any dreams. Only the faintest hint of anger that carried him into the darkness. There was nothing around him. Whenever he opened his eyes, it was still dark. Wherever they were going it was a long way away. Then he felt the vehicle stop.

He snapped wide awake, well rested. Now he might have a chance to escape. A chance to escape, and get word to Viyar, and the very fact that he was seizing on the Special Investigator said so much. Or a chance to get more information. Which did he choose?

Viyar had asked him to risk his life. Now he was about to be at that point. He had no idea whether he really would or not.

48

Ly LOOKED both ways along the docks. People were running, but not in any particular direction. Ly yelled "Stop!" at the top of lin voice.

Apparently, ly projected some reasonable amount of authority, because at least some of the runners stopped moving.

"Stop running until we know what happened!"

Ly wasn't paying any attention to the yacht.

"I don't know anything," a male dockworker said, bowing his head a little.

"I don't expect you to. I expect you to find out before you panic and run around like a herd after a large woman jumped into the middle of them."

The man looked distinctly uncomfortable. It hadn't been on the docks, not this time. So, an explosion somewhere.

Ly frowned then started to head for the embassy level. Fortunately or unfortunately, lin sense of purpose caused lin to develop an entourage as ly moved through the station. Ly did not take any lifts, not wanting to risk being stuck in one if there was another explosion. Or a malfunction. This could all be some kind of accident.

Ly hoped so. Ly was tired of the low level conflict; true, most people didn't even really know it was going on. However, it lingered on and on.

"Somebody blew up the tyrar embassy."

"The one that is currently empty." It was a message, Viyar thought. Probably a message to the missing tyrar.

Of course, ly had no idea which ones were trustworthy victims and which were bad guys. Even the survivor didn't seem entirely clear, although she had given them descriptions.

At least tyrar were not too hard to tell apart. Viyar made lin way into the embassy. The explosion had not managed to breach the outer hull, but had certainly done some damage to the interior of the embassy. Destroying evidence, then. Or getting attention. Or distracting attention.

"Special Investigator?" came after a while.

Or at least that seemed to be what the person behind him was trying to say. Ly turned.

"The yacht is gone."

"Of course it is." The distraction had worked. Ly had screwed up yet again, in the same way, but ly had learned long ago not to beat linself up over it.

Even with lin experience, ly had been more concerned with the explosion. "Let it go."

"We put a trace on it, but it's interstellar capable."

"Has it jumped yet?"

"No." The security person looked down slightly at lin. "Should I let you know when it does?"

"Set up an alert, put me on the list for it."

That way nobody would have to worry about it. Now, though, they knew that their fridge was gone. Had they put a trace on that? Ly had checked, but could ly be sure?

THE YACHT WAS OUT THERE. The humans had the samples. Ly had lost an opportunity to do something which might have worked, but which was also probably completely stupid.

They had a trace on it. They would know where it went until it jumped. Even if it jumped they could find it if it was in system.

Viyar had to rely on that for now. Ly did not have access to a ship to follow them. Ly did not have jurisdiction to follow them. Ly had only the recriminations ly was thankfully good at not feeling and whatever information the humans could get.

Whatever information Dhyanil could get, and ly didn't want to rely on that. Ly had already asked him for too much. Far too much.

So, ly did what ly always did when stumped: Went and got something to eat. In a restaurant on the promenade, where there were people. Stimulation, which might lead lin brain to go in an actually useful direction.

If not, then at least the soup was good. And not poisoned, which was a bonus right now. The tyrar had blown up their embassy then taken the yacht. That ly should have predicted. The human ship...had the stuff that could be used to destroy them. Ly was definitely second guessing that.

Except they were very smart and while ly did not entirely trust them, *any* beings could be trusted to look out for their own interests. Ly could make the reasonable assumption that the crew of the ship were sane by human standards, which presumably venn diagramed with sane by ky'iin standards. Ly had just finished lunch when lin computer beeped. The human ambassador.

Presumably...had they found something already? Ly finished lin drink and headed over to the embassy.

The station seemed very subdued. People had finally worked out some kind of power struggle was going on. Ly suspected anyone who could get back down to the planet was doing so; that the shuttles would be full and they would have to run extra ones.

Ly could not, of course, blame them for that. Ly would be leaving linself if ly could. Of course, was there really a point in staying?

There was, and she was the other side of that door.

THERE WAS a different faint floral scent in the embassy this time. This time, Viyar was sure, it really *did* come from one of the Ambassador's plants.

She was sitting on the couch, looking very small, but stood as ly entered. She was trembling slightly.

"What did you find?"

"In vitro, that virus infects human cells quite handily. It wouldn't be enough...for what they had in mind, but it has a long incubation period. It would have been a *pain* to eradicate."

"Is it altered?"

"Thankfully, yes." She smiled weakly. "Thankfully, because the tyrar have asked for human help."

"They *have*?"

This was news to Viyar.

"We can explain...by the way, we're going to destroy what of that virus is not needed for evidence."

"We'll finish the job after we've finished investigating. Thank you."

She moved to pour a liquid beverage. "Safe for ky'iin," she promised, then offered lin a cup.

Ly drank it carefully. It warmed lin from the inside, with a faint herbal note. "So..."

"We screwed up Earth. We screwed it up quite badly. Uncontrolled industry, pollution. Wrecked the climate. Colonized Mars...that's the planet I'm from...as a backup. Eventually we fixed it, but it took a lot of work and effort."

"And *we* screwed up Tyranis."

"Exactly. They want our expertise to fix their world."

"Not every tyrar does." It all suddenly fit together, pieces of a picture ly had not even known existed.

Tyrar working with ky'iin isolationists to destroy the humans before they changed Tyranis forever.

"Why..."

"You'll change their world forever. Asking for your help guaranteed that. Some of them would rather fix it themselves. Some people..."

"Are afraid. I *know*." There was something in her voice, an emotion

Viyar could not quite recognize. "I know, but if they don't do something Tyranis is going to become uninhabitable."

Ly knew that. "That's why they've been building such huge ships. That's *their* backup."

"Out system colonization. Which isn't a bad idea if we, or they, can find unoccupied planets." She looked, abruptly, tired. "You're right. Some of them would object. And of course some would object to the Destroy All Humans level."

She emphasized three of the words in a way ly didn't understand. Ly didn't, at least for now, ask. Asking seemed like it might get lin in trouble. She was already angry enough. And some of it *was* at lin. And deserved.

Ly fell silent, letting her calm down while ly sipped at lin drink. It was the tyrar after all.

No. The tyrar were being used.

49

Dhyanil opened his eyes again.

Now there was some light in the room and he shook off the heavy sleep the darkness had instilled in him. A protective measure, that, for a diurnal species.

An annoying reminder of evolution. Of their evolutionary past. Of times in the past of Kyx when the ky'iin could not have dominated because of it, for so much of the world had been in darkness, winds howling past their primitive, huddling ancestors.

One day the world would be like that again, the inevitable shifts and changes in axis and rotation. But now, they were civilized people who could deal with it, could light the world. Biologically, though, they had not changed. Culture adapts faster than evolution.

Bright light! The door opened and two women came in, dragging him out.

There was no sign of Garil.

"Sorry, but we had to grab you as well," one of them said. "We had to make it look good."

A fake kidnapping to hide the fact that the amiable professor was a mad scientist. Of course.

He fantasized about escape, now he knew that, until he looked around. While he slept, he had been taken further than he thought. The grey walls, the metallic tang to the ear said it all. He was on the station. No. He was on a *ship*. There was a faint vibration under his feet. This was no shuttle. The room was larger than any he had seen pictures of, oversized along with the door. This was a tyrar ship.

"You'll be returned to Kyx safely when this is all over...and when it's too late for any conscience you might have to prick about the humans."

He tilted his head to her. "So..."

"The snatch was to grab Garil and, of course, the virus samples. We trick the humans into taking the samples onto their ship. They get infected. Very long incubation period."

"It won't work," Dhyanil said, finally. "They have at least as good medical science as we do. They'll beat it."

"Best case scenario, they don't. Worst case scenario, they're so busy beating it that we don't have to worry about them for years."

Dhyanil mused on that and could see the logic. "And if they realize where it came from and start a war?"

"The military then finish the job for us. Several of the captains would love an excuse to do a nice orbital bombardment of their homeworld."

Dhyanil elected to pretend he didn't realize this was a tyrar ship. He had no idea why they were involved.

The ones who had wanted to book a holiday through him. Were they on this ship? Why would the tyrar be involved in destroying humans? He had no idea. But he said nothing more. Apparently, now he was on the ship, he was a 'guest,' not a 'prisoner.' A guest who couldn't, of course, leave.

Which meant he could find out more. He just had no way to tell anyone.

"You made the perfect..." Garil lifted a shoulder at Dhyanil.

"Patsy." Dhyanil wanted to glare at him. It would be appropriate to glare at him.

But there was something about him that seemed so sad, enough that he wondered if Garil was regretting what he was involved in.

Dhyanil let out a breath. "I'm not in agreement with your methods, but if we can get rid of the humans..."

There was the oddest flinch in the other man's features. Dhyanil was not sure what it meant, but he took note of it. Was Garil planning on double crossing them? He hoped so. He wished he could somehow signal that if that was the professor's intent, he would help.

"We can," Garil said firmly. "And we can fix all of the problems."

Dhyanil didn't like the sound of that. What did Garil consider to be problems? "Problems?"

"We have lost touch with who we are, and sooner or later that will destroy us as a species."

Dhyanil considered that. "We've improved as well, though."

"Have we?" Garil turned towards him. "I like being a scientist, but I feel...I felt...pushed. Pushed to prove that men can do anything women can, that ly'iin can fight, that..."

"You're a good teacher. Your students love you." Maybe that was the problem, though.

Whatever was going on with Garil, he was clearly not in the best place, mentally.

If he thought...

They were on a *tyrar* ship.

"You...wouldn't..." He whispered.

"Once, we lived the way we were supposed to. Then something happened. Something happened and the ly'iin were born."

This was a confession. This was a confession that was about to come bubbling out of Garil. "That was before we were *ky'iin*. Without them..."

"Without them we would still live in harmony as predators."

"Without them we would *die* the next time the axial tilt shifts."

"But we would die as natural creatures, not twisted ones."

Dhyanil tried not to show his horror. He was fairly sure... "It's not just ly'iin, at this point. It's the suppressors, it's..." Ly'iin were essential, were vital. And also were *natural*.

"Yes. It took a three-pronged approach. The tyrar were glad to help. We will never bother them again."

Cold settled in Dhyanil's belly. He thought of his mother. If she wasn't in on this, it was because she didn't know about it. If she knew about it, she would want in. Or failing that, she would die happy knowing he was involved. This was what he had been working for.

"How does it work?" he found himself asking.

"IT'S QUITE SIMPLE," Garil explained, the stars behind him. It made him seem like a halo. "Ly'iin are *not* a third sex. Ly'iin are females that don't develop properly in the egg."

Academically, Dhyanil knew this. But ky'iin had been seen as the third sex for so long that they were at every level that mattered.

"The virus will rewrite the genetic mutation, ensuring that all future ly'iin children develop as they should, as women. The ly'iin will naturally die out."

Dhyanil pretended to be fascinated by this, while inwardly being horrified. "And..."

"And it will also slightly adjust the sex coding of those children such that our current suppressors will no longer work." Garil spread his hands. "The new generation will be freed to embrace their biology rather than fleeing from it."

And civilization would collapse, but it appeared this was not a bug in the code of Garil's plan, but an intentional feature.

"And we'll go extinct," Dhyanil said, grimly. "You *really* think this kind of social change is survivable?"

They wouldn't even go back to being hunter-gatherers. Garil intended to literally turn back the evolutionary clock, remove the key thing that made them ky'iin. Push them back past the point of the primates. Because offworlders managed without... He intended to destroy their myoran, and he saw it as a good thing.

Dhyanil had to get out of here. No, better. He had to get a message out.

"We will adapt as we always have. Our grandchildren will have better lives, Dhyanil. Cleaner ones."

A message, because nobody could be allowed off this ship. Dhyanil had read about the Red Plague in school, the quarantines. He didn't know that they had infected him with this virus, but it would be a logical thing to do.

"We won't be ky'iin any more," he tried, knowing it was the last thing he had to say.

"Maybe we don't deserve to be." Garil turned and left the room, thus ensuring he got the last word.

Dhyanil turned to the observation windows, oversized as everything was on this ship. Void. He could see only one course of action. Would he risk his life for this? He hadn't been sure.

Now he had a feeling he was going to have to give it. The ultimate goal was in front of him, and it wasn't what he wanted after all. He wanted stability. He wanted *safety*.

He wanted his grandchildren to live.

50

VIYAR WAS MOVING to leave the human embassy when the lighting turned purple.

"What?" the Ambassador asked.

"Red alert. Stay here. It's a shelter area."

Presumably she had species-appropriate pressure gear somewhere. She nodded, and abruptly ducked into a side room. Probably looking for it. Viyar considered.

This was, indeed, a shelter area. Ly should stay here. Ly was not sure, though, that ly *could* stay here. Mentally. Emotionally. Ly needed to know what was going on. Full alert on the station. She came out of the bedroom, not with a pressure suit but with a personal computer of slightly unusual design.

"The *Challenger* is undocking. There's a huge ship in orbit."

"Tyrar," Viyar said. "Tell them it's tyrar. They build large."

And a full sized tyrar ship, possibly a warship? This was incredibly bad. This was *unimaginably* bad. This was, quite possibly, war.

"What should they do?"

"Liaise with the station commander. Undocking is smart." No captain wanted to be sitting prey at a time like this, and it seemed the humans shared the same instincts.

"I'm going to need to translate, then."

Viyar considered, then. "It's irregular, but I think we should go to C&C."

Her head dipped. The gesture appeared to be human assent. "One moment."

When she reemerged, she was wearing a pressure suit and carrying the helmet. Good. There wouldn't be human-suitable gear anywhere *but* here, at least not yet. Viyar, meanwhile, could raid a locker in passing.

"Come on."

The human would be noticed, but hopefully not have too much attention paid to her in all the chaos that would be going on. Transients who would *not* stay in shelter areas being the worst. They had four warships in system. Plus the human ship. The *Challenger* was a warship, something the humans had been careful not to emphasize and the ky'iin had been careful to ignore.

But it meant they had extra firepower, albeit of an unknown quantity and quality. And station C&C would be where they coordinated. She was right. They needed the translator up there.

She reached for lin hand, hooked hers into it like a child who did not want to be separated from sy father. She already seemed childlike enough. But it was a good idea. Ly set off at a speed that the shorter human should easily be able to match, keeping a firm grip on her.

The corridors were utter chaos.

SOMEBODY RAN PAST LIN, a hatchling in their...his?...arms. There were people milling around. A glen was somehow clinging to the ceiling. Viyar knew they could climb, but ly didn't know they could do *that*.

Ly was faintly envious, just because the ceiling was about the safest place to be right now. Making lin way through this with a fragile-seeming human clinging to lin. Ly shook lin head. "This isn't working. Ambassador, may I?"

"Yes."

She released lin hand and tucked the helmet firmly against her chest. Ly scooped her up in lin arms and started running. It was much easier, if far less dignified for the poor human.

This wasn't a time to worry about one's dignity. Probably how the glen had ended up on the ceiling. Not worrying about one's dignity would lead you to...shoulder through a crowd. Pushing people carefully aside.

Station security was trying to get the crowd under control. Ly ignored them. Was this war?

It didn't make sense for anyone involved to up and attack when so far everything had been subtle and honorable. Even the tyrar were doing things in ways that were...the tyrar did *not* consider infecting people with a disease to be honorable.

Void!

The picture was starting to form. It was a jigsaw puzzle with ten thousand pieces. Tyrar could be dishonorable too. Anyone could be. And everyone had a different idea of honor. And dignity. Nobody had any dignity left.

Ly made a turn into a service corridor and left most of the crowds behind. With lin arms full of ambassador, ly couldn't really say anything. But ly could catch lin breath and keep moving, through the dark corridors of the station. The purple lighting of full alert still flickered and glimmered. It was enough to give lin a headache.

Ly carefully set the ambassador down. "There's a ladder. Can you climb it?"

"Yes," she said.

"You go first."

The ladder led up to the "back" entrance to C&C. Ly wasn't technically supposed to know about it. Ly had made *very* sure to know every way of getting through the station. At the top, she hopped off the ladder. Despite her size, she'd moved quickly.

"Okay. So...the tyrar ship is likely a warship and likely did *something* to trigger the alert."

"I don't feel like a war today."

"Neither do I. The tyrar are faster to resort to it than ky'iin are."

"Carnivores have more social safeguards to keep from fighting than herbivores," was what she said, oddly.

Ly thought about that.

Ly had never thought about that before. "But how this ties into the virus, we don't know."

"We identified the virus," she said. "It's not meant to attack humans. It's a genetic engineering vector. And it's aimed at you."

THERE WAS no time to deal with that bombshell. C&C was behind a bulkhead. The door probably wouldn't have opened for Viyar. It opened for Suza.

She stepped onto C&C like she belonged there before it had even opened all the way. Ly scurried after her before anyone could think better of it and shut it in lin face.

"I'm here to translate with the *Challenger*," she said.

The station's commander merely indicated a place she could stand. Viyar stayed back by the bulkhead. Ly wanted to know more about the genetic engineering vector. But for right now, the commander was filling Suza in.

"A tyrar warship that was not expected jumped in. They claim they are chasing fugitives. We have yet to locate the fugitives."

That made sense.

This wasn't the people with the virus. This was the tyrar authorities and, Viyar suspected, they were pissed.

Suza did that head dip. "I will tell the *Challenger* to stand down. It's our operating protocol not to stay docked when on full alert."

"They weren't the only ones," the commander said smoothly. "It's understandable. Just keep them standing down unless we actually need help."

Viyar cleared lin throat.

The commander turned. "And..."

"Special Investigator Viyar. You're aware of the incident in the tyrar embassy."

"Ah. *Those* fugitives."

"Those fugitives indeed."

"I don't want you on my bridge, Investigator, but I suppose I have to use you."

"Just get me a liaison with the tyrar so we can exchange information. We also have a tyrar in medbay who needs..."

Most ky'iin weren't sympathetic. The commander was no exception. She stayed just as cold. "Please leave my bridge, Investigator. I will have the tyrar contact you."

"Thank you."

Ly left the bridge. The ambassador, for now, was apparently allowed to stay. Outside, ly caught lin breath. The purple lights faded to green.

The tyrar ship wasn't a threat, but it was very like them to come in acting like a threat. Display behavior, ly supposed. Herd behavior. Instincts lin could not understand, but could learn to accept.

Slowly, ly made lin way back to lin quarters. Ly had to trust that the tyrar would, indeed, be in touch. That ly would start to get answers.

51

THE SHIP WAS MOVING. That was not being kept from Dhyanil. He experienced his first jump, the faint and jarring sensation that was faster than light travel when you weren't the one flying.

He wasn't sure where they jumped to, but it was short. In system, then. Hiding? Going to get something? He had to work out how to get out of this situation. Or perhaps how not to. He could not go back to Kyx. Even his corpse could not go back to Kyx.

Jumping out of an airlock might be the only solution. Getting a message to Viyar, to anyone, was impossible. He wanted to apologize to his mother. He wanted never to talk to her again. The latter wish was going to be the one which was granted. She had warned him.

Maybe she wasn't dying after all. Maybe that had been her way of trying to get him out of this.

Or maybe it wasn't so small a planet and she had no involvement, or knowledge. That was more likely, but he wanted...

He wanted his father. His father was dead, had been dead for years. Dhyanil had grieved and got over it. When you are facing death, you want your father and your clutch sibs. You want your egg, even if you can't consciously remember being held within it.

Dhyanil wanted a hug. He had some limited freedom of movement

on the ship. The observation lounge, though, was closed off. That probably told something about where they were to somebody who knew
more about ships and being on ships. Not being that person, he didn't
find it helpful. The ship had a kind of arboretum area. He went there
instead, ignoring tyrar. It wasn't large.

Tyrar built big, but this wasn't one of their giant carriers. This was
an ordinary ship, one which might be used to move a mix of people
and cargo. Not a warship. A warship would have been noticed. A
trading vessel? Not so much. He wanted to prick himself and see if he
still bled.

He was moving past being afraid. A message to Viyar. If the virus
was on this ship, then there was another solution. *If* he could get a
message out. He couldn't. Not on his own. Was there anyone here who
was not part of the conspiracy?

He needed an ally. And he knew exactly how to go about starting
the search for one.

THERE WAS A CREW LOUNGE. It was not locked. It was also almost
completely empty.

Dhyanil found a place to park himself and studied those there.
Those not on shift and not wanting to tuck themselves away. Three
tyrar. He didn't understand tyrar. No, if he found a co-conspirator, they
would have to be ky'iin.

He couldn't even *hear* the tyrar without a frequency transformer.
This was not going to work. It was not going to work at all. Any ky'iin
on the ship were going to be deep in the conspiracy. The tyrar in the
room huddled as tyrar were known to do, their fur mingling at the
edges where they touched. They ignored him. That was, perhaps, his
superpower.

But he had no technical skills. He was not a spy. Any tracker Viyar
had put on him was either removed or, of course, useless. Space was
awfully big.

What he did have was a perfectly good brain, if not trained in the
right way to solve this. Maybe that was his advantage. So. He was

on a ship. He did not have control over where it was going. He might or might not be infected with a destructive genetic engineering vector.

If he was, then there might or might not be a cure. If he was *not*, then the picture was quite different. That was the first question he needed to answer. They'd had plenty of tme to infect him.

If the virus was ready and on the ship, he had to assume he was infected. If it was *not* then he could reasonably assume he was clean.

He had to get that information out of Garil, without clueing him in. That part shouldn't be too hard; the male liked to talk and liked to brag. He would definitely brag if it was here. And if it was here, then this ship had to be destroyed.

And that, Dhyanil thought, he could manage. He hadn't sabotaged anything in a long time. That didn't mean he wasn't capable of it. You didn't need much knowledge to destroy something. And it was a lot easier if you didn't need to be out of the blast radius.

An odd sense of calm came over him. If this was how it was going to go down, then he didn't have to worry about... anything.

HE WENT BACK to his quarters. He didn't have to worry about anything. All he had to do was get into the engine room and find something important to break.

He forced his thoughts into something resembling a straight line. If he could blow the ship up, he could do something else to help the authorities catch them. But he could only do one or the other. How vital was this ship? He stayed put until Garil called for him. The professor wanted company for dinner.

"So, how close is the...viral vector...to being ready?" Dhyanil asked, once he had well and truly stuffed his maw.

The meat was probably vat grown, but he didn't really care at this point. It was fuel.

"Want to know how long you'll be stuck here?"

"Wouldn't you?"

"It's ready," Garil said, dismissively. "Unfortunately, part of our supply was captured. A large part. We're going to have to go with plan B for dissemination."

That wasn't good news. "And if they captured it, they'll know what it does."

"Oh, well. They think...if we set things up right...it's a variant on verian fever designed to kill humans. That's half right."

Verian fever was self limiting in ky'iin. Did that make it a good vector? "I would have thought an established disease..."

"We wanted something with no risk of killing anyone. We're not monsters."

Yes you are, Dhyanil thought. You are a monster, you are a regressive being who longs for the days when somebody else made all of your decisions. The fact that Garil was male somehow made it worse. A woman seeking to return to the glory days of full blown matriarchy? That would make sense.

A man? He couldn't see it. He couldn't see why anyone would want to go back to being, best case, a third (no, wait, second) class citizen. At worst, property and breeding stock. Ah, but Garil was from the mountains, where men had ruled. *That* made it make more sense.

"What's plan B?" he asked, finally.

Garil shrugged. "A few carriers. A crowded public place."

That settled it in his mind. Dhyanil had to destroy this ship. He didn't want to, but he had no choice. It might not be enough. He had to trust that the other samples would be identified and destroyed.

But he had to destroy this ship.

52

OF COURSE, once back there, what the ambassador had said came back to lin.

Suza had said it was a genetic engineering vector for ky'iin. The humans must have ky'iin DNA samples. Honestly, they probably had *lin* DNA from lin visits to the embassy. Viyar didn't really mind that. But of course they wouldn't have the expertise to know what the virus actually *did*. Not a virus to kill humans.

Had ly fallen for a massive red herring? Or, worse, were there *two* viruses?

Ly very much feared the second, but right now there was nothing Ly could do about it. They could destroy this virus, although ly hoped they would stop to understand it first.

It might even be something they could learn from, could make useful.

A genetic engineering vector. From the tyrar. The tyrar had every reason to hate ky'iin and some of them also had reason to hate humans. Most of them did not want to *destroy* the ky'iin. They wanted compensation. They wanted help fixing their world. Or they wanted to be left alone.

But this wasn't isolationism. This was an attempt to, what? Ly didn't know.

It was an attempt to win a war they would not have to actually fight. *That* was what it was, and there was nothing wrong with that. Except for the scale. You poisoned people. You didn't poison entire waterways. But this wasn't terrorism, not if it was the tyrar. It was war. Unless, of course, they were being manipulated. Lin terminal pinged.

The Ambassador, standing back from her terminal. "I'm back," she said. "The tyrar have agreed to work with us."

Us.

Ky'iin, humans, tyrar. The authorities against... "Good. Because if it was the tyrar government, this would be war. I don't like war."

She made that sharp sound again. "I don't either. But some people seem to enjoy it as a hobby."

She was right there, sadly. "Do you know what the virus does?"

"No. We're going to have to trade data with ky'iin scientists. We can tell it's designed to insert viral DNA into the genome."

"I...I'm not a scientist."

"Neither am I, so let's just say this thing is meant to induce permanent genetic change in ky'iin, and for that change to pass on to offspring."

"Void."

That was irresponsible. That was beyond irresponsible. Altering an individual's DNA was fine. But you didn't let it go into the germline. This thing could cause ky'iin extinction.

Ly decided. "Share the data, but if the samples were to..."

"...fall out of a convenient airlock?"

"Exactly."

"We'll make them go away. It's a good job you sent it to us. It shouldn't affect humans; we don't have the DNA strands it's targeting."

Ly was relieved by that. But also, for the first time in a long time, ly was scared.

ONCE SHE WAS GONE, Viyar considered a stiff drink, still on the case or not. A very stiff drink.

Ly wanted to get so blind plastered drunk ly could forget this had happened until the morning. A genetic engineering viral vector designed to reengineer the entire ky'iin species. Ly could only assume it was also highly contagious. It was a good thing the humans were sequestered on their ship except for the Ambassador, who hadn't been there in a while. There was essentially no risk of it getting onto the station. It did need to fall out of an airlock, but ly wanted to know what it did. What it was meant for.

To destroy them, that was obvious, but why something so convoluted. A fatal disease with a long incubation period would be much more effective.

Unless your goal wasn't to destroy the ky'iin, but to enslave them. That had to be it. Ly made another call. Dhyanil had not been seen in some time. Ly hoped that meant he had elected to disappear himself. Ly doubted it.

"We haven't found him, but we know what happened. Professor Garil was abducted. Dhyanil appears to have been with him at the time. The kidnappers must have decided to take him along so he wouldn't raise the alarm."

That was good and bad. They hadn't killed him, which was always good. So, they had Garil. Even though they didn't need him. Which meant...there was one obvious thing ly hadn't thought of.

"Get protection details on all of our top virologists. And tell them some data is coming their way from the station."

"All of them?"

"Anyone who might be capable of creating or neutralizing a new disease."

"You think that..."

"I think our conspiracy may decide to neutralize everyone who can stop them. And it isn't the humans under attack after all."

Ly was looking at this all wrong. Ly was thinking that the tyrar would love to eliminate the ky'iin. But what was in it for any *ky'iin* working with them? What would both make a traditionalist happy and please the tyrar? Answer, some way to confine ky'iin to their planet. Could you do that with genetic engineering?

Ly would have asked, ironically, Garil. Without him being available, ly was left to speculate and think of other names. Could you make a species dependent on their planet?

If ly was an isolationist, how would ly want to change the ky'iin to keep them away from other species. There was, of course, one obvious answer.

THERE WAS one scientist on the station ly could talk to. One ky'iin scientist, that was. There was a retired virologist who had elected to live where she could control the gravity in her quarters. It was set to about half what was normal.

Higher than the human embassy; although the Ambassador had told him the gravity on the human homeworld was about two-thirds that of Kyx. Her colony world was smaller.

So, it didn't feel as light as it might have without that experience. "Thank you for welcoming me, Syahin."

"No trouble." She was withered with age, a once formidable woman now oddly shrunken, her skin wrinkled in excess over muscles long wasted. That was what age did to you, eventually. "So..."

"So, you will get the data soon. Somebody created a viral vector designed to make permanent changes to the ky'iin genome. I'm trying to work out what it could possibly do that would interest isolationists."

"Hrm."

"My first thought was to make us all allergic to tyrar."

She laughed.

"It's funny," she explained after a moment, "Because I *am* allergic to tyrar. I can't be around them without drugs."

"I'm...sorry...I..."

"It was an obvious example. But they would also have to make us allergic to glyn, and glyn exoskeletons are barely biological. I don't think you could do that in one alteration."

Viyar tilted lin head. "So, what would you do?"

"Hrm." She started to pace. "Germline alteration?"

"Don't worry, the samples we have are on the human ship, which is barred to ky'iin, and they're pitching them out the airlock once all the data is gathered."

"Oh, good. I'd like to see a sample, and I don't even cycle anymore, but it's not worth the risk." She made more hrm noises. "It could reduce tolerance for altered gravity, which *might* cause us to stay on Kyx more. But I don't see it. It's got to be more indirect."

"Reduced aggression?" Viyar considered. "Make us more like..."

"Tyrar don't *actually* have reduced aggression. I've heard stories."

"I was thinking of certain animals."

"Also, we wouldn't survive."

"They might not think that through. This isn't *meant* to destroy us as a species, there would be easier ways to do that." Unless the tyrar thought it was. This was at *that* level of complexity, where each side believed different things about the other.

"Maybe." Her maw twisted for a moment. "This might not have *any* symptoms."

"I hadn't thought of that." Then it would spread through the planet like wildfire. If they hadn't found out about it. "Sterility would be the easiest if they were trying for that."

"We'd fix it," she mused. "But if it's about removing us as a threat..."

Lowering the population could do that. "The issue is that there are ky'iin involved."

"Some people are crazy enough for voluntary extinction to be a concept they buy into."

"It doesn't feel right."

"I'll look at the data. I'll tell you what it does."

"But we need to..."

Viyar didn't finish that. Ly knew what else ly needed to do.

53

DHYANIL'S EXPLORATIONS of the ship gave him little hope that this would be easy.

But it was easier than trying to escape. *That* was impossible, even if he thought it was a good idea.

If he had been infected, how would he know? He might not. If he was designing a disease to spread through the entire population quickly, he would make it have few or no symptoms. That slight headache he'd had could be that or it could be, well... Anyone in his situation who *didn't* have a headache would either have nerves of steel or just not get that particular symptom of stress. The lighting and the grey walls and the overall sterility of space did not help. Nobody could be in a situation where their death was the best possible outcome and *not* be stressed.

But as people got used to him, he was ignored more and more. Finally, he found it. A way into the service areas of the ship. The tyrar used robots more than ky'iin. Probably everyone used robots more than ky'iin. But the corridor still had life support, if only dim lighting. It was a way to move about the ship more easily, especially for a relatively small man.

It was potentially a way to engineering. He didn't know what the easiest way to destabilize a singularity drive was, but he did know that sabotage in engineering was one of the biggest fears on a warship. So it had to be possible. What he was looking for right now was a way to hack into communications. Physically getting close to the array with a device was how they sometimes did it in thrillers.

His life was a thriller. He wasn't sure it was a particularly good one. If it was ever made into a movie, they would no doubt improve things. Make him more of an action hero. Maybe threaten his kids. His kids would be fine. His line would go forward.

Even if this happened, it would. Just not in a world he wanted his grandchildren to live in. Especially his grandsons. Deep breath. He studied the array and tried to remember his electronics engineering classes. If he was caught he would be locked up. But if he could get a signal out first that might be enough.

If they killed him; well, he wasn't planning on surviving anyway. He just had to assume all the ky'iin on this ship were infected. Including Garil himself.

That was the bypass. He made the connections quickly, being exceptionally careful of the bare wire. He didn't want to electrocute himself. He couldn't die *yet*.

DHYANIL COULD NOT SEND out a lot of bandwidth. He could not get a message to anyone.

What he *could* do was broadcast a fake distress signal. It went out into the void, echoing, and they would not be able to, he hoped, turn it off without coming down here. It would tell everyone in the system where this ship was. The problem was they would come with rescue in mind. So he had to do something else. Patterning. The human Ambassador.

The books he had asked her for. They had a way of signalling that was designed for this situation. The humans would know what it was. He pulled out his phone. Pulled it up. Dash, dot, dot, pause, dot, pause, dot dot dot...

It was obviously some kind of signal, and he wished he could thank her for it. He would never be able to thank her. Pause, dash, dot, dash, dot. Would they *believe* the message? He would try and he would be caught and locked up, and then he would have to break out.

He didn't want to die. That was at the heart of it, but doing this was divorced from that. No matter what message he sent, it wasn't like putting a bullet in his own skull. He would die because of this, but he wouldn't know when.

Or he would have to put that bullet in his own skull. Which wouldn't help, but it would be... It would be the thing he could do. Or it would be the guilt of his failure.

He finished the message with dot, dash, dash, dot. Then paused and repeated it. He would repeat it until they found him. They wouldn't know what it meant either, or would they? He had found it in the Ambassador's book by accident. Somebody else could have too. Human signaling methods. Humans.

The irony of the situation struck him, rolled up inside him as hysteria. He, an isolationist, was likely to die at the hands of offworlders and he was likely to be glad of it. Everything had led to this point. There were footsteps in the corridor. He dropped everything and ran away from them like the coward he was.

He was not a coward.

But he could not afford to be caught.

IT SEEMED as if he might, well, not make it. At least delay it. Hopefully they would stop to stop the signal first. He found a storage closet.

He swore that the cleaning robot inside gave him a startled beep as he opened it and threw himself inside amongst the equipment, both manual and automatic. Closed the door. A broom nearly hit him on his head. Of course, they might decide to deal with the saboteur by closing the bulkheads and evacuating atmosphere from the area.

Would that be better or worse than being caught? He wouldn't be able to keep working towards the next stage, but if he was lucky the next stage would not be needed. The closet was dark and cold and smelled only of metal. This was where he was going to die. He was never going to smell the sea again. He was never going to feel the hot tropical sun...or the sometimes equally hot tropical rain.

He was never going to run laughing for shelter from the rain which came without warning, when you thought the rainy season was not with you yet, but it was. Oh, how it was! He was never going to see his grandchildren.

It was worth it. The calm light within him told him it was worth it. If it worked. If not, then he had tried. Because what he wanted to preserve was that beach and those grandchildren.

Was the small, sleepy town he grew up in, where the population doubled at the height of the dry season. Where people came to laugh and spend time with their friends and teach things to their children.

But it was also Meruhin's chance to be who she was without being a slave to her cycles. His sons' chance to be who they were without being a slave to a woman. Those things mattered too.

As much as he feared the offworlders would destroy the relationships between men and women, he still wanted biology to be tempered by freedom as much as freedom by biology. He drew his knees to his chest and waited for the inevitable. They would find him. They would not kill him. They needed all of the infection vectors they could get. They would lock him up and then...

He had to work out, as his last backup resort, how he would die before he got back to Kyx.

54

FIRST, they had to quarantine the station. It probably wasn't necessary, but it was a good safeguard.

The interstellar transports to the colony world salso had to be halted. If the worst happened and the virus got loose on Kyx they could at least protect the colonists. They would have pure ky'iin without the alterations. Whatever they were. Anyone who got infected would have to be kept from having children.

That was draconic, but there was no other way to control it. There was no myoran to that solution. There was no myoran to letting it spread through the population, especially if it was well enough engineered to be a dominant trait. None of this could be voiced.

The humans would destroy the samples and ly could hope they were the *only* samples. But if this thing was contagious enough it wouldn't take much. One infected individual, without symptoms. The multiple vials would be for multiple points of infection to make it harder to contain. Ly didn't have the jurisdiction to order the quarantines.

Lin superiors did. And they agreed. The temporary economic loss would be worth it. It shouldn't take long to find them. The tyrar ship was scouring the system. So was the *Challenger*. The humans had volunteered to help search the system for fugitive ships. Nobody had the heart to turn them down. Besides, their ship apparently had pretty good sensors. Its commander was coordinating well. The Ambassador was up in C&C again, translating.

Ly was at a loose end. Station security could search the station as well as ly could, of not better. The scientists were the only ones who could work out what the virus did, and at some levels it wasn't that important. The people on the ground were better positioned to find Dhyanil.

There was nothing Viyar could do. Ly *hated* feeling that there was nothing ly could do.

Lin computer pinged. Ly was expecting Syahin. It was the station commander.

"Special Investigator, I would like your professional opinion on something."

"Always."

"We picked up a message from in system. It's on tyrar distress frequencies, but uses a human form of signaling."

"A distress call?"

"A *hacked* distress call. It's actually kind of brilliant. The humans have a way of signalling that's just light and dark. Or sound and silence."

"What does it say?"

Her tone turned grim, her body language angular. "It says 'Destroy this ship.'"

"Can we find the ship?"

"I'm sure we can. But what would you do?"

Destroy this ship. Who would send that as a message using human signaling...a signal no ky'iin or tyrar could translate? Somebody brilliant. Somebody not afraid to die.

Or rather, somebody who knew their own life was not that important in the grand scheme of things.

"Let's start with *finding* the ship."

Destroy this ship. Why? There were several reasons. Ly liked none of them.

THE HUMAN SHIP had been smart enough to stand off even as it stood down. They weren't caught in the quarantine. That, Viyar thought was a good thing. They were helping look for the ship. It was deep in system, likely as close to the primary as it could safely get. A military move, that, to come out of the sun. It worked as well in space as it had ever done on planet. Even animals knew to do it.

But in this case they were just trying to hide. Viyar did not want to think about what might have happened to whatever brilliant person sent that message. Who would have thought to use a human code, one which the tyrar and ky'iin on that ship could not understand? They must have had the code with them. Which meant it was somebody in contact with the humans. Or perhaps it *was* a human, although they had not admitted to missing one. Perhaps whoever it was had stolen the information from the ambassador, but...

Ly could not know it was Dhyanil. Ly could only suspect in a strange level of certainty, the certainty that came from not being able to think of anyone *else* it could be. Ly suspected he was now dead. Certainly, in their place, ly would have killed him. Unless, of course, they had some other use for him. Ly could hope for that. Ly had not, had never thought that...

No, ly had known ly was putting a civilian in danger and by rights ly should answer for that. It had been a fool's game, a stupid move. Ly had *known* it was a stupid move and had done it anyway. Maybe it was time for ly to retire to that teaching position, in which ly could use this as a very solid example of what not to do. Except that Dhyanil was an activist, not a civilian. Ly had assumed he knew what he was doing. In fact, he *did* know what he was doing. A trained agent could not have done better.

A trained agent would almost certainly be just as dead. There was not much ly could do about it, in truth. Ly could only hope that they had some other use for him. Then fear for what that other use might end up being. None of this was good. None of this was good at all, and ly was not sure what ly could do about it.

The human ambassador admitted to feeling the same way. Of

course, she was primarily a translator; she had little experience with intrigue. They needed to find her a spy. Maybe the ky'iin could lend one, but no, she would not trust any agent they lent her. She needed a full staff.

Ly, for lin part, needed a plan.

"WE FOUND THE SHIP. It's a tyrar freighter."

A freighter. Any ship in system could take it out unless it held some nasty surprises. Which it might; there were not uncommonly nasty surprises. Sometimes they were for legitimate reasons. Piracy in space was difficult, but some people tried it anyway. More often they indicated that the freighter concerned was designed for criminal activity itself. A bit of extra engine speed. A weapon or two. Just in case.

Viyar lowered lin hands. "Are we sure it's a freighter?"

"You mean, as opposed to a well-disguised cutter? No. We aren't sure. But if it's a disguised cutter, it's done *very* well."

Any ship they had could take it out. "Interstellar capable?"

"Yes."

"Then we don't want to spook it."

A really good pilot could track a jump by following the reverse wake that a ship produced in hyperspace. But it took a *really* good pilot. The humans had a really good one. Ly wasn't sure about anyone else in system.

"No, we don't."

Destroying the ship was not going to be as easy as just flying a warship over there and blowing it up, Viyar realized. Of course it wasn't. Nothing was ever that easy.

But it also wasn't his talent. "Sorry. I don't mean to do your job for you."

"You must be going stir crazy," the commander said, finally. She glanced at the human.

Suza stood there at the edge of the bridge, quietly listening. In one hand she had a small object she was fidgeting with, turning it over and over. Part of her thought process, likely. Her alien mind might have insights they didn't, and something of a vision went through Viyar's mind.

Instead of fearing their differences, perhaps it was time to celebrate them. Make use of them. Help everyone survive by putting them together.

The commander turned to her. "Ambassador, could you please make sure your ship *knows* that if they spook the freighter..."

She spoke with confidence. "If it jumps, we'll find it."

"You trust your pilot."

"I trust Iterk with *everything*," Suza said, simply.

Iterk. The aquatic. Ly knew that he would be a good pilot, living in three dimensions. He was not surprised.

"Then I trust you. But..."

"Should we destroy the ship or capture it? We already destroyed the virus."

"Viyar's agent on the ground..."

"Could be seeing the small picture," Suza said, finally. She then fell silent, going back to fidgeting. She seemed even more childlike than normal.

Perhaps that was how she reacted to stress. Perhaps it said something about humanity. No, Viyar thought. It said something about *her*.

55

DHYANIL WAS DRAGGED from his hiding place. Garil stood facing him.

Ah, so the first stage of the punishment was to be professorial disappointment.

"I suppose I should have known..."

"You really expected me not to try something?"

"We didn't expect you to try that." Garil lifted a hand, but not in threat. "I'm actually impressed. What does it say?"

Dhyanil's maw turned into a slit, just enough space to breathe through. He wasn't saying anything. He wasn't saying anything if they beat him up. He probably couldn't beat whatever truth drugs they had. But he could try and he could stall.

If they found out what he sent, they would jump to another system. But they had to come back. Sooner or later they had to come back.

"You're fortunate we need you alive."

No, Dhyanil thought. He wasn't fortunate. He was highly unfortunate that they needed him alive, because they would *keep* him alive. They weren't going to let him die, not when they could drop him naked in a major city, drugged so he wouldn't know that he was supposed to hide and die. That was what he would do. He was an explosive, a bomb to be planted.

So was Garil. So were all the ky'iin on this ship. He didn't know how they'd been infected, but they had to be. He kept his maw half closed, kept his hands by his sides, hoped not to give away anything in his body language. That was all he could do.

"Going to play the silence game, I see. I hoped..." Garil sighed. "I really hoped I could get you on board in truth. You would..."

Don't say anything. He pretended he'd been arrested and anything he said could be evidence against everyone he loved. The cops weren't supposed to listen, but they were only ky'iin and imperfect and sometimes in enough of a rush to close a case that they screwed up.

He pretended that any word from him would get Myahin killed. Eventually, they put him back in his quarters. Except now he heard the lock click from the outside. Maybe they thought a bit of solitary confinement would get him to talk. Or boredom. They'd taken his personal computer, although he'd factory wiped it. They weren't going to get the meaning of the message from it.

The terminal was also locked. With nothing else to do, Dhyanil curled up on the bunk and tried to sleep.

AN UNKNOWN AMOUNT of time passed. Dhyanil spent most of it trying to find a way out of a room which had, thankfully, never been designed to be a brig. They had three people open the door to pass him food. He didn't touch it; he could go for several days without eating if he had to. It was almost certainly drugged. There was no timepiece in here, but if they had just visited he could, perhaps, trust that they would not be back. Which meant he could get to work on the panel under his bunk. It had been *designed* to be opened, or he would never have tried it.

It had not really been designed to be opened without tools. He had no choice, though. For the first time in his life he wished he was female, just for the added strength. Not really. He just wished for added strength. The human ambassador had worn an exo when on planet for the memorial to Haniyar. He wished for one of those. That was better. An exo, like a construction worker might wear, or some-body who grew up in low gravity. It would give him strength and...

Wait. Leverage. Was there anything in this room that he could use as a lever. It was pretty bare. The bunk, secured to the wall and capable of folding in. Bedding. A terminal with a chair in front of it. The chair was bolted down.

You couldn't trust artificial gravity, so everything on a ship was bolted down. Everything he could use was bolted down. He wanted to scream in frustration. He needed out so he could do something. So he could do what hadn't been done. His message might not even have gone through. Or the humans hadn't translated it.

Or, most likely of all, they were still arguing about whether it was the right course of action, not knowing what he knew. Not under-standing what he understood. They thought they could just capture the ship, likely. He was terrified of that possibility. If they captured this ship, then whoever boarded it would be exposed and...it was airborne. He was sure of that. Or perhaps he was paranoid of that; he had to assume that it was. They wanted it to spread rapidly.

They wanted it to spread universally. Airborne, and using an alien virus so nobody would have resistance. It wouldn't work, part of him thought. It wouldn't actually *work*. But he couldn't risk it.

Success! The panel came away with a pop. And yes, he could fit through. This was a tyrar panel, designed for their size. He was through and into the workings of the ship. Where he could be the vermin in the works.

Time to go chew through a few cables.

———

DHYANIL FOUND himself in a sort of junction box. He didn't know what any of the cables did. The temptation to *literally* chew through, or rather rip out, a few cables to find out what they did grew. But if he alerted them to his location, they would evacuate the air.

They wanted him alive. They would sleepy gas him. And then likely *keep* him asleep in medbay until they could dump him back on

Kyx. He might only get the one act of sabotage, if he even got time for that.

This place was designed for people to be in it. Tyrar people, true, but people nonetheless. There might... ...paydirt! The suit locker contained tyrar suits. They were far too big on him. The gloves had the wrong number of fingers. But until he worked out what he was going to do, the ill-fitting suit would protect him from being sleep gased or having all his air evacuated. It would keep him alive even if it wasn't going to be comfortable. He didn't deserve to be comfortable.

No, that wasn't fair. True, he had in many ways put himself in this situation, but a good part of it was on Viyar. Whom he could have turned down. Should have turned down. He thought he knew what he was doing. Maybe he did. He moved away from the junction box. Where was engineering? He needed to find engineering. Vibration. When the engines burned for station keeping, the ship vibrated slightly. Maybe he could get a directional sense from that.

There was a regular pattern to it, he'd noticed. If that pattern changed, it meant they were moving from their tight-in orbit around the sun. It meant that they were doing something, whether it was going back to Kyx or preparing for a jump. Why *hadn't* they gone back to Kyx? What were they waiting for? Had his signal at least achieved that much?

Vibrate.

Vibrate.

The second one was longer. As if it had been caused by his thoughts, the ship was moving. The ship was moving. He didn't know where to, but he moved as quickly as he could. He could feel the vibration. He couldn't hear anything, but he saw small puffs of air or smoke. Sleep gas, as he'd predicted. Hopefully the ill-fitting suit would still protect him, even as it slowed him down. He would get one act of sabotage. He had to make it count.

56

THE SHIP WAS MOVING. It was probably going to jump. Or make a run for it to its destination in real space. It *had* jumped.

Could the humans track it? Their ship had been creeping inwards, making it look almost like a failing orbit. Trying to be sneaky. Perhaps not sneaky enough. Or perhaps this had been their plan. They had been flying casual, refusing to be spooked, refusing to change things... That seemed foolish and stubborn. Tyrar spooked easily, but Viyar was not convinced that ship, despite its manufacture, was being run by tyrar. Ly was convinced it was being run by ky'iin. An unholy alliance.

"Investigator." The male voice came at his elbow. Ly glanced around. "Captain Kerehin requests your presence."

Captain Kerehin, likely to be an Admiral before too long after her performance in the war against the humans...and in the peace. Ly wondered what she wanted with lin.

"Alright."

"Bring an overnight bag."

The young man left him to pack such and lin's maw tilted. She wanted an investigator on her ship, and ly trusted she had already got the required clearances.

In lin quarters, ly found another message. This time it was from a virologist, a video recording.

"Please have the humans destroy the virus. I don't want to learn anything more from it." She took a deep breath, her tongue quivering inside her maw.

"I believe the intent was to...engineer us back to the Stone Age. The goal was to remove the mutation that creates ly'iin and make certain other changes in reproductive biology."

No more ly'iin. By traditional belief, that meant no more civilization. Ly listened as ly packed.

"However, I am fairly sure that the actual impact would be, in addition to ensuring no ly'iin hatched, to render the second generation infertile."

Genocide.

Was it a mistake or was it the tyrar intervening? It didn't matter.

Destroy this ship.

The virus was on the ship. The virus was loose on the ship. Or at least somebody on the ship feared it was.

Destroy this ship. Destroy the virus. Guarantee it would never be released.

They were right, whoever they were, but there was always the desire not to waste life which had myoran. Ly sent a response to the virologist. Asked her to work on a cure or a vaccine, just in case. Hopefully it wouldn't be needed.

The most brilliant of them was with the enemy, but Garil was far from the only ky'iin capable of creating this. That meant he was far from the only ky'iin capable of destroying it. He'd screwed up because he'd tried to make it too complex. Viyar had screwed up many times for similar reasons.

Ly finished packing. Sent the message. Told her to send the response to Kerehin's ship. Then made lin way to the military docks. That Kerehin was going after the ship was clear. The humans claimed they could track the jump. Ly hoped they really could.

Of course, Kerehin had a good pilot too. Lin wanted to believe a better one, but that was mere species pride, with no evidence to support it. Ly reached the docks. The door stood open, guarded by two female crewmembers. Ly stepped on board, although to what ly did not know.

THE SAME MAN who had come to lin quarters escorted Viyar to a small room. Thankfully, it wasn't shared, but it made transient quarters on the station look truly palatial. Ly left lin bag on the bunk.

"Where does she want me?"

"For now, stay here until called. Strap in. We're going to burn hard when we leave dock."

Viyar nodded to that. The only place to strap linself in was the bunk. Military ships had no spare space for creature comforts. They only had space for ky'iin and weapons. Ly put lin bag in the locker without unpacking it and then waited.

This was not lin first rodeo. Ly felt the burn, and it was as hard as allowed next to the station, then increasing as they got out of the speed restricted zone. Ly trusted the pilot and navigator knew where they were going. The ship had probably shown up again.

The burn eased. Ly unstrapped linself cautiously, glancing around. There was a terminal, but ly had no doubt that it was locked out of anything truly interesting. Ly resisted the temptation to poke at it. You did not argue with a ship's commander on her ship, not ever.

Then the man showed up again. Escorted lin up a deck. The diplomatic deck, as it was sometimes called, was more spacious. The human ambassador would have stayed here while they negotiated the peace. This ship was history now. Up one more deck to the middle deck where the bridge was. Wet ships had the bridge at the top so they could see.

Starships had it in the center, seeing through cameras and lookouts. The bridge was the safest place to be. And ly had never seen one before. Ly had been on military ships briefly, but ly had never been permitted into the holy of holies. It was smaller than station command and control. But there was enough space at the back for lin to stand, watching the backs of the crew as they worked.

Kerehin stood from the command chair, turning to face lin in a smooth, predatory manner. They were of similar age, but she had chosen a very different life path. "Investigator. I apologize for the minor abduction."

"I figured we were in a hurry, ma'am."

"Do you think we should destroy the ship?"

"In my professional opinion, yes, and we should give no quarter." Ly let out a breath. "The ship may be carrying a genetically engineered virus intended to destroy the ky'iin as a species. While we can probably beat it..."

"It would cause far fewer casualties if we stopped it now."

Ly thought about that. The virus wasn't designed to kill anyone. For a moment, ly wondered what it would be like to be a woman. Every ly'iin did that at least once, usually during adolescence. Once they had not understood what made ly'iin. Now they understood it was a defect, but one which had been of so much value to their species it had spread.

"Not casualties. It causes infertility."

That got a sharp nod from her. She did not ask further.

Ly did not want to explain further. The virus would not kill anyone, and they would have time to fix its effects. Maybe. But ly did not want to risk it.

"The humans disagree. They have a stronger value for individual life than we do."

"No. Just a different one."

It wasn't that Viyar *wanted* to sacrifice those lives. But everyone on that ship had chosen to be there. With one possible exception.

And if ly was right, ly would carry that for the rest of lin life.

AT THIS POINT, the ship was in transit. There was nothing to argue with the artificial gravity. Kerehin dismissed lin from the bridge, but told lin to explore as long as, of course, ly stayed out of sensitive areas.

Ly went to the diplomatic deck. Ly looked at the quarters there; larger than the one she had put lin in. That was a message. She could have put lin here. Ly would have been assumed to prefer it. Instead, she had given lin crew quarters. That told lin that she valued lin input. She thought of lin as part of the mission, not a visiting dignitary to be coddled.

Ly looked around. Ly could almost hear the human voice, speaking the human languages. English and Mandarin they were called, the primary languages, the equivalent to Central. There were no doubt thousands more languages. Dialects and accents. Ways of speaking that drifted, changed, came apart and braided back together.

Destroy the ship. Was there an alternative? Anyone on that ship who survived would have to be quarantined, possibly for the rest of their lives. Certainly for the years it would take to develop a cure. Ly thought about that. Given the choice, ly would choose quarantine.

But the message that had been sent; that came from somebody who was willing to die. Somebody who didn't trust science? *No*, ly thought. Somebody who knew that science sometimes failed. Who would rather die than quarantine for the rest of their life. Who couldn't take the minuscule risk of this thing getting out.

If it was Dhyanil, this was on Viyar. Except it was also on Dhyanil. Perhaps, Viyar thought, ly was respecting the man's choice when ly spoke for the ship's destruction. Ly shook lin head and left the diplomatic deck for a place where ly could find out more of what was going on.

The crew mess was the perfect place to hang out. Not the officers, who would know more but say less. The mechanics, the technicians. The working class part of the crew. They would know less, but they would tell lin what they knew. It was a comfortable place to hang out, spartan yet homely, with bright pictures hung on the walls. Pictures of Kyx. Ly wanted a feel for this ship if ly was going to be on board when the fight started.

If there was going to be a fight.

57

Such lighting as was in the corridor abruptly flickered lurid green. Green was a safe color.

Maybe it wasn't a safe color to tyrar. Or maybe it looked quite different to them; they might not even have the same color vision. But the lurid flashing told Dhyanil what he needed to know. The ship had just gone to some stage of alert. He wished he knew what was going on. Of course, had he stayed in their good graces, he *would* know. He was still trying to map the corridors without being caught. He was still afraid of being caught.

They wouldn't kill him. Maybe he could get them to kill him. But he had hope; hope that the alert status meant that somebody had found them. And that somebody knew his message, got it, took it seriously. The idea of dying as the ship was torn apart...or, worse, being thrown into space in this ill-fitting suit and surviving until his air ran out...terrified him.

It did not terrify him as much as taking this virus to Kyx. Or maybe it terrified him more, but he had made his decision and had to accept it. The alert lighting was giving him a slight headache. He wondered if he could polarize his suit visor.

He wasn't going to mess with the controls on this suit; who knew what they would actually do. He was going to find engineering and start breaking stuff. The ship twisted. The artificial gravity failed for a brief moment, just enough to make him hope he wasn't about to throw up inside a suit helmet. That was the last thing he wanted. That was an evasive maneuver. The ship was in a fight, a fight he prayed to the Void they would lose.

He was not sure he believed in an afterlife. He had once. Now he wasn't so sure, perhaps there was something, perhaps there was nothing. What he truly hoped for in that moment, hoped for with all his being, was that the old animists were right and souls were recycled, reborn. Then perhaps he would see White Fish again, not remembering this life. He wanted nothing more than to walk that quiet beach, watch the waves lap lightly against the shore. Enjoy the long summer of axial stability, which would last well beyond his lifetime. Enjoy the rest of his life and then go to peace. Instead he was going to die violently here. Another evasive maneuver threw him against the wall. He felt a bruise start almost instantly, or perhaps it was the assumption of a bruise.

The future memory of one. He moved quickly and cautiously. On the bridge, he knew, tyrar and ky'iin crew would be working together to keep this ship alive. They would be trying to flee, not fight, if they had any sense. They apparently couldn't flee.

He expected, any moment, the shuddering movement of a jump. You didn't want to be up and moving during a jump. He had no choice. Another twisting shudder. The odd silence of the inside of his helmet.

He was an idiot who *deserved* to end up in the void. The toggle would be in the helmet. He found it. He turned on the radio.

MOSTLY, he still heard silence. Tyrar communication in frequencies well below what he could hear. But there was the occasional word in ky'iin intercom pidgin. It gave him tantalizing hints. Just hints of what was going on.

The ship, shuddering and moving, and there. *There* was engineering, and there was the wires that ran out from it. He didn't need to do much. If he could compromise the ship's mobility, they would almost certainly be hit and this would be over. Better yet if he could violate the integrity of the artificial singularity that powered the jump drive. Then it would be *very* over, ship and crew pulled into the implosion, turned into energy in a moment that was supposedly faster than your nerves could carry any pain signal to your brain.

The Void consuming them. But he had no idea how to do that. He had no idea how to do anything but what he did; start to pull wires out with gloved hands. He didn't worry about electrocution; the suit would protect him from that quite nicely. And in any case, it didn't matter.

He was going to spend the last moments of his life here, right here in this place. Tearing at wires as if they were the soft belly of a large prey animal he and his pack had brought down. Imagining that made it a more ky'iin moment. He would never run in a hunting preserve again. But he could bring down this one last prey. There was shouting on the radio system.

Likely there was more in engineering. He moved. The more damage he could do before they tore him out of this suit, the better. It would, somehow, be easier if he knew. If he had a countdown to the end. If he could accept it and prepare himself for the oblivion he rationally knew was coming. There was a tyrar in the corridor in front of him. Their eyes met. She was going to kill him. Or worse.

He grabbed another wire and thrust it into her unprotected face. Time slowed. He'd killed people before; at a distance, and seldom intentionally. This was face to face, in self defense. Electricity and plasma rushed through her form. Her mouth opened, but he could not hear any scream through the suit. Or they even screamed in infrasound. He would never know. He kicked her body to one side. Scrambled past it. Didn't check to see if she was really dead. It didn't matter.

Space was starting to twist. The corridor went triangular then square again. Drive containment was leaking, space and time were bending. Dhyanil swore.

If that happened, it was supposed to be instant. Clearly it wasn't, clearly the universe was not going to be nearly that nice to him. Twist. Instinct and panic took over. He ran. He ran at full speed away from that twisting, feeling it come behind him, feeling the ship distort. The *air* was distorting, he had moments when he couldn't breathe. He knew he couldn't escape.

But even a predator will panic and run. His mind went blank, there was nothing but the run. Nothing but the desperate need to escape.

THEN SOMETHING KICKED Dhyanil in the back, something which knocked the breath out of him. Smears of vomit appeared on the inside of his visor. He tumbled, and the distortions pulled him one way, then the other. He screamed.

And then he was pushed again, thrown away from the distortion, tumbling down the corridor.

He was in space, the ship distorting away from him. He was in pain, he was tumbling through empty space. He was going to die now. It hurt, because of course it did. There was still air in the suit. Maybe he could turn it off, end things faster.

He could not quite bring himself to do so. He spun slowly, a piece of debris barely out of the range of the implosion of the tyrar freighter. Two ships were visible.

He hoped they did not find him in the debris. He could watch the stars and wait to run out of air, and somehow he was okay with that. What mattered was that Kyx was safe. White Fish was safe. They would work with the offworlders, and they would change.

But they would change in the right way. He would not have to see it, but Meruhin would. She would command her starship and perhaps she would command a starship with offworlders amongst the crew. They would reach out, to the new species the humans had found, to other races, and they would work out how to preserve what was ineffably ky'iin. It was probably hypoxia, but suddenly he *believed* in that future as he spun amongst the stars and waited for the curtains to fall on a life well lived.

He only regretted that his children would never know what happened to him. He regretted not saying goodbye to his mother. The waves were lapping around his feet now and the stars were dimming into darkness. It was over.

He had...won?

58

JUMP.

Viyar had never been in a space battle before; but this one would likely not last long. The human ship, Kerehin's ship, and one freighter with a nasty surprise; a keel-mounted railgun. A slug from it striking the ship, taking out artificial gravity and damaging their engines. Because *everything*, ly had been told, took out artificial gravity. That was why ly was strapped in, in a spare seat in the rear of the bridge. Safest place on the ship.

Ly was to be *very* quiet. Don't interfere with the stalk, the hunt. The freighter darted to and fro with remarkable maneuverability. Neither ship had gotten a solid hit on it yet, although the *Challenger* seemed to have avoided the railgun.

"Whoever's flying," said the pilot in pidgin.

No doubt she'd explain later when she could talk properly, when her hands weren't occupied with steering the ship. It shouldn't last long, but it felt as if it was lasting forever. As if this fight was an eternity. Just like a bar brawl. Fights *always* took longer while you were in them. The ship shook again. Another hit.

If that thing took them out, it would embarrass all of their descendants and kin. The Challenger did an abrupt spin and twist and somehow, almost as if it had microjumped, it was on the far side of the freighter. Which was powering up its rail gun again. The thing hit hard, but it was slow.

Then it happened. The rail gun glowed and powered down.

"Weapons failure," said weps. "Let's finish them."

Destroy this ship. It undoubtedly was the ship. They were sure from the distress call it had sent during the fight, the same transmitter. It wouldn't be answered. They had made sure of that.

The freighter was now starting a slow tumble. Somebody had finally got a good hit.

"Us or them?" Kerehin asked.

"Neither!" weps declared.

So they'd had a malfunction.

No. They'd had sabotage. It was clear as day. Whoever had sent the message had sabotaged the ship. Had made it a sitting duck for them. Whoever it was should be a spy. Was a spy.

Then both ships fired. At the same time. Plasma beams intersecting from different angles. A killing shot.

A shot designed to implode the drive. It didn't quite work. Instead of instant implosion, the ship twisted, spacial distortions extending out from it like ripples from a pond.

Then it was gone. Viyar let lin head sink. Unnecessary loss of life. No. Very necessary loss of life. It was over.

59

DHYANIL SHOULDN'T HAVE WOKEN up at all. There was no questioning of the fact that he was still alive. If he was dead, surely, he wouldn't hurt. Where did he hurt? *Everywhere.*

His body felt like a giant bruise and it faintly hurt to breathe. He was supposed to be dead. He opened his eyes. Tried to sit up, only to discover he was under restraint. For a moment, he started to panic, then he forced it down. If he had been rescued, then he was most likely on a ship. Which would now have to be quarantined. Probably.

His brain fogged over again and he drifted back out. Drifted into a place where he was neither awake nor asleep, where odd dream fragments never came together into a coherent narrative. When he came fully awake again, he was more able to deal with his surroundings. He was, indeed, secured in a bunk. They had also secured his wrists so he couldn't unstrap himself in a moment of delirium. He was definitely in a metal room. He was definitely on a ship.

Void.

It wasn't contained. It wasn't contained as long as he was alive and slow panic dawned within him. The metal was a kind of greenish gray. He focused on it, on the ceiling which was all he could see. It wasn't a color ky'iin would pick. It wasn't a color the tyrar had used either; they preferred the soft reds of their homeworld. He tried to talk, but nothing came out.

Then he heard a voice in a language he didn't know. The bunk tilted upwards. For a moment he had no idea what the being in the room with him was...a brown-skinned biped wearing a green coverall. Then as his eyes focused, he realized it was a human. Just not of the same ethnic group as the ambassador; much more pigmentation on the skin and the close-cropped hair was tightly curly. He couldn't expect them all to be the same shade, that would be silly. They had a cup, and carefully poured water into his maw.

He tried to talk again. This time it worked. "Thank you."

The human dipped their head. They were more angular than the ambassador too, and it slowly dawned on him that this was likely a *male* human. Or at least a different gender. They then turned and babbled in purely verbal speech into the intercom. He was on the *human* ship.

And the virus he carried...what would it do to humans? He didn't know. They didn't seem worried. He didn't know any human words. No, wait.

He knew the silly signal thing he'd studied. He started to tap on the bunk. The human's eyes widened. Then his head dipped again. He untied Dhyanil's wrists, then abruptly fled the room.

No, he fled the room as soon as Dhyanil moved. The human fear of ky'iin. Later, food came on a tray carried by a robot. They should have used a robot in the first place. He ate. Then he slept.

Dhyanil was not sure how long he was in the room. He was too exhausted to want to leave it even though he could now unstrap and move around. No doubt they were watching him through cameras.

Then the door opened and another human stepped in. It took him a moment to recognize her.

"Ambassador," he said.

Somebody he could talk to. Void, somebody he could *talk* to. "You should not be in here."

"Don't worry. You're..." She paused.

"Am I carrying a virus?"

"Yes, and a nasty little thing it is too, but it doesn't affect humans. We don't have the genetic receptors for it to latch onto. They had a different one for us, and that one we should be able to get a vaccine for quickly enough."

He relaxed. He trusted that she was telling the truth. "Except...that..." He had to quarantine for the rest of his life.

"We'll fix it," she promised. "We've fixed a lot worse. If nothing else, we should be able to find something to get your viral load down to the point where you aren't contagious."

He lifted his hands. "I thought you were a translator."

She gave a sharp sound. "I'm trying to translate from medical."

He laughed. It was the first honest laugh that had come to him in a long time. He knew *exactly* what she meant by translating from medical. Jargon was universal.

"So, we think we can make you not a danger."

"But in the meantime, none of the other humans can stand to be around me, and..."

He would have to live in a room. He thought about it. Was it better than dying? He suspected that if he asked in the right way they would let him die. But if he was dead, it could not be fixed. Something about her optimism infected him.

She stood there for a long moment. Her chest rose and fell with the pattern of her breathing. She seemed like a child. Or she seemed like a legendary messenger, from the Void or the old gods. Waiting to see if he could stop being afraid before she spoke again.

Waiting to see who he was, what he was. What he was made of. "What are you going to do with me?"

"How would you like to be the first ky'iin to see Sol?"

He froze. How would he like to be the first to visit the human home system, to be the one who reached out to them... "You can't..."

"Stand to be around you? We have to fix that."

"I don't like offworlders." To live surrounded by them...

...to live as she had before the Challenger came, as she would until a team could be put together for her. To live amongst predators knowing how easily she could become prey.

He closed his eyes. "I just wanted us all to leave each other alone."

"Contact can't be unmade, Dhyanil." She sat on the edge of the bunk. "History repeats itself, over and over, but that's one lesson we've always learned. Contact changes you. Even if we all withdrew, we would not be the peoples we were before."

And she was right. He had been willing to give his life to this. Was he willing now to give his principles? He could not go back to Kyx without destroying everything he valued in the world.

"How are we going to work on it?"

"How well, Dhyanil, do you dance?"

EPILOGUE

THE SKY WAS a rich shade of blue. The water reflected it more deeply. The colors of a yellow sun.

A boat was pulled up on the beach, turned over for careening. The sand was soft white, gentle under bare feet. Waves lapped against the shore with force, the lines of massive tides showing in seaweed and other debris. A dark gray hand reached down, picked up a shell that had been washed up. Turned it over.

Dhyanil set the shell back down where he had found it; it might be a harmless thing to collect, or not. His minders were up the beach. It was not White Fish. It was a tropical island, a place where people went on vacation or where they lived in rhythms that he could fall back into so easily.

It was a place so much like his home that his heart hurt, and so much unlike that he finally saw what he had been missing all along. People are people. Myoran lay in the things they did to one another, and there was no more arguments about who had it.

What they needed to do now was understand the forms it took, the shapes it formed. How human myoran was not ky'iin and was not tyrar and was not glen and was not...

...there might be an infinity of peoples out there, a diversity of life-ways, yet they all came back to the same thing.

A tyrar might walk along this beach and pick up a shell. A glen might. Because this was universal and it was beautiful. He had only wanted to be left alone.

Now he was the first of his kind to walk an alien world. That was not so alien after all. He turned, walked up the beach to his minders and asked the question so many would ask in this situation.

"Where can I go fishing?"

And everything was, despite it all, okay. No, more than okay.

Everything was good.

AUTHOR'S NOTE

First of all, I have to start this with an apology. This book was supposed to come out some time in mid to late 2020.

Yeah.

On top of the global pandemic, which did a number on my mental health, the last three years have seen me fall off a horse and break my dominant hand (not the horse's fault) and put my father in a care home. It has *not* been a good three years.

My goal was to write the entire series and then put them out so the long gap would be before, not during. But I didn't plan on a gap this long.

For which all I can do is apologize. Hopefully it will not happen again!

On top of that, I got 20,000 words into this book thinking it was a sequel to *Transpecial* and an extension of Suza's story. I got stuck. It was not an extension of Suza's story. I love Suza. But her story is done and told. I didn't quite have to start over, but it was close!

This novel is the first of five books that explore the different alien races I've created for this universe in more detail. I hope you all enjoy your trip to Kyx. I promise there will not be as long a wait for book two!

ACKNOWLEDGMENTS

As usual, acknowledgments go to my wonderful editor, Jennifer Melzer, to fantastic cover artist Rachel A. Rosen, and to my husband and primary proofreader, Greg Pearson.

I'd also like to thank Charlie Jane Anders and Our Opinions Are Correct for making me realize that my first attempt at this book was stuck because I had the wrong protagonist. You saved this entire series! Thank you!

OTHER BOOKS
OTHER BOOKS BY JENNIFER R. POVEY

The Silent Years (Mother, Crone, Maiden)

The Ky Federation novels
Transpecial
Araña

The Lost Guardians Series:
Falling Dusk
Fallen Dark
Rising Dawn
Risen Day
The Secret History of Victor Prince (prequel)

Daughter of Fire

The Lay of Lady Percival

The Friar's Tale

Tales of Yirath:
Firewing

EXCERPT FROM TYRANIS

Read on for an excerpt from Council of Worlds Book 2: Tyranis

1

YOSHI

THE SOUND WAS TREMENDOUS. Dust raced upwards into the surrounding atmosphere to join that which was already making the sun thin and wan.

The concrete building swayed as fire and smoke rose from its base. It collapsed in on itself, falling into rubble, vanishing among the dust in a matter of moments. An acrid smell spread through the area, the scent of explosives and of bits of dust. Despite her protective gear, Yoshi sneezed, almost blowing the mask from her face. Even at this safe distance, even with ear protection, her head was starting to ache, but it was done.

The last of the buildings *they* had put here to process the ore was a heap of rubble, everything useful already having been removed. Now it was clean up, but it was clean up everywhere, all across the face of Tyranis where they had left scars.

Scars that Yoshi herself bore, thin lines of white that ran through her fur from the time in her youth when one of their machines had failed, shattered, and sent shrapnel through the factory.

The time when she had studied at night, illicitly, not for ways to fight them but for ways to repair the damage. She had been young then, a girl. Now she was a woman and her children were in school, learning what they needed to know.

Hopefully they would live to see the sun again as she feared she might not. To see it as it should be seen, from the surface of this poor, ravaged world. Her love for her world was strong.

Strong enough that she had to watch the implosion, but now she headed back to the site office, the dust settling on her fur such that she wished for a brush. She shook herself, sending some flying, but it didn't help, it was in the air, and it was their dust. Not toxic, because they'd stripped the toxic crap out. But it was of them and they still flew and still lived and loved and part of her wished things were otherwise.

She knew better than to cling to that thought. It would not hurt them, only her. It would fester until she became one of the bitter, angry old tyrar who shook ancient muskets and had yet to leave the revolution behind.

She had no desire to become one of them.

No desire at all.

INSIDE THE SITE office there was the smell of tyrar sweat and, yes, a little of dust. She shook herself again before actually entering, trying to track in as little of it as possible.

It was inevitable, though. Reclamation sites were always dusty, and the rain that should have come was still missing in action.

Rain where there shouldn't be rain, no rain where there should be, and the snowpack in the Verias Mountains not remotely close to what it should be for the season. She wondered if it would ever rain in these hills again. Even if it did, would it do anything other than wash the soil into the valleys, leave bare rock with stick like dead trees, until the trees burned.

Until the world burned.

It was all their fault and she pushed down the anger again. She would *not* become one of those tyrar, as much as she wanted to.

Chiran rumbled a greeting and she turned to nod to the man after a moment. The frost of age that dusted his dark gray fur was something to be respected. He was an administrator, not a scientist, but it was natural to respect those who were older.

And, of course, those who were good at what they did, who played their role in the herd with aplomb. There was *no* arguing that Chiran was an excellent administrator. He even occasionally made his work sound interesting.

Occasionally.

She went back to her desk, listening with one ear swiveled towards the engineers who were talking numbers. The implosion had been a success; no part of the storage building remained standing. The rubble could be recycled.

But being engineers, they were still talking about how they could do better next time and what they could learn from it. Their voices rose and fell quietly in the background. Something comforting about that, the presence of a herd, even if she wasn't involved in their conversation.

It reminded her that she was not alone. Never alone. Once she'd been alone, only once, and the thought still scared her.

She didn't need to be in the conversation, she could get on with her own work. But she needed it to be there, that soft reminder.

Sometimes she wondered what it would be like to be one of them. To be a predator. To not need the safety of numbers, the protection of the herd.

Maybe that was what kept her from becoming one of those tyrar.

But she went back to her numbers.

Her numbers were not good.

Not good at all.

YOSHI COULDN'T MAKE the numbers any better by staring at them. Instead, she got up and slipped her respirator mask back on. She walked back outside into the dust. What had been thrown up by the implosion had now largely settled. Suited engineers examined the rubble, in preparation to haul it away for recycling or disposal. It might be contaminated, too toxic to reuse.

She did not go that way. She walked over to the old tailing pit, the waste pit where she had been growing the phytoremediation algae. It looked like the numbers suggested; not a healthy purple but a dulling blue. Yeah. This batch had done no better than the last batch.

Too many heavy metals. Too toxic for any plant she knew of or could think of to deal with. She was not sure what to do about it, either. Her instinct was to take a deep breath, her stronger instinct was to drift back to the others.

Yoshi engaged her willpower and did neither. She wasn't entirely alone, she could convince herself of that for long enough to take a sample. Taking a deep breath get her a nose full of even more unpleasant smells and potentially toxins off gassing from the pools and the dying algae.

She knew better than to ever take a deep breath, much less curl her lips up in flehmen as if she was looking for a strong male to sire her next child.

There would be no more children. She had decided two was enough years ago, and five years ago she had had it all taken out before it could cause the problems sometimes experienced by older women.

Two was definitely enough. Some days it was too many.

The instincts had not completely gone away, though. She headed back to the site office with her sample, sealing the bottle carefully, and she didn't relax until she was there.

Next time she would take somebody with her, but she wasn't a child, to need to cling to a parent's fur.

Or maybe she was.

Maybe they all were, these days. Maybe they were all children, struggling towards maturity alongside the rest of their species.

But she was not going to *act* like one. So she kept her dignity as she went back into the office.

"That batch failed too?" Chiran sounded entirely supportive.

"They've all failed. I don't think we have many things left to try."

They could cap it, bury it, put the problem off for a few years or decades or centuries.

She wasn't willing to do that, not yet.

"There's always something to try."

She wrinkled her lips at his optimism, but went past him into the lab building. In there, two of the younger scientists were working on something, heads so close together that she could not hear them speak, language transmitted bone to bone in the old herd huddle.

She didn't need to.

All she needed was to work out why it had failed...and what she could try next.

2

BEVERLY

BEVERLY HAD NEVER IMAGINED that she would leave Earth; let alone that she would leave the solar system.

Of course, she hadn't even thought it was possible until relatively recently. Now she was sitting on the observation deck of the *EFS Endeavour*, looking out at a completely alien solar system.

The system held a singleton star, similar to the sun in color. It was larger; everything in this system seemed to be just that bit larger, but it was still a main sequence yellow dwarf. The exact kind of sun around which one expected to find a habitable world.

She couldn't quite see said habitable world yet. Not quite. It was there, though, and it was her destination. About which she was decidedly nervous. An alien world inhabited by aliens. Not the ky'iin, who's brief war with Earth had seen casualties and fear but, thank God, nothing like some of the on planet wars of the past.

No trench warfare, no destroyed cities, just a relatively clean fight in the skies and a peace treaty. A peace treaty that also included these people, who were not at *all* like the ky'iin. She pushed her chair back slightly and looked at the view again.

Maybe it was avoidance. She was not looking forward to working with aliens. No, she would never have called herself xenophobic. It wasn't xenophobia.

It was some very real concerns about how *they* would view *her*. They were herbivores, would they see her as a predator and get nervous?

Or would they see her disability and...

The first sign of civilization is a healed femur. It wasn't actually true, Mead never said that, but it was one of those seductive lies that people wanted to believe.

And it had a point. Social creatures supported those who could not contribute in one way to ensure that they could contribute in others. She suspected that disabled Neanderthals had been the babysitters and the storytellers.

But she had no idea how these people would react. Would they feel they had gotten a "defective" human?

The ship gave a slight shudder. They were normal, but they made her tense. If the artificial gravity cut out she might end up in a quite embarrassing situation.

Maybe it was time to go.

Soon it would *definitely* be time to go.

As she rolled back to the elevator, she saw the head pilot, Lt Lauxon, moving in the other direction. The French-Canadian woman smiled at her. "You should stick around. You'll be able to see Tyranis soon."

Beverly hesitated. "I'd say I'll be seeing enough of the place."

"Not from orbit."

She turned around. The ship had changed course.

"There," Lauxon pointed to a sphere that seemed...

"It looks redder than Earth." Maybe that was the purple hue the vegetation had, thanks to the slightly different combination of solar radiation and atmospheric composition.

Maybe it was the pollution.

"It does, doesn't it. Larger, too."

Another thing Beverly wasn't looking forward to. Larger planet meant higher gravity and while she would adapt, she would probably feel kind of miserable for a while. That was the warning.

Kind of miserable for a while. It was probably an understatement, but it wasn't like she wasn't used to pain, the pain that still occasionally shot up her spinal cord or flickered through her legs.

"Half again as big. And apparently everything down there matches." Beverly heard the wryness in her own tone before she really grasped that it was coming out.

"Send pictures."

Now she laughed. "You mean you aren't going to come down and see the sights? Try the local cuisine?"

"The cuisine, maybe."

The tyrar were herbivores but they did still apparently cook and prepare their food. Hopefully they would...

...well, Beverly was not one of those people who got sick if she didn't eat meat. She'd still need supplements, though.

She was going to be down there a while.

She was going to be down there for as long as they needed and wanted her. She was hoping they wanted her. It was not going to be an easy, or entirely pleasant, duty. But it was a duty and she suspected, no she knew, that it would feel good when it was done, just like the last project.

The projects that had restored a struggling Earth to a new balance.

How much of that red hint *was* pollution?

She didn't want to know.

THE *ENDEAVOUR* GLIDED INTO ORBIT. Beverly was packed and ready. Her luggage and an exo that she hoped she would not need were already on the shuttle.

Just her and the chair, the one with the all-terrain tires. She had no idea what she would be facing down there. Where she might have to go. She was envisioning rocky trails and muddy fields.

She rolled onto the shuttle and one of the crew expertly secured her into place. It worked better than most planes she had flown on. People had gotten much better at catering for wheelchairs until the neurological web had made most of them obsolete. Much better than the bad old days when disabled people had been out of site, out of mind.

Now, she was a rare bird, a failure everyone stared at. Something of a bygone age. The c word, spoken entirely too often in her hearing.

The looks of pity.

Maybe the aliens would be better after all. The other scientific advisors were strapping into their own seats. Then the shuttle was away. The small windows showed little, but somebody had tuned the view screens to a pilots' eye view of the descent. The curve of the planet.

Oxygen-nitrogen atmosphere, breathable if it wasn't so polluted. She had a mask that she was to wear whenever she was outside . She had cartridges for it. She'd had to wear masks before.

But never because the entire planet was polluted. Earth had pulled back from that fate only to run headlong into another, into climate change and the megastorms and coastal flooding. Into mass extinctions.

In this case, the planet was dirty.

Dirty *and* starting to warm up.

They roared into the upper atmosphere and she could see the heat rising around the shuttle. Some of the others looked away.

She trusted to the craft's design. It was meant to do this and it would be more of a problem if she couldn't see it, she had been told. Well, for the moments before they blew up.

Heat. Rattling. And then the shuttle was an airplane, gliding down towards whatever the planned landing site was. To the spaceport. There it was. There, in the middle of a cold, high desert, with a city nearby that no doubt had not existed before somebody put a spaceport here. The city looked more like something in the Middle East than her native North America.

Well, except without people sleeping on the roofs. And then they were turning towards the runway and they were touching down. She pulled her mask on before they opened the door and waited to be unstrapped.

A helpless moment. She could probably do it herself if she had to.

She told herself she could do it herself if she had to.

Then the cool air of the planet was rushing in, and with it the acrid smell of death.

3

YOSHI

HOME AND HERD. Yoshi was tackled by two children as she reached the house, they wrapped themselves around her as if still small enough to cling into their mother's fur.

They were Varsha's children, both of them nearly black in color. The older, the boy, had a white line down the center of his back.

They were two years apart, a good gap in ages. The girl almost *was* still small enough to cling into fur and ended up wrapped around Yoshi's leg as she walked into the house. "Varsha!"

Varsha laughed and ran to retrieve her daughter. "Come on Sree."

The girl, thankfully, switched her attention to her mother.

"Shankar's making dinner."

That was good news to Yoshi; Shankar was an excellent cook, and she trusted him to provide a good meal. "Good. I'm starving."

"Not too much, I hope."

"Don't worry. We imploded the storage facility today, the site will be clear soon."

"But clear for what?" Varsha voiced her own words.

Not that Varsha, a poet, knew all that much about Yoshi's work. Like any good herd, they were no two of the five in the same profession, not counting the children.

When Varsha sat down, Raju, the boy sat next to her. "Are the algae growing?"

She shook her head. "Not yet."

He was smart, and she suspected he would go into science. In the old days, that wouldn't have been something people thought a male capable of; their sex hormones tended to get in the way.

Of course, that had proved to be bullshit. *They* had weird ideas about that kind of thing too.

Her terminal beeped.

She considered not checking it, but she knew full well that it could be an emergency.

She checked it.

No emergency, just a notification about an all hands meeting in two days, in the middle of her shift. She added it to her calendar then firmly turned the terminal off.

She was home now, with her herd and her family, and unless it was a genuine emergency, they would get her back in the morning.

Leela and Naveen came in together, practically clinging to each other, gray and chestnut fur combining into an interesting pattern.

They often managed to time that arrival, given they worked in the same part of town.

They were also lovers, which Yoshi tried to forgive them for and mostly succeeded. You generally didn't do that kind of thing inside a herd. Even if it was the kind of loving that *didn't* result in babies. But this was the modern world and the rules were made to be, if not broken, at least tweaked to allow for freedom the ancients had not known.

Raju nudged her, and she turned to the boy and started to answer his barrage of questions while the lovebirds went upstairs to change out of their work clothes.

Despite everything, life was good. Or at least, life was *meaningful.* This, she thought, was what she was fighting for.

SHE WAS THINKING the algae were a dead end, but she had no idea what to try instead, what to even *think* about trying.

If they couldn't clean up the heavy metals on this site and others, then they would be unusable for generations. Literally. Some people thought that the best future for the tyrar was to colonize some other world.

She thought that was not a bad idea, but as *well* as fixing their own, not instead. Looking at the numbers from the last assay she sighed.

There was just too much for them to deal with and also the weaker sunlight was affecting photosynthesis...and thus food supplies.

Lights? What about sun lamps over the pools? It was worth a try and she set the AI assist to run the numbers on the cost, to see if it was potentially feasible.

So many of their limited resources had to go towards making the air more breathable, the water more drinkable. Except that it all tied together. She *had* to solve the algae problem.

Her frustration made the all hands meeting a welcome interruption rather than a source of dread. Yoshi hated meetings, but it would at least force her to think about something else for a while, force her to let the less conscious parts of her brain work the problem.

She lumbered into a room which smelled pretty much entirely of other tyrar, a comforting smell. Herd-smell.

Never alone.

Chiran talked for a while about inanities, then he dropped the bombshell. "Now, here is the big one. If you have been following the news, you know we have signed a treaty with the ky'iin, glen, and two newly discovered species."

The humans and...there was an aquatic species on their world too, but the name escaped her.

This was about the aliens?

How could it be about aliens?

"The humans have offered scientific assistance and expertise."

There was an immediate rumble of, "We don't need more aliens." And "We don't need them telling us what to do."

He lifted a paw. "Oh, I understand, but they have promised they will *only* act as advisors. One of them is going to be coming to look at the site.

So, they had to have an alien here. An alien who might...

No.

Even the ky'iin had not done that, but it always felt like they might.

"When are they coming?" she found herself asking.

"Next week."

IT WAS ALMOST AMUSING to see who was scrambling to be on site and who was scrambling to be anywhere but on site.

Yoshi volunteered to be on site. She would rather see the alien than hear about them second hand. If they ended up sticking around for a while, she would have to learn to deal with them.

They would all have to learn to deal with aliens. It would probably be easier for the children.

Probably.

Kids were tough and kids dealt with change better than adults, they didn't get so anxious about it.

One alien.

Like the ky'iin, then, they didn't turn into anxious messes without a herd. It was a *strong* advantage to be able to spread out like that, to be able to send scouts who were less easily seen. Probably predators then, like the ky'iin.

That made her nervous, but she would rather meet this person, this alien, than hear about her. So, she made sure she was scheduled to be on site. Watched the others. There was excitement and there was fear and there was the natural concern that the alien would...

Would act like *them*. Would pretend to know what was best for them, would not listen, would make things worse.

Did the alien understand that they...she, apparently...had to be careful? Yoshi didn't know. She didn't know anything about humans.

So, that night, she decided to try and find out what she could. She used the large screen in the office.

Humans, like tyrar and ky'iin, had a four limbed bilateral body pattern, walking on their hind legs to free the forelegs for tool use. They were furless like the ky'iin, but had separate breathing and eating orifices...a much more sensible arrangement.

Definitely predators, with their eyes set forward for maximum binocular vision. Even more forward than the ky'iin. Were they...well.

She wasn't the kind of biologist to speculate. They covered their bodies with clothing, but she was able to pull up naked versions. Male and female, like the tyrar, but the females had grotesquely swollen teats, a pair of them at the top of their chest. To *them* no doubt it didn't look grotesquely swollen.

To her, it made them all look like they were in the throes of nursing. It was almost weirder than the oviparous ky'iin.

They did have fur, on the top of their heads, and longer on the females. Then she realized that, no, some individuals trimmed it and the fact that more women didn't was probably culture or fashion.

They were predators, but not like the ky'iin. Humans were apparently *omnivores*. Which meant they could probably manage a tyrar diet, maybe with some supplementation. That would make things easier if this scientist stuck around.

She wasn't satisfied.

They were still predators.

4

BEVERLY

EVEN WITH THE MASK, Beverly could tell how bad the air was, but they had her inside a building quickly.

It was a hotel, recognizable as such on any planet. Everything was a little bit larger - the native tyrar averaged seven feet tall, and door-ways, elevators, and furniture were all made for them. Her room was huge.

In fact, her room was clearly designed for the kind of occupancy that on Earth generally occurred only during conventions that attracted people without much cash. Anime cons, for example.

She was going to be there for a couple of days and sharing this huge room with Rosa Lawrence. Rosa had already claimed her bed and half of the room and was, in fact, flopped on said bed, fully clothed and snoring.

Beverly managed not to wake her. The bathroom was easy enough to deal with; they had set up some rails for transfer to the toilet and the fact that everything was so big made it *much* easier to navigate. Also, they didn't believe in over the tub showers.

The shower looked like it was designed to be shared too.

The tyrar were herbivores and herd animals. Did they like to sleep in cuddle piles? At least there was more than one bed.

Or maybe they'd switched the furniture around for the humans because somebody had told them humans *didn't* like to sleep in cuddle piles.

Sometimes she thought sleeping in a cuddle pile would be awesome. This wasn't one of those times.

Unlike Rosa, she managed to get herself undressed and under the covers, chair parked next to the bed, before she passed out.

She was woken by a knock on the door, but thankfully Rosa answered it while she was transferring herself back to the chair, pulling her legs into position. Two tyrar were outside. Both seemed a little nervous and the slightly smaller one was sniffing the air.

Beverly worried a bit. Did she smell of meat eater to them? She wasn't going to eat meat while she was here; it seemed peculiarly disrespectful to do so in front of people who had been prey for so much of their evolution.

Of course, the ky'iin had no choice, but she was not a ky'iin.

Maybe that was it.

The ky'iin were why this world was the way it was.

And humans were their allies.

THE TYRAR WERE escorts and translators, and the place they escorted Beverly and Rosa (once Beverly was dressed) was the hotel restaurant. Beverly could not speak their language, but she had taken a crash course on understanding it. It required a frequency transducer to hear everything they said; tyrar voices were designed, like those of elephants, to carry over long distances.

Some kind of pidgin would probably develop, but in the interim she had studied klion, a dominant tyrar language and they had studied English, so they could each speak their own language and be more or less understood.

Dinner consisted of an assortment of unidentifiable vegetables, some kind of grain mush and a selection of pills.

The tyrar slid a glass over to her. "I hear humans drink alcohol."

She sniffed at it. It smelled like wheat beer. "We do." She took a cautious sip, and was rewarded with a pleasant ale-like taste, but she could also tell it was rather more alcoholic than regular beer. "This is a little potent. But thank you."

She would just drink less of it, and hope they understood and were not offended. Tyrar were larger and had a digestive system designed for browsing.

No doubt this was their idea of a normal strength beer.

Rosa, on the other hand, took a large swig of it.

Was her roommate a lush? It didn't matter, it wasn't like they were going to be in the same place for that long.

And if Rosa got a hangover, Beverly would offer help but no sympathy. She had been there, most had.

The food was good too, and it didn't make her sick, although her stomach was perhaps a little disturbed. No doubt because it *was* food from a different planet.

They were lucky they could eat the food here at all, she thought wryly. Honestly, they shouldn't have been able to. It shouldn't work like that. Fortunately, it did. After they finished eating, or at least finished the actual meal...there was still food on the table and the tyrar occasionally nibbled, the tyrar explained their assignments.

Rosa was going to liaise with two dolphins that had come on the expedition for a marine exploration to check the health of an analog to a coral reef.

Beverly was going to start her "tour" at a mine reclamation site. That should be interesting. With a sigh, she decided she might end up needing the exo after all.

She would very much prefer not to. It was uncomfortable, it made her ache in places she did not want to think about. It was something that made *her* uncomfortable so she could fit in with others. She would not do that, not until and unless she absolutely had to.

But before that they were being offered a tour of a different kind. A chance to explore this city and these people, and what they had salvaged of their ravaged past.

THE CITY WAS NOT BUILT for humans, but it was built better for wheelchairs than most.

"Why do you not use a powered chair?" the tyrar guide asked her.

"First of all, they might break down. Second of all, it keeps me fit." She smiled up at him; he loomed above her even more than a human would, and the tyrar males were a little smaller than the females.

"Ah, I can see that."

It hadn't felt like an intrusive question. She did see some tyrar using mobility devices; she hadn't seen a wheelchair, but she had seen a grey-furred elder walking with a cane and another with something akin to a walker.

He was guiding her to a museum, and held the door for her. That made her flinch, but she probably wouldn't have managed it, not in this gravity and not the size it was. She did wish he had asked, though.

Once inside, though, she found herself in a riot of exquisite blues and greens. Stained glass covered the roof of the atrium, not in a picture, but in a pattern clearly designed to flow down into the room. Not much red in it. The tyrar didn't see red. But it didn't matter. She couldn't resist a gasp of delight.

"This is the Venora Cultural Institute, and the atrium roof was designed by Yoshi var Bevrit." He gave a date that meant little to her.

Yoshi of the herd Bevrit. To distinguish them, no doubt, from any other Yoshis. "It's beautiful."

"I was a little worried. The ky'iin do not always appreciate our art."

"I've seen ky'iin art."

The ky'iin would have filled this place with murals of triumph and death and of families and mating. Their art had to tell a story.

Perhaps they just didn't have a strong cultural appreciation of this abstract beauty.

"What about human art?" He turned towards her.

"We brought a lot of data files. And one day, perhaps, you'll be able to come to Earth and get a tour of, say, the Louvre. But our art varies a lot."

"So does ours. It's just..."

"The ky'iin like all art to tell a story."

"They like all *life* to tell a story. They don't just sit and be. Perhaps..."

"Perhaps it's because they have to hunt all of their food." Well, they didn't have to, but she knew the ky'iin homeworld held large hunting preserves where ky'iin could deal with their instincts.

"Perhaps. But please, come this way. I have more loveliness to show you."

She wasn't sure loveliness was the right translation, but nonetheless, she followed to see what beauty lay in the galleries.

www.ingramcontent.com/pod-product-compliance
Lightning Source LLC
Chambersburg PA
CBHW021206250626
47155CB00008B/2690